Burnt Mountain

Burnt Mountain

A NOVEL

ANNE RIVERS SIDDONS

GRAND CENTRAL
PUBLISHING

NEW YORK   BOSTON

On page 221, the excerpts from the poem "Labysheedy" ("The Silken Bed") by Nuala ni Dhomhnaill, are from her book entitled *Rogha Dánta/Selected Poems*, published by New Island Dublin. Used by permission.

Yeats quotes throughout are reprinted with the permission of Scribner, a Division of Simon & Schuster, Inc., from *The Collected Works of W.B. Yeats, Volume I: The Poems,* revised by W.B. Yeats. Copyright ©1933 by The Macmillan Company, renewed 1961 by Bertha Georgie Yeats. All rights reserved.

Grand Central Publishing
Hachette Book Group
237 Park Avenue
New York, NY 10017

www.HachetteBookGroup.com

Printed in the United States of America

First Edition: July 2011
10 9 8 7 6 5 4 3 2 1

Grand Central Publishing is a division of Hachette Book Group, Inc.
The Grand Central Publishing name and logo is a trademark of Hachette Book Group, Inc.

The publisher is not responsible for websites (or their content) that are not owned by the publisher.

Library of Congress Cataloging-in-Publication Data
Siddons, Anne Rivers.
   Burnt Mountain / Anne Rivers Siddons.
      p. cm.
   ISBN 978-0-446-52789-7 (Hardcover)—ISBN 978-0-446-56695-7 (Large Print)
1. Camps—Fiction. 2. Marriage—Fiction. 3. Georgia—Fiction. I. Title.
   PS3569.I28B87 2011
   813'.54—dc22
                                                                    2011000854

For Annie Simmons, Tom Higgins, and Bob McDonald
Heart friends

Prologue

We heard it first on an early morning in June. I thought then that it might have been going on for many mornings, but given what we know about it now, I realize that this must have been one of the first times that it sounded, perhaps the very first. This year, anyway.

It wafted into our bedroom on a soft green wind, along with the sleepy twitter of songbirds and the heartbreaking sweetness of wild honeysuckle from the woods behind the house. We had had one of Atlanta's not-infrequent and unadvertised long, cold springs and had only slept with our windows open for the past month.

We had moved into our house just recently, and the sounds and smells of our new neighborhood were still unfamiliar to us, exotic in their strangeness. But we were learning. The sleep-murdering a.m. roar down the street had become the Suttles' scowling teenage son starting his motorcycle; the choking miasma that often drifted over the lower end of the street was old Mr. Christian Wells, who had a widely known fear of West Nile virus, spraying his extensive lawn with a virulent pesticide; the shrill shriek that set every dog on Bell's Ferry Road barking was Isobel Emmett across the street, who had forgotten once again that she had armed the house alarm.

This morning's sound was different, though. This was the sound of children, many children, far away. Singing.

I lay for a moment without opening my eyes, trying to see if the sound tasted of dreams. It didn't; the singing children seemed to be coming nearer, from somewhere in the west, and their song grew louder. I could almost make it out. It was a raucous shouted noise, somehow a summer song. I felt that. I knew it.

I turned over and looked at Aengus. He did not move, but his eyes were open. Even in the dimness, they burned the banked-fire blue that I had fallen in love with, the blue of the hot embers of coal. His crow's wing of black hair fell over one eye. I had fallen in love with that, too. And the straight thick black eyebrows. I even loved the scattering of black freckles across his nose and cheeks. Aengus at the time I met him was as unlike any of the other young men in my small southern town and only slightly larger southern college as a raven to a flock of sparrows. The fact that my mother was appalled by him when I first brought him home from school lit my budding infatuation into a bonfire.

"Angus," she had murmured sweetly, looking up at him from under her celebrated inch-long lashes. "Like the cows?"

"I wouldn't be surprised," Aengus said agreeably, in the rich lilt that could not have been cultivated in the Deep South or possibly anywhere else in the country.

Mother lifted her perfectly arched eyebrows and smiled.

"I don't believe we know any Anguses, do we, Mother?" she said to my grandmother, who lay reading on the chaise on the screened porch where we had gathered.

"He has fire in his head," my grandmother murmured, not looking up from her magazine.

We believe she's starting Alzheimer's, Mother mouthed confidently to Aengus. *Don't mind anything she says.*

Grand gave a disgusted sniff, still not looking up. She was wearing one of the bright silk caftans she had brought home from India, and her vermeil hair was piled on top of her small, elegant head. I thought she looked beautiful.

"Well, she certainly knows her Yeats." Aengus grinned. "I spell it that way, too, Mrs. Wentworth. With an *A* before the *e*. Nobody uses it like that but my mother, but there it is. Will you come dance with me in Ireland?"

"I have no idea what either of you is talking about," my mother said dismissively. "Thayer, go get us some iced tea. The sweet, in the pitcher. There's mint in the fridge."

I got up, but before I left the porch I saw my grandmother lift her head and give Aengus her dazzling full smile. She had been a great beauty; everybody said so. When she smiled like that she still was.

"I will dance with you anywhere, Mr. O'Neill," she said, and from that moment on she loved him almost as much as I did, until the day she died.

5

Aengus looked over at me now, half-smiling in the dimness.

"Do you hear that?" I said.

"Yep."

"What on earth do you think it is?"

"The children of Llyr," he said, stretching luxuriously. "Grieving for the human children they were before the Dagda turned them into swans."

"I don't want to hear any more of your damned Irish bog fairy tales," I said. "Really, what do you think that is?"

We listened for a moment. The singing children were coming closer. Their song was a real shout now. Its familiarity tickled my tongue.

"Kids having a good time. They're obviously going somewhere in a car or something, the way they're moving closer."

Another moment passed, and then I said, "I know what it is! It's 'The Cannibal King'! It's a great kids' song; we used to sing it endlessly on the bus to camp and coming home...."

Just then we heard the *shushhhh* of air brakes and the grinding of big gears changing.

"It is a bus," I said. "Where on earth are those kids going this early in the morning on a bus? There aren't that many kids around here...."

"Isn't there a camp or something that all those assholes in Happy Hollow whomped up for their little darlings?" Aengus said peevishly. "God knows there are enough toddling scions and scionesses over there."

Our street, Bell's Ferry Road, ran through the hilly river forest surrounding the Chattahoochee River just to the west of Atlanta. Many of the big old houses had been summer places for well-to-do Atlantans for decades—ours was one of those—and the newer ones were gracefully and conservatively built to blend in. It was a cool ribbon of a street, winding its way down to the bridge that spanned the river.

On the other side of the bridge there was a gated community of houses so jaw-droppingly expensive and baroquely designed that first-time visitors were often stricken to silence—the few who were invited into the enclave. It was called Riverwood, and it gleamed, as my grandfather used to say, like new money on a bear's behind and was as impenetrable as Gibraltar. It was a mark of distinction among many people we knew not to know anyone who lived there.

To get anywhere near the city or the freeway, the Riverwoodies had to drive back east up Bell's Ferry Road toward town, and it was all I could do to stop Aengus from throwing rocks or squirrel turds at their Jaguars and Land Rovers and chauffeured limos. I don't know why Riverwood and its denizens riled him so. Aengus had no temper to speak of, and had never seemed to care who lived where.

But Riverwood maddened him.

"I think it does have a camp," I said now. "Up in North Georgia near Burnt Mountain, maybe. It's private; only their kids can go. This would be the time of year for it to start and that *was* a bus, and that song..."

He grinned again.

" 'The Cannibal King'?"

"Yes. I don't think there's a southern kid alive who doesn't know it."

"Sing it."

"Oh, Aengus…"

"Sing it, Thayer. I'll perish if I can't hear it."

So I sat down on my side of the bed and sang:

Oh, the Cannibal King with the big nose ring
Fell in love with a dusky mai-ai-aid,
And every night in the pale moonlight
Across the lake he'd wa-a-a-ade.
He'd hug and kiss his pretty little miss
In the shade of the bamboo tree-ee-eee,
And every night, in the pale moonlight,
It sounded like this to mee-eee-eee:
"Aye-oomph! Aye-oomph! Aye-oomph-tiddy i-dee-aye…
Aye-oomph! Aye-oomph! Aye-oomph-tiddy i-dee-aye-
    aye-ay!"

"You were supposed to give your arm a big sloppy smack after all the 'aye-oomphs,'" I said. I was smiling slightly; I could feel it on my lips. The hot, dusty cocoon of the yellow bus, and the blue and green young mountains of North Georgia flying by, and the smell of suntan oil and Popsicles, and sweet young voices shrieking at the tops of their lungs. Camp. Going to camp.

He laughed.

"I'll never hear 'The Cannibal King' again without thinking of you," he said.

I looked over at him, and suddenly, unaccountably, my eyes filmed with tears and my chest and throat constricted, and I saw, not Aengus's dark, sloe-eyed face but another one: tanned nose peeling, sun-bleached hair hanging over gray-green eyes, chipped front tooth, a slow smile that made my breath stop. Always.

This is where we should get married, a deep voice said from the other pillow. A top bunk, I remembered…

I jumped to my feet and went to the window and looked out, not seeing the tender new green or smelling the sweet honey of the sun dappling through the branches onto our lawn. I was stony with pain and surprise. I had buried it all so deep. . . . It was so long ago. . . .

Up at the end of the street I heard the bus's air brakes hiss again and the gears growl as it made the turn onto the road that would take it to the freeway north. A last banner of song floated behind it: "Oh, the Cannibal King with the big nose ring…"

It did not sound cheeky and summer-day and young now. It sounded somehow menacing. Knowing, in a crawling, terrible way. Wrong.

I turned and ran across the rug and slipped into bed and buried my face in Aengus's neck. He pulled me close to him, holding me hard against the long length of him.

"What's the matter?" he said. "You're shaking."

"Cold," I whispered. "Just cold."

He held me that way for a long time, but I did not get warm again. At least not that day.

CHAPTER

1

"You don't know my mother."

Once, in my freshman year at Sewanee, I lay in the infirmary shaking with influenza and tried to estimate the number of times I might conceivably have said those words to someone. Within five minutes I realized that even without the burning forehead and the throbbing bones I would have had more luck tallying stars.

"Why are you still wearing shoes? It's the middle of June."

"You don't know my mother."

"Those pigtails are geeky. I wouldn't wear them if I was dead."

"You don't know my mother."

"You told Sonny Etheridge you didn't want to go to the prom with him? Are you out of your mind?"

"You don't know my mother."

"Sewanee? Nobody even knows where that is! Everybody

11

else is going to Georgia. You could be a cheerleader without even trying out."

"You don't know my mother."

I stopped there. It was a rhetorical statement, anyway. By that time almost everybody in my world knew my mother. Everyone except, perhaps, me.

She was the prettiest girl in Lytton. Everybody said so. Even today there are still people who will tell you that there was never a prettier girl in town than Crystal Thayer, and for all I know she still may be. I don't go back to Lytton now and it has been a long time since I have seen my mother, but by the time I came along it was one of those small-town dogmas that had been repeated so often that it had passed into local mythology, like our toehold on history ("All them rails was twisted into knots by the Yankees; Sherman's Neckties, they called 'em") and the obligatory haunt in our cemetery. ("Nat Turnipseed. Folks have seen him skulkin' around in that graveyard since he passed, and that's been eighty, ninety years now. Wring your neck soon as he'd look at you.")

And so: "Crystal Thayer is the prettiest girl we ever had in Lytton, and everybody thought we'd up and lose her when she married that schoolteacher from Atlanta. Reckon she kept him on a short rope, though, 'cause they never left there."

They were right. Finch Wentworth never took his pretty bride back to Atlanta with him. Everything that came after turned on that, like a ball bearing.

My grandfather Thayer was a druggist, a kind, absent-minded man who would have run a prosperous small-town drugstore if he had not been so bewildered by his flock of clamoring daughters and so apt to hand out healing potions free of charge to afflicted neighbors who could not pay for them. I don't remember much about him; he died, still kind and still bewildered, when I was four. But I could remember the smell of the lemon drops he kept in his shirt pocket for my older sister, Lily, and me and feel on my cheek the white stubble of his chin.

My grandmother Leona I remember not at all. She slid away on the wings of one of her famous vapors before I was born. It was said around town, I heard later, that many of the women thought the sheer grandeur and excessiveness of my mother's wedding to my father simply sank her.

"Don't know what she expected, Crystal marrying one of those highfalutin Atlanta Wentworths," was a consensus, if not the general one. "Ought to have known she couldn't just put around some flowers and light a few candles."

But in truth it had been my mother, and not the high-falutin Atlanta Wentworths, who had insisted on the spectacle of her marriage to Finch Wentworth III.

"Half the Piedmont Driving Club was there," I heard my mother say silkily more than once. That they were there out of a sort of wincing allegiance to their Wentworth friends and not because "that's the way they do it in Buckhead" never occurred to my mother. My father must have known, but he was oblivious to almost everything but the pretty, rose-gilt creature in his bed and was nearly as absentminded in his own scholarly way as my grandfather Thayer had been in his. If the thought struck my father, he never mentioned it.

And my mother's open-armed welcome into the fabled

Piedmont Driving Club, to which the baroque wedding was the springboard, never happened.

That she never thought to blame my grandmother Wentworth for that came to surprise me, for by the time I was old enough to speculate on the motivations of the adults in my family I knew that she blamed Grand for everything else that was awry in her marriage. But her most corrosive disappointment was aimed, always, at my father.

"We could have moved there," I heard her say to him over and over. "You know your mother wanted you there with her. Everything in your world is there. All your friends. All your clubs. Your relatives back to Adam. It wasn't me who wanted to stay in this one-horse town; I told you that over and over. You think I wanted my daughters to grow up where they could marry dry cleaners, or ... *feed* sellers, for God's sake? There's not even a Junior League here."

"I like Lytton," my father would say in his mild, slow voice. It was a voice that I loved; many people did. I think it may have been one of the reasons he was such a good history teacher, and later such an effective school administrator. His voice promised, somehow, safety and acceptance.

"And," he would go on, "I need to live where my school is. There's no question of that. How would it look if I taught at Hamilton and lived in Atlanta? It would look like I didn't think Lytton was good enough."

"It isn't!" I have heard my mother nearly scream, in exasperation. "Your precious mama would tell you that, if you asked her."

But in truth my father's mother had told him just the opposite.

"Your life is in Lytton with your wife and your work and your children," she told him, even before he and my mother married. "Believe me when I say this. Crystal is a girl of great strength and purpose, and she would never be able to exercise those qualities effectively in Atlanta. She can at home; it's her turf. She's already a princess there. In the long run she would be bitterly disappointed here. And I believe you and perhaps your children would suffer for that. You have just the temperament to fit perfectly into a small town; it's not as though you'd never see Atlanta again. You'd be plenty close to keep up with all your friends. And we'll visit back and forth often."

"Mom," my father said, "she wants a big house. She wants nice things. For some reason she thinks we can't have them in Lytton...."

"She shall have them in Lytton," my grandmother Caroline said to her son, hugging him. "Your father and I are going to give you the grandest house we can in Lytton, and see that it's fittingly furnished. Wouldn't she like that?"

"*I'd* love it, Ma, but I just don't know about Crystal...."

"Crystal cannot live with us on Habersham Road," his mother said crisply and finally. "Nor, I don't think, anywhere else in Atlanta."

"I just don't see how I can tell her that," my father said miserably. "She's practically packed up already."

"Don't tell her," Grand said. "Let her find out when we

tell her about our wedding present. Surely a lovely furnished house of her own right there at home, where everyone can see how well she's done, will take her mind off Atlanta."

"You don't really like her, do you?" my father said, and his mother hugged him harder.

"No, I really don't, not much," she said into his soft hair. "But you love her, and I'll do anything I can to see that she's happy, so that you will be, too."

"Except have her here," he whispered.

"Yes. Except that."

(All this I learned later, in a talk with my grandmother Wentworth before she died.)

"So it was you all along, and not Daddy." I smiled, picking up her thin hand.

"Oh yes," she said. "But I really don't think she suspected; do you?"

"No. Otherwise she'd have been all over you like a duck on a June bug. You were smart not to let her know."

"It wasn't because I was afraid of her, Thayer," Grand said, reaching up to trace my face with her forefinger. "I've never seen the day that I couldn't handle your mother six ways to Sunday. No, I did it for you. Believe it or not, Lytton is a much...*sweeter* place to grow up than the Northwest of Atlanta; at least as it was in those days."

"But I wasn't even born yet. How'd you know there would even be me?"

"I knew," she said very softly. "I always knew there'd be you."

Somehow, I always believed that she did know. I didn't believe that of anyone else, though. I was born nine years after my older sister, Lily—the afterthought baby, the accidental child. Not that anyone ever called me those things, but I overheard my mother's fluting laughter more than once, at this bridge game or that dinner party: "Oh, Thayer, my little wild child. We'd resigned ourselves to the fact that Lily would be an only, and then, poof! Here she comes, our little redheaded caboose. Didn't even look like any of us; Finch used to tease me about the mailman. I was planning Lily's wedding before Thayer even needed a bra."

And she would ruffle my carroty hair and laugh, so that everyone would know it was our little joke. I learned to laugh, too, a dreadful, false little trill as much like my mother's lilt as I could manage.

It did not occur to me until much later that being the family joke was not really anything to aspire to. It got you fond laughter but little else.

My father didn't think I was a joke. My earliest memories are of him walking around the house or the garden with me in his arms and later riding piggyback on his shoulders, choking by then in a miasma of makeup and perfume and wet stockings and slips hanging corpselike on shower and towel rails, his naturally soft voice drowned under dinner-table talk of boys and dates and clothes and the shalts and shalt-nots of burgeoning genteel womanhood. I knew that he meant it when he said, "Come on, Red. Let's get some fresh air and spit tobacco and tell lies."

"You'll be sorry when she grows up thinking she's a boy!" Mother would call after us.

"Not in a million years!" my father would toss back. "This one's going to leave them all in the shade."

"Yeah, like that's going to happen!" I heard Lily call after us once.

"What does she mean?" I asked my father, reaching up from my perch on his shoulders to snatch a chinaberry off the tree in our garden.

"She means she doesn't want you to turn out prettier than she is," Daddy said. "Think she's scared you will."

I could not get my mind around this. Nobody could be prettier than my mother and my older sister; everybody knew that. People called them the Wentworth girls, and indeed, they did seem of a piece, silkily blond and gentian eyed, with incredible complexions. In those days of "laying out" slathered with a mixture of baby oil and iodine, my mother and sister never let the sun fall on their faces if they could help it. Their skins were the translucent milkiness of Wedgwood or Crown Derby. My own face was, almost from the beginning, dusted with freckles. My hair burned in the sun like a supernova. My eyes were not blue but the amber of sea glass.

"Your grandmother Wentworth's eyes," my father would tell me. "Hair, too, before hers got the gray in it. In fact, you look almost exactly like the photos I've seen of her when she was your age."

"That's good, isn't it?" I said. I did not see a lot of my grandmother Wentworth in those days. She spent a great deal of time traveling abroad, usually alone, to places with names like songs and poetry to me...Samarkand. Galapagos. Sri Lanka. Dubrovnik.

"Outrageous!" My mother sniffed. "What on earth do people think of her?"

"That she's rich enough to do what she damn well pleases," my father replied once, weary of it all. "And I very much doubt that she is alone, usually."

"That's just what I mean," Mother said, but scarcely loud enough to be heard. My father would brook no complaints about his mother.

"Oh yes, that's good," he said to me that day in the garden. "That's the best. Your grandmother is a great beauty. Always has been."

"I thought that was Mama."

"Your mama's very pretty. It's not the same thing."

"You think that's why she doesn't like me?" I said. "Because I look like Grand? I don't think she likes Grand very much."

He swung me down and we sat together on the stone bench that overlooked the fishpond. It flashed with fat orange shapes, some black speckled. My mother called them koi. My father called them goldfish.

"Your mother loves you," he said into my hair as I squirmed on his lap. "Don't ever think she doesn't. It's just that she's more tied up with Lily right now because Lily's at an age when it's really important to get things right. You don't need that kind of fussing over. You're a pretty easy little customer to deal with."

"What would happen if Lily didn't get things right?"

19

"God knows. She might run off and join the circus."

"Cool! We could all get in free!"

He laughed.

"So we could, my funny valentine, but I don't think that's what your mother has in mind for her. Best we just go on our way rejoicing and leave them to it."

"Okay." I shrugged. "But if I look like Grand I don't think Mama will like that much. She thinks Grand looks like one of those women Pisossa painted, all neck and eyes. I heard her tell Mrs. Etheridge that."

He laughed again. "She does, does she? Well, in that case, you'll be a raving beauty. His women are famous all over the world. It's Picasso, by the way."

After that, none of my mother's carelessly chirped little darts hurt me. I looked like my grandmother Wentworth, and she looked like a lady this Picasso painted. We were famous all over the world.

There are maybe ten small towns and communities orbiting Atlanta like dwarf moons. Most of them are close enough to the city to lie, figuratively, under its canopy, like fruit dropped from a great tree. Since their settling, many of them have had a love-hate relationship with the city, insisting on their own uniqueness and autonomy but fed by the life force of the mother tree. If you could have bitten into one of them, like an apple, I think you would have tasted first Atlanta. But few Lytton dwellers ever admitted to wishing they lived in Atlanta instead.

"Too big, too loud, too smelly," went the litany of my

acquaintances. "Either Yankee tackpots or too good to piss in the same pot as anybody else. I wouldn't live there for a million dollars. Lytton has everything you could ever want, without the traffic."

Fully half of them shopped weekly in Atlanta, though, and sometimes more often. Dressed defiantly in their Sunday best, gloved, hatted, and handbagged, they surged into the city in waves, on Greyhound buses and in newly washed family sedans. A few of the Lytton men who were not merchants or farmers or makers or repairers of objects worked there. A scattering of lawyers, a big-town banker or two, airline personnel, toilers in the huge industries that besmirched the municipal skies with smoke and stink. But my father was the only Atlanta native I ever knew who chose to leave it and live and work in Lytton.

The Alexander Hamilton Academy, a well-endowed and -regarded boys' preparatory school on Lytton's northern outskirts, drew students from all over the South. The school was known to have been founded by an eccentric Atlanta millionaire who believed that the bucolic drowsiness of a small town would be the best atmosphere for learning, unfettered as it was by such distracting amenities as movie theaters, soda shops, or gaming establishments. Most students boarded, and undoubtedly would have mutinied and fled in droves except that the educations they received were first-rate.

To a man—or boy—they howled at the lack of recreational amenities, but most went on to colleges of their choice, and so, in turn, they sent their scowling sons there.

Lytton boys did not attend Hamilton Academy. Not that

there were none qualified; a few would have done well. But the school was still owned by the family of the founding millionaire, and the curse of Atlanta still hovered over it. Lytton High had been good enough for generations of Lyttoners, and it was good enough, by God, for their sons. Or maybe that nice military school down in Newnan that was said to be stricter than the army itself.

How many Lytton boys might have found their futures smothered and shaped by Hamilton Academy will never be known.

I still wonder if any of the other Atlanta satellite towns could possibly have had the sheer animus toward it that Lytton pumped out. After all these years I still don't understand. But it did not surprise me that none of Hamilton's faculty lived in Lytton; no rental opportunities were ever offered them. I imagine most of them figured they were well out of Lytton, anyway.

And then came my father.

It was his great-grandfather, known to his associates to be crazier than batshit, who had founded the academy, and the family down to and including Finch's mother and father had kept it viable, not as much for fun as for profit. Hamilton added a nice heft to the bag of profitable endeavors that the enterprising Wentworth men had cobbled together. By the time young Finch Wentworth, the only son of his generation, graduated from Princeton, the Wentworth clan was coining money and living at the top of Atlanta's scanty social heap, on Habersham Road. Finch, who had studied history at Princeton and wanted only to teach it, was a natural for Hamilton, not only for a faculty position but also as incumbent owner of the school.

He had been teaching for scarcely two weeks, living at home on Habersham Road and beginning to think he should be nearer to Hamilton, both in fact and spirit, when he walked into my grandfather Thayer's drugstore on Lytton's main street and asked to see the owner. My grandfather Owen sauntered out from behind the drug window and asked what he could do to help him.

My mother, Crystal, sampling colognes behind the gift counter, sauntered out to see who this tall stranger might be.

My father saw my mother and forgot what he had come for.

"I think I need some Band-Aids," he said, still looking at Crystal Thayer. In the soft artificial lighting of the gift department, smelling of My Sin, she burned on his retinas like a solar flare.

Recognizing the symptoms of his affliction—for she was by then almost MGM pretty—she smiled at him and faded back behind the counter. But she kept her ears open. Not too many tall, well-dressed strangers walked into her father's drugstore.

My father jerked his head back around at my grandfather Thayer, waiting politely beside him, and stammered, "...Uh, uh—Oh! And some iodine and Mercurochrome, too, and aspirin, and a whole bunch of first-aid stuff, and soap and things like that, and I guess vitamins and cotton swabs... lots of those..."

My grandfather lifted his eyebrows.

"I'm buying them for the school," my father said. "For Hamilton Academy. I guess I'll be buying a good bit of stuff in bulk every month. Maybe I should open an account...."

"And your relationship to the school would be...?" my grandfather said a trifle coolly. This addled young man could be setting up a field hospital for terrorists, for all he knew.

"Well," my father said, "I guess I own it. Or at least my family does. And I teach history there. Finch Wentworth," he added hastily, putting his hand out.

"Owen Thayer," my grandfather said, taking it.

My mother came out from behind her counter and wafted up beside her father.

"I'm Crystal Thayer," she said, cocking her head winsomely up at my father. Her silvery hair swung over her cheek like a bell.

"You're from Atlanta, aren't you?"

"Ah...yeah," he said. "But I'm thinking I really ought to find a place here, you know, with the school here and everything."

"Well." She dimpled. "That shouldn't be any problem, should it, Daddy?"

"I don't know of any places right off, honey," Dr. Thayer said, "but I suppose I could look around...."

"Oh, shoot, Daddy, I can think of one place right off. You know our garage apartment's just been sitting here since Memaw died. You were saying just the other day we ought to do something with it."

"Well, you know, your mother..."

"I'll talk to Mama."

My grandfather went back behind his window to start gathering up my father's supplies. He knew a done deal when he heard one.

CHAPTER

2

Even now, with all that has passed between and around us, I sometimes think that I am not entirely fair to my mother. Is any daughter, ever? What girl child can ever see the woman who bore her whole? The mask of mother is a totality; there are no fissures in it where the vast complexity of otherness can show through. I think comprehension can come later, on both sides, if both mother and daughter are willing to do the work. I never was. I think I simply grew too comfortable with the role of victim—dependent on it, really. It defined me so early that I never had to search for a legitimate self until much later.

But my mother was never simply a victimizer; she was a wife, a lover, and a mother in the best sense of the words, as well as the worst, a daughter and a dreamer, a yearner. Oh, a great, great yearner. As a larva might, if such things were possible, yearn for the completion of butterfly wings and endless nectar, my mother yearned for the perfect complexion and habitat for her specialness.

No one had ever told her that she was not special; from the time she could understand words, her mother told her of her beauty, her gifts, her talents, her destiny. She was to be, though I doubt if my grandmother ever came right out and said it, all that plain, frail little Leona Brumby was not and never had been. My grandmother Leona was in one respect a very tough cookie. I think she could have bent silver spoons if it had been her will. That will got her a handsome, well-born druggist husband and one of Lytton's more substantial homes. And as for all the other things...the looks, the vitality, the promise...she would have them. She knew this. If not for herself, through this last, porcelain daughter.

Like my father, my mother was a late-born child. Her clamorous older sisters were away at school or, in one case, married, so there was no competition for Crystal Thayer's throne. She had childhood virtually to herself.

Leona Thayer was by then often bedridden with the frightening spells that left her white and gasping and kept Owen Thayer's worried attention constantly upon her. The son of a physician, he adored medicine and he would have studied it himself if his IQ had matched his father's. The drugstore was the next best thing, and fussing over Leona came as naturally to him as breathing. No doctor had ever seemed to diagnose her debilitating spells with any degree of certainty, but there could be no doubt that Leona Thayer was chronically and gravely afflicted. Most of Lytton thought she was lucky to have a handsome, attentive husband, a beautiful youngest child, and free medicine all her life. And everyone said how sweet that pretty child was to her mother, not going away to school as her sisters had done but staying close to her mother's side. Crystal often politely refused invitations with a shy smile.

"I promised Mama I'd read to her this afternoon," she would say. "We're reading *Wind in the Willows*. Mama's Ratty and I'm being Mole."

By the time she was grammar-school age her bewitched father had offered boarding schools in six states, but Crystal refused to leave her mother.

"There's plenty of time for that *later*, Daddy," she would say tremulously, the "later" tolling like a funeral bell with import. And Owen Thayer would hug her with tears in his eyes. He knew that his wife would not live a great deal longer, even if he was not and never would be quite sure what it was she died from.

"You're our special angel," he would say to his daughter. The special angel would hug him back and go, sighing audibly, back to her classes at the little Lytton school. The truth was, she loved being head cheerleader, homecoming queen, best all-around everything, booked up months ahead for every dance, and being courted by every eligible young man in the area. Achieving all this in Lytton was a cakewalk. She was not entirely sure how she might have fared elsewhere.

She knew where elsewhere would be, though.

"Atlanta," Leona would say to her over and over. "Atlanta was just made for you. You could have the richest husband and the biggest house in town. The Piedmont Driving Club, that's where you belong. You can have it all without lifting a finger; you just wait and see. It won't be too long now."

Both Thayer women would allow tears to stand in their eyes for a moment. Both knew what Leona meant.

"What's the Piedmont Driving Club, Mama?" Crystal had asked early on. "What do they drive?"

"It's one of the fanciest private clubs in the world," her mother assured her. "Everybody who's anybody in Atlanta belongs to it. They don't drive anything; it's just an old-fashioned name. But there's no other club like it."

Leona Thayer had never been inside the sacred walls of the Piedmont Driving Club, but she had read the *Atlanta Journal* and *Constitution* society pages until she memorized them, every day.

And because she heard the litany so often and there was no one to disabuse her of it, the Piedmont Driving Club shone in Crystal's not-too-capacious mind like the names of Paris, London, and Monte Carlo by the time she was in her teens. She also knew the names of the streets she would choose from to have her showplace of a home, and even the family names of some of the young men she might, with impunity, consider marriageable.

She did not recall at the time she met Finch Wentworth in her father's store if his had been among the names, but she knew with her infallible butterfly antennae that this was what she had been bred and groomed for. The white satin knot was tied before the first feathering of My Sin smote my father's nostrils.

He did indeed, without much coaching, rent the apartment

over the garage where Crystal's grandmother Thayer had lived. It seemed an arrangement made in heaven. For him my grandmother Leona rallied herself and wore crisp cottons and kitten heels and cologne, though never My Sin. She had her hair done and her nails lacquered pale rose at Ginger's Beauty Nook, and hung on to my father's every syllable with a murmuring interest Crystal had never seen before. In fact, she had never seen this woman before at any time. She could see now exactly why her father had married Leona Brumby; she had always wondered.

For Finch Wentworth, my grandfather lit up like a harvest moon and told seemingly endless stories of his own boyhood in Lytton, and took him duck hunting in the rich swamp of the Chattahoochee River where it cut in close around Lytton on its way to join the sea. I could never imagine my father hunting anything, but I know that he went. For him my grandmother's cook, Bermuda, set dinners upon the mahogany dining room table that he still talked of when I was a child. No more meals at the yellow breakfast room table. Mahogany and starched linen for this young man.

For him my mother untied her pale hair from its ponytail and let it brush her shoulders. And doubled up on My Sin and shone like a pearl. It was all she had to do.

Finch Wentworth took her home to Buckhead to meet his parents before that quarter at Hamilton Academy was a month old. He may not have been able to read his future in that jewel-like October afternoon around his parents' pool, but Caroline Wentworth did.

"I knew the minute she walked in that she was going to be my daughter-in-law," Grand told me while I was still small.

"Were you excited?" I asked.

"Oh yes." She smiled, putting on her sunglasses so I could not see the slanted amber eyes. "I was very excited."

Whatever else she felt she never told me, but later I came to see that evening in Fellini-like detail. I did not know how, but I knew I was right. I've never had cause to doubt that.

My mother wore her black silk sheath, matchstick slim, that bared her golden shoulders, and her mother's pearls around her neck. She had black high-heeled silk pumps to match, and a slim black satin clutch dotted with rhinestones. My grandfather took a picture of them as they got into my father's modest blue Plymouth to leave for Atlanta. Daddy looks like just what he was: a tall, gangly young man in gray slacks and a blue blazer, his nice Coca Cola–ad face tilted down to my mother, beaming. My mother looked like a *Vogue* model out for a shimmering evening at the Pierre or the Carlyle.

My grandmother Leona had taken her daughter on many excursions to Atlanta, to shop at Rich's and J.P. Allen and to drive the length of Peachtree Road, out to where it lost itself in the tangle of Buckhead. There were many fine and even palatial homes to see along its length, but they had never turned left off Peachtree and onto Peachtree Battle Avenue and the warren of quiet, curving, deep-forested streets that made up what Atlantans called, simply, the Northwest. I imagine my mother's chatter slowing and finally stopping as Finch Wentworth turned the car onto Habersham Road and drove slowly up it.

Habersham, of all the golden streets in the Northwest,

still shines brightest. It is a beautiful road, winding, swooping up small hills and down over little bridges, arched over with magnificent old hardwoods that have been fed and pruned almost since their birth. Deep emerald lawns sweep far back to large houses set like jewels into perfect flowering shrubbery and vibrant borders. More huge trees mass gracefully beside and behind them, spilling not a leaf anywhere and hiding, but hinting at, magnificent gardens and pools and who-knows-what-else...statuary, fountains, gazebos, guesthouses...all pristine and camera ready. There is nothing raw or raucous or ragged in the Northwest.

My father parked on the circular drive before the big gray stone house and carefully decanted my gaping mother.

"Everybody's out back," he said. "Let's cut through the house."

"Everybody?" squeaked my mother.

"Well, some friends of mine and I think Mom and Dad's, too," he said. "Everybody wants to meet you."

"How nice," Crystal said. It came out in a sheeplike bleat.

He took her hand and led her up the curved marble steps. The carved mahogany doors were closed but opened silently as he turned the knob. It flitted foolishly through Crystal's head that she would never leave these doors unlocked if they were hers. She looked up and saw an ivy-covered turret with deep shuttered windows on either side of the house, decided then and there she would sleep in one of the rooms one day, and followed Finch into the cool dimness.

She could scarcely see but got the impression of a vast drawing room with dark, gleaming furniture; a silvery-green papered dining room with the largest oval table she had ever seen, shining like a skating pond, and two great cabinets holding intricate crystal and china in patterns that reminded her vaguely of the Renaissance; an enormous kitchen, all blinding white and as clean as an operating theater. The entire house had an indefinable smell, one she had never smelled but would never forget: rich, deep wood polish, the museum-like scent of old and very good fabric, a diffuse sweetness like the breath of flowers, and something else...money?

"Hi, Corella," Finch said to the smiling black woman at the stove, who wore the only honest-to-God maid's uniform Crystal had ever seen, complete with little frilled cap.

"This is Crystal; you be sweet to her. She's special," Finch said.

"She sho' is," Corella said. "Tell that by lookin' at her. You mama 'n' them are out by the pool."

Crystal put out her hand and the black woman took it slowly, looking down at their joined hands, then back up with a wide smile.

"It's nice to meet you," Crystal trilled, realizing by Corella's look and Finch's small pause that one apparently did not shake hands with the help in Buckhead.

They stepped out onto a large, cool back porch carpeted with a faded Kilim and set about with flowered, deep-cushioned wicker sofas and chairs. Great bouquets of garden flowers and foliage—zinnias, asters, sunflowers, chrysanthemums, eucalyptus stems, feathery grasses—sat on the low glass tables. Small, shapely potted trees gave the porch the appearance of being nestled into an intimate forest. A ceiling fan turned lazily. Beyond the porch, down another flight of steps, lay the garden...and the pool, and the fountains, and the statuary and gazebo, and the guesthouse. It was the largest garden Crystal had ever seen outside *House Beautiful.* The sounds of splashing water and tinkling ice and low, amused conversation floated up to her. When it stopped, she knew that they had seen her.

There were perhaps ten of them: a striking woman sitting under an umbrella who looked nothing like Finch but was nevertheless undoubtedly his mother; a squat, dark man with a thick mat of wet hair over almost every inch of him, with a face like Julius Caesar's and wet bathing trunks, who had Finch's dark hair and profile and was, of course, his father; another couple of adults, deeply tanned and in swimsuits with half-filled glasses of something lime garnished; two tall, bronzed young men with crew cuts, also in tartan and madras swimsuits; and four girls with perfect white smiles, glowing tans, and little makeup, in swimsuits or sundresses. Every foot in the group was bare or sandaled. Most hair was wet and slicked simply back.

Every inch of Crystal felt as though she had had hot, shining black tar poured over her. The silk shoes seemed to have been suddenly magnified to Clydesdale proportions. She was able to furtively toss the flossy clutch into a potted ficus tree beside the back door, but otherwise there was no salvation at all for Crystal Thayer, come to be presented to the world of Habersham Road and the Piedmont Driving Club looking, as Bermuda would have said, like a mule dressed up in buggy harness.

"*Why didn't you tell me?*" she hissed at Finch, who had taken her arm preparatory to leading her down into the fatal garden.

"Tell you what?" he asked, mystified.

But his friends were streaming up the stairs to meet them and she did not reply. She herself did not know quite what she meant, only that her otherness was bone-deep and ineradicable, and always would be no matter what she wore.

They were wonderful to her. Never by so much as a raised eyebrow or the faltering of a smile did they let their condescension show. But Crystal heard it in every drawled syllable, saw it in every attentively cocked head. Perhaps it was not even there, but by the time the evening was over it did not matter. Hatred and a determination of a degree she had never known had been born in her breast. It did not truly die for as long as she lived.

"You're just as pretty as Finch told us," Caroline Wentworth said, hugging her lightly. Caroline's skin against Crystal's cheek was sun warmed and satiny, and she smelled of sun oil and tuberoses, and her amber eyes swallowed you whole. Her body, in a faded copper racing suit, was small and curved and neatly muscled. Crystal had never seen a muscular woman in her life. If a Lytton girl was so unfortunate as to have chiseled shoulders, she covered them no matter where she was. There was a vivid white scar like a lightning bolt that ran down Caroline's polished calf; she did not seem to notice it.

The imperial-faced, frog-bodied man who was indeed Finch's father hugged Crystal, too, a trifle too long and hard,

35

and said, "No wonder that boy didn't let you wear a bathing suit. You'd cause a riot."

Crystal went hot all over, at both his frank appraisal of her body and what she wore on it. The lack of respect was like a pinch on a buttock. She could not imagine her father saying it to anyone, most certainly the person his child was in love with. She could not imagine anyone saying it, for that matter, except maybe Sonny Prichard and his crowd in Lytton, who hung around Buddy Slattery's gas station and only dated girls from other towns, and only certain kinds of girls at that.

She darted a look at Finch, to see if he was going to defend her honor, but he only laughed, and the rest of the crowd did, too.

"Don't mind Finch's horrible father," Caroline Wentworth said, raising her beautiful coppery eyebrows and flicking her husband lightly with the corner of a towel. "His testosterone level is sky-high. He's been on the road too long."

Everyone laughed again, so Crystal did, too. The dialogue might have come straight from a Cary Grant movie. No, not Cary Grant. Steve McQueen, maybe. Nobody in Lytton...

They ate at a long table under two vast umbrellas beside the pool. It was laid with a vividly colored runner Caroline Wentworth said was a tribal scarf from Morocco. Tiny white lights fringing the umbrella sparkled off heavy, square crystal tumblers and the heaviest and most ornate silver Crystal had ever seen. Japanese lanterns glowed from the low branches of the nearest trees, and the candles were set about everywhere. It was a lush blue velvet night and the mothy, warm darkness was fragrant with the thick scent of ivory magnolias in a bowl at the table's center.

"Ron at Quelques Fleurs got them for me," Finch's mother said. "God knows where this time of year. But the garden at night has a kind of Moorish feel to it, I've always thought, and that thick, waxy smell always seems to me sort of exotic and Oriental. Besides, it covers up the bug spray. Wouldn't you think the damned mosquitoes would be gone by now?"

The evening did seem out of the world entirely to Crystal. Shawls and soft sweaters had come out to bloom over the women's shoulders, and the men had drawn polo shirts over their swimsuits. There was absolutely no sound besides the gentle lap of the pool and fountains and the droning of cicadas and the talk. Not a single street noise penetrated into the enchanted duskiness behind the house. There was not even the chink of silver on fine china. The perfectly broiled filets in mustard sauce Corella passed around were served on paper plates.

"Nobody but you, darling," said one of the older women to Caroline.

"Well, it's just a little backyard cookout, after all," she replied.

The evening seemed endless to Crystal, stopped in time. Swimming in candlelight. She sat near one end of the table, with Finch opposite his mother at the far other one. His friends were grouped around them. They drank what looked to be endless glasses of a pale green wine, and leaned in to talk to one another so that the candles underlit their sun-flushed faces, and laughed, and chatted, and laughed some more. Crystal smiled brilliantly the entire evening. None of the talk seemed to be about her.

Oh, they tried. She could see them remembering, breaking off in mid-warble and turning to her and saying something like, "Are your men in Lytton as awful as they are here? Well, of course they are. All men are awful."

And Crystal smiled.

All of them were, like Finch, out of college and into their lives. Crystal caught mention of bond sales and law clerking and volunteering at the Junior League. But all the talk seemed to center on schools.

"Do you remember him from freshman year? He told everybody his father was in oil and it turned out that he ran a gas station in Opp, Alabama, for God's sake...."

"...no, no, he did date her for a long time, but he ended up marrying some girl he met at his cousin's debut in Newark. I didn't know they *had* debuts in Newark...."

"...swear to God she did; I saw it with my own eyes. She was at the Old South Ball with Corny Jarrett and they were doing this really fast jitterbug and he swung her around and one stocking just popped right out of her bra and dangled down the front of her dress to her waist. It looked like somebody was stuck down in there trying to get out...."

A long silence fell into the candlelight and they all stopped and wiped their eyes and shook their heads and then, as if given a cue, looked over at Crystal.

"Oh, my God, we are all so rude," chirped a curly haired,

snub-nosed girl who was, Crystal thought, some kind of docent somewhere, whatever that was.

"We've just been sitting here all night yucking it up about our own precious selves and leaving you out completely. You must think we're barbarians...."

"No, no," Crystal said, still smiling. "It's all so interesting."

"So where did you go to school?" the docent said, seeming to quiver slightly with interest.

They all looked at Crystal.

Crystal played her ace. She had been wondering desperately how to work it into the conversation. Her smile faded slightly and she looked down.

"I haven't gone. Not yet. My...my mother is very ill and I've just sort of been, you know, sticking close. She...I... don't think it will be forever...."

There was a hush, and then they flocked to her and hugged her and kissed her cheeks and murmured what an angel she was, and how brave, and how hard it must be.

"I don't know how you do it," one of the other girls whispered.

"Oh, you'd do the same, if it was your mother," Crystal said softly, letting her gentian eyes slowly fill with tears and looking away.

When they said good night they all hugged her again and said they hoped her mother would be better soon and that they would look forward to seeing Crystal whenever Finch brought her home. More than one pair of eyes glistened.

Crystal smiled shyly around at them, stopping when she came to Caroline Wentworth. There were no tears in those amber eyes. Instead they sparkled with what appeared, incredibly, to be suppressed mirth. Slowly she inclined her head to Crystal.

After the good-byes and the plans to meet again and another too-hard, too-long hug from Finch's father, Crystal and Finch got into the car and ghosted down the drive and back down Habersham Road. It was true dark and smelled of honeysuckle, and a few of the huge houses had lit windows, but the purring of the motor was the only sound that broke the sweet autumn night. They rode in silence until they turned back out onto Peachtree Road again and the world flowed abruptly back around them.

"Well," Finch said, taking her small, warm hand in his. "What do you think?"

"About what?" she said carelessly, hugging herself in secret glee. No matter how it had started out, this night was hers.

"Oh, everybody. You know. The house..."

"I thought it must be like living in the Taj Mahal," she said with a rich little hill of laughter in her voice. "What happened to your mother's leg?"

"Oh...she fell off a racing camel in Kabul. It was a long time ago. I'm still not sure where that is."

Crystal threw back her head and laughed, a throaty little laugh of sheer exuberance with a sort of purr in it. In a moment he joined in, hugging her hard. She knew he had no idea under the sun why she laughed but loved the laughter anyway. And she knew that when they got home, before they went into her father's house, Finch would ask her to marry him. She knew that as surely as she knew that the sun would rise the next morning, or that the night would follow.

And of all the scenes from the jeweled, faultless tapestry of her life that unrolled before her, this was indeed her finest hour.

But she did not know that.

CHAPTER

3

About an hour and fifteen minutes above Atlanta, on State Highway 575, a smaller road, Talking Rock Road, cuts east and up into the ragged edges of the Blue Ridge Mountains. These are old mountains, among the oldest on earth, and they have been gentled by aeons of weather so that their peaks, though high, are rounded, voluptuous, instead of jagged like the newer, more savage, and often still-smoking mountains of the West. You will not drive long before you come to Burnt Mountain, the last of that dying chain, a great, wild excrescence that did not go gentle into the good night as its sister hills did but raged against the dying of the light.

Burnt Mountain is high, smoke blue from far away, a wild disgorged green when you are upon it. Its right flank, facing the distant bowl that holds the city, is gentler, the spiraling road open to wide vistas and scenic overlooks and friendly little lanes leading off through the woods to undoubtedly even friendlier places. For the first part of your ascent, the hollows and the foothills themselves are drowned, throttled in virulent seas of kudzu. It has taken houses, barns, cars, whole farms, a few telephone poles. Even these toy topiary habitats are beautiful, in a surreal way, if you don't think of them as ever having harbored life, ever having been slowly strangled by the inexorable green.

The left slope of Burnt Mountain is an almost sheer drop of shale and gravel ledges and great green cliffs to the valley floor. In that valley robust signs of human enterprise—gated communities, tiny strip malls—flourish. If human life flourishes up on that slope of the mountain proper, there is very little sign of it.

It was to Burnt Mountain that Finch Wentworth brought his bride, still in her car-spilling soufflé of seed-pearled white satin, for their honeymoon. They were headed for a small colony of old cottages in an enclave called Burnt Cove that rode the ridge of Burnt Mountain down to an icy little blue inlet of War Woman Lake. Burnt Cove had been the wilderness retreat for a small number of Atlanta families for many generations. There had always been Wentworths in the Cove, Finch said.

"Is it private?" Crystal asked when he told her about it, envisioning gates mounted with carved eagles and a discreet log sentry house. Beyond it, bridle paths and a low stone clubhouse.

"Jesus, no...or I don't think so, anyway," Finch said. "It's just kind of always been the same bunch of people. I don't guess all that many new people would appreciate the Cove now. It's seen better days. But I've always loved it. I used to come here with Dad a lot when I was a kid. You know I told you it's not fancy, honey, but it's all I have time for in the rest of Christmas break. Later on, in the summer, I'll take you anywhere you want to go. Mexico, the Caribbean… anywhere."

"The Piedmont Driving Club?"

"Food's awful and the nearest wildlife are the mosquitoes on the tennis court."

He laughed, liking it that his new wife was relaxing enough to joke about the lares and penates of his privileged life.

She wasn't.

A gravel road dipped down into the hollow that sheltered the approach to Burnt Cove. The road wound around a kudzu-garlanded shack—"caretaker's place," Finch said—and past a small, canted white board church. Its bare, swept yard had a hand-lettered sign that read: *Holiness Church of the Pentecostal Fire.*

"Isn't that great?" Finch said, looking over at Crystal. Her face was blank.

"Is that where y'all go to church?" she said finally.

"Well, no," he said, looking closer to see if she was still making jokes. It was impossible to tell.

"It's just an old mountain Pentecostal church; I'm not sure who goes to it. I'm sure of this, though: Whoever they are, they holler. It's been there as long as I've been coming up here. I just kind of like it."

"We could have gotten married there," Crystal said, and this time she was smiling.

44

He laughed aloud with relief. "Oh, right. That wedding would have blown the roof right off old Holiness."

"It was pretty, wasn't it?" Crystal said dreamily.

"It was spectacular," he said.

The little gray stone Methodist church in Lytton sat on the corner across from the post office. It was as old as the town, well over a century. Crystal had fretted when her mother insisted on having the wedding there.

"It won't hold half of Finch's friends and family," Crystal said. "And everything inside is all dull and...*old*. And Reverend Lively snorts when he inhales."

"It won't look dull and old when I'm through with it," Leona said. "And Reverend Lively won't have enough to say to snort. Besides, a woman is *always* married in her own church. Where were you thinking of having it, the Piedmont Driving Club?"

"Well, the Wentworths go to St. Philip's Cathedral in Buckhead...."

"You would be laughed out of Atlanta," Leona said, and that was that.

True to her word, the Methodist church looked neither dull nor particularly old on the day of the winter solstice, when Crystal Thayer married Finch Wentworth. It looked, as Caroline Wentworth said privately to her friend Ginny Hughes, "like a Christmas sale at Rich's. A good one, of course." The old wooden pews were garlanded in pink poinsettias and the altar was forested with them. Ruby the florist had almost lost her mind rounding up enough pink poinsettias to satisfy Leona Thayer.

"They all go to Sears and Kmart," Ruby said aggrievedly. Leona persisted, and the church billowed in a froth of pink, accented with fragrant evergreen boughs and garlands of smilax. Before the altar great crystal vases held huge, blooming magnolia boughs, their green leaves shining in the light of hundreds of flickering white tapers. ("And if you think it's easy to find blooming magnolias in December...," Ruby huffed.)

As a nod to the festivity of the season, Leona had tucked sprays of holly here and there in the greenery and woven tiny twinkling white lights through the altar magnolias.

"Where's the goddamn Santa Claus?" Big Finch groused in Caroline's ear, none too softly.

But the church glowed in the winter dimness and smelled of candle smoke and cedar, a really lovely smell, and Gladys Abbott on the ancient organ did not produce a single wheeze or squeal. When Crystal swept into the sanctuary on her father's arm in many yards of pearl-seeded white satin, carrying calla lilies with a few chaste holly berry stems, a great sigh rose to the eaves and hung there like a cloud. She looked, Finch thought, truly angelic, a vision of Raphael or Fra Angelico. Crystal had been born for this moment. In her chaste bridal glory she had moved even herself to tears, before the full-length mirror in the dressing room. They floated down the aisle on white rose petals strewn by her sister's youngest child, finger in nose, and ten bridesmaids—fellow cheerleaders and her two married sisters, one vastly pregnant—turned incandescent faces to her. Their holly-green velvet gowns drifted just so. Beside and behind Finch, his best man and groomsmen, most of them prep school friends, looked black and white and elegant, and stunned. The tiny tuxedoed ring bearer, looking like a grotesque munchkin, dropped the ring and wailed, but it was retrieved in one neat swipe by the best man and slipped onto Crystal's finger as if fitted for her, which of course it was. The Reverend Lively did not snort when he pronounced them man and wife, and when Gladys Abbott boomed out Mendelssohn the church bells pealed as if to salute a new millennium.

And so they were married.

There was no reception.

"Let us give you one when you get back," Caroline Wentworth said. "You're both worn out and you really don't have much honeymoon time. I promise we'll pull out all the stops."

"Where?" Crystal asked, envisioning once more the Piedmont Driving Club, with flowers and candles, all eyes on her.

"Surprise," Caroline said, smiling.

So it was that when they drove over the small, rattling bridge that spanned the inlet and into Burnt Cove, Crystal was still in satin and Finch in his tuxedo. In their bags, in the trunk of Finch's father's Mercedes, there were only jeans and slacks and sweaters and boots, because, Finch said, Burnt Cove gave new luster to the word "casual" and it would be cold. Crystal, however, had tucked in some velvet pants and a long wool skirt, for the club. Just in case.

But there was no club. In fact, there was no sign of life in any of the rambling old houses that crowned the ridge nestled next to the long meadow that ran down to War Woman

Lake. They were faded board and batten or age-scummed stone, and the trees leaning close in around them lifted straggling bare fingers to the steely sky. No chimney spouted sweet wood smoke. There were no cars.

Crystal looked over at her husband. Husband...? He was grinning with pleasure. She composed her face into a smile of anticipation.

"Is it just us?" she said.

"Probably. Nobody much comes for Christmas. But there'll be some people up afterwards, over New Year's. There's always a holiday hunt. Are you sure you really don't want to spend this Christmas with your folks? I know what we said, but..."

"Oh no," she said, squeezing his arm. "I want this Christmas to be just Mr. and Mrs. Finch Harrison Wentworth the Third."

She got her wish. The Wentworth house sat near the top of the ridge, looking far down on other houses and the muddy road and the frigid gray lake. It was large and sprawling, painted a weathered green almost indistinguishable from the moss that clung to its roof. Dead vines that would be luxuriant in the summer snaked up its small entrance porch and onto the steeply sloped roof. Behind the house the crest of Burnt Mountain beetled darkly against the wide, empty sky. A cluster of small buildings and sheds were scattered among the saplings behind the house. For one horrified moment Crystal thought one of them might be an outhouse. But then she saw that the windows were cheerfully lit and smoke curled from the stone chimney, and reason prevailed.

"This looks cozy," she said.

Finch got out of the car and came around and helped her out, and swept her up, satin and all, and carried her up the steps. Sharp spits of sleet hit their faces.

"Poor baby." He smiled into her hair. "It looks like six miles of hard road in winter. All the Cove does. But it *is* cozy. You'll see."

There was a swag of fresh cedar on the back door, tied with a bright red satin ribbon. And the kitchen, when he carried her in and set her down on her high satin heels, shimmered with warmth and smelled like heaven. A battered copper kettle on the equally battered stove simmered and sang. Crystal breathed in cloves and cinnamon and other spices, things that spoke of the mysterious East, and smiled in spite of herself.

"Russian tea," Finch said. "I don't really know what's in it, but Corella makes it every Christmas. She and Mother were up several times this week, and she came back up today to fix us some supper. Oh, she's not here now; she and Osgood have gone to Macon to see their kids. But I'll bet there's plenty of food in the fridge. Come see the rest."

Shadows leaped on the high living room walls, cast by the roaring fire in the great blackened stone fireplace and the lit candles set around the room. They were great, leaping things that seemed alive; the light didn't extend to the corners or the ceiling. There was a threadbare but once good Oriental rug on the floor, worn through to the boards in places, and sofas and chairs slumped around the room, none of the fabrics discernible in the dim light. Big islands of tables and trunks and benches and—Was that a piano?—loomed, and the walls were hung with what seemed to Crystal to be many kinds of violins and fiddles, plus a moth-eaten deer's head, forested with antlers, over the fireplace.

Crystal winced. Finch followed her gaze.

"Don't worry about ol' Buckhead. He didn't die at Wentworth hands. My father couldn't hit the side of a barn, so he bought him in a gun place somewhere in Alabama. We never said it wasn't his, of course."

"I'll remember," Crystal said faintly, looking around. There were wreaths and garlands of fresh greenery all about, and urns of holly bright with berries, and on the table behind the spavined couch stood a small fresh cedar tree trimmed in pinecones and strings of cranberries and popcorn, with apples and oranges for color, and white lichens for snowflakes. There were no lights, but on top rode a great, misshapen tin star, with shear marks still on some of its points.

"I made the whole thing, including the star, for the first time when I was about ten," Finch said, grinning. "We always said it was our Cove tree."

Under the tree were piles of wrapped packages. A couple of large ones sat by the fireplace. On the coffee table, which looked very much like a great barrel top, was a platter of cookies in the shapes of stars and bells and angels, all frosted with glittering white icing.

"Corella again," said Finch. "She always makes them, whether or not anybody wants them. Let's take a look in the kitchen."

The tiny, pine-paneled kitchen was darkened with the smoke of a hundred fires, and on one side many-paned glass doors looked out into blackness. The other walls were hung with an astonishing array of pots, pans, knives, cleavers, spoons, strainers, brushes, brooms, flypaper, and other things that Crystal could put no name to. A bulletin board held elderly messages, stained recipes, yellowing photos of adults and children on the hills and by the lake, accompanied by numerous dogs of no particular breeds. In all of them it was summer. In all of them everyone was laughing. Crystal wondered if she would ever know who any of them were.

The pine counters were stacked with bowls and toasters and brown paper bags and foil-wrapped bundles. When Finch opened the door of the chugging antique refrigerator she saw that it was overflowing with food: ham, roast beef, several pies, eggs, milk, bacon, butter, casseroles of every description, many bottles of wine, and one of champagne, with a red ribbon around it. A tag on the ribbon said: *TONIGHT!* On the middle shelf, alone, sat a small, beautiful wedding cake on a crystal plate, frosted and shining and embellished with flowers and tiny Christmas candies. On its top were a miniature bride and groom of spun sugar. Around the cake, more vivid holly rimmed the bowl. A note in Caroline Wentworth's distinguished back-slant hand said: "You'll have a much grander one at your reception, but you must go to sleep on your wedding night with a slice of wedding cake under your pillow." From the oven came the smell of something rich and winey and buttery.

"Isn't Ma something?" Finch said happily, and put his arms around Crystal and pulled her close to him. She put her arms around his neck, tipped her face up to be kissed, and then stopped. All of a sudden something—everything—the smells, the food, the leaping, lurching shadows, the utter blackness and stillness outside . . . all congealed at the base of her throat and she retched.

"Oh, Finch, I'm going to be sick!" she wailed, pulling away. "Where—"

"Here," he said swiftly, and jerked a door open. She stumbled into a small bathroom, with only a toilet and a washbasin in it. She just had time to see that the room was papered with *New Yorker* covers, most of them yellowing, before she jerked up the toilet lid and began to vomit.

She vomited for a long time. It felt as if she would never stop, that there was nothing inside her that would not be heaved from her stomach into this toilet on Burnt Mountain. But finally she did. She leaned weakly against the wall and finally gathered the strength to look at herself in the speckled mirror. Then she began to cry.

Her beautiful coiled blond hair hung in her face in wet, lank strands. He face was swollen and blotched. As much of her chest and shoulders as she could see was splotched with vomit, and the white pearled satin bodice had come unfastened and hung, splattered and stained, off one shoulder. She closed her eyes again, and cried and cried.

Finch hammered at the door.

"Baby! Let me in! God, Crystal, you sound like you—"

"No! Don't come in! Don't you dare!"

"Then come out—"

"I am not ever coming out!" she wailed, and he wrenched the door open and stared at her.

"Oh, my God, darling, what's the matter? Come here and let me see you!"

"No! I smell!"

He leaned her back against the wall and stared at her. Then murmuring and crooning, he held her close, rocking her as if she were a child.

"Finch, you'll get it all over you! Please just let me..."

He let her go and picked up fresh towels, wrung them out in hot water, and mopped her face and neck. With a damp washcloth he cleaned her hair and hands. He turned her around, carefully unbuttoned the tiny round satin buttons of her bodice and caught it when it fell to the floor, and put the whole satin bundle into the dirty-clothes hamper. Crystal stood, shivering and crying, her hands over her eyes.

"Step out of your shoes," he said, and she did, and then he unhooked the satin bra and slid the silk and lace panties down her legs and off and tossed them after the dress into the hamper. With warm, wet towels he continued to clean her beautiful naked body until it was polished, and had her wash her mouth out with a glass of icy springwater, and when she finally turned to him, white and shaking and unable to speak, he reached into the closet and pulled out an enormous terry robe, its fluff worn away but smelling of bleach and sweet soap, and wrapped her in it. And then he picked her up and carried her into the living room and lay down with her on the sofa before the fire.

For a while he simply held her. Then when the shaking began to subside and she began to whisper horrified apologies, he pushed himself up on one arm and looked down at her.

53

"Do you feel better?"

"Yes, but...I must look just so *terrible*...."

"You are the most beautiful thing in the world to me," he said, and kissed her face all over, and her neck.

"But I looked so pretty...."

"Well, you look just like you did, only you're naked. Do you think you weren't going to be naked on your wedding night?"

"Not like this! And you've still got all your wedding clothes on...."

He got up, stripped off the clothes and tossed them behind the sofa, and stood for a moment looking down at her in the fire- and candlelight.

"One way's as good as another," he said.

She stared up at him, this tall, lean man who shone in the light like a young pagan god, who looked to her just as she had imagined he would in the long nights in her bed in Lytton, when she could not sleep. Deep in her stomach, something old and slow turned over, curled, stretched. It was warm, almost hot. She opened her arms to him and, without even knowing she did, raised her hips on the prickly old sofa cushion, and moved them slowly.

"Yes, it is," she whispered.

It was.

I gave my mother her honeymoon. I gave it to her, backward from the future, not long after my own. By that time so much had been corrupted by her discontent, scalded by her bile, that it occurred to me, shamefully for the first time, that of all of us, her pain must be the worst. She lived so long with it, could not, as others could, walk away from it.

"My God," I said to the man who was my refuge, "she must be scarred on the inside from her brain to her stomach. Why didn't I know that about her? All this time and I didn't even know...."

"I don't imagine you were much in the way of being healed yourself until recently," he said. "Couldn't look till then. Now that you can, do you think you might begin to see her a bit differently? I don't think it would help her much, but it might do you a mite of good."

"I just honest to God don't know. I don't even know if I want to. It's not like there's ever going to be some great, tearstained reconciliation scene. We can't be anything else to each other than what we are. Can't you see that?"

"Yep." He breathed in a great, sweet-smelling lungful of smoke from the pipe he had recently affected and blew it back out, watching it curl into the twilight dimness of our back porch. The pipe had annoyed me at first, but I didn't think he liked it very much himself; he seldom smoked it. There was no sense fussing about it.

"But," he went on, in the thick, soft lilt that was like music to me still, "p'raps it would give you closure. Isn't that the word they're usin' now? 'Closure'?"

"P'raps it would," I said. And from then on, every so often, tentatively, as if I were afraid the memory might burn me, I began to look back at my mother, metaphorically narrowing my eyes so that the naked sight of her would not sear my retinas.

Not long after that I lay in my bath and opened my mind
to my mother. I stirred the popping bubbles in the eucalyptus bath salts with my foot and consciously thought about
her. I would, I thought, begin with her in a place I knew she
was happy and see where that woman led me.

"I'm starting with her honeymoon," I told my husband
when he ambled in and sat down on the edge of the tub, as he
often did. "Then, at least, I assume she was happy."

"Sure of that, are you?" he said, popping bubbles with his
long fingers.

"Well...why wouldn't she be? She'd just had that
humongous wedding and she was alone with him for the first
time, up in that mountain cabin...."

"You must remember as vividly as I do how she talked
about her honeymoon," my husband said, grinning as the last
mass of bubbles disappeared.

I looked at him.

"You know, 'That dinky little cabin up there on that god-
awful bare mountain, and cold as hell, and I threw up all over
my wedding dress and it never came clean and I wanted Lily
to wear it, and then it iced and we couldn't get out for days,
and I read old Mary Roberts Rinehart novels till I thought
I'd scream, and of course with nothing else to do we got Lily,
I bet by the second night....'"

"She was just talking...you know how she does, when
she tells a story about herself or Dad...."

He continued to look at me, a deep blue-eyed stare.

No. My mother had not had a happy honeymoon. So I
lay back in my vanishing bubbles and gave her one.

*   *   *

It did continue to ice and snow lightly on Burnt Mountain. In the dark early mornings, before the gray winter light came creeping into the bedroom, they could see the dancing stipple of snow light on the old ceiling and hear it ticking softly against the old glass panes and they would turn in to each other under the deep-piled quilts and the old goose-feather mattress would take them deep and they would make love again, sleepily, deeply, their skin hot against each other's. And they would cry out in joy and contentment, and go back to sleep, and when they awoke again, it was mid-morning and they would race, yelping, into the icy little bathroom and pull on soft sweats and socks and sweaters, and build up the living room fire that never really went out, and put on coffee to perk and then they would lie, intertwined, on the old couch under the thick old Chief Joseph blanket that belonged to it, and look up through the skylight at the opaque sky and watch the snow fall. Softly. Softly.

And my mother was happy. She had not really expected to be. Oh, she knew that her feelings for Finch Wentworth were strong and that she loved to look at him, and feel the hard pressure of his arms around her, but she had thought that their first coupling would be in a different bed, a sweet-smelling one with satin coverlets, perhaps at the Cloister at Sea Island, where so many young Atlantans honeymooned, perhaps even in the big tower room on Habersham Road that she had decided long ago would one day be their bedroom. Perhaps even there.

She had not expected Burnt Mountain, and she had not

expected that the long body next to and around and inside her could give her so much abiding sensation and ecstasy. She had not expected to willingly, even eagerly, spend so much time in bed and on sofas and even kitchen tables with him. It was the first great gift of her marriage, his to her. Those first few landlocked days she was steeped in him, tasted of him, swollen with him, aching for him. She, who had hoped to get the matter of where they would live, among other things, settled while they were on the mountain, thought of nothing but the next time he would take her into bed.

Days passed thus.

On the morning of New Year's Eve she woke up and looked over at him in bed. Before he could reach for her, she said, "Darling, I want to go home. I want to spend New Year's Eve at home. We always have scalloped oysters and eggnog and set off fireworks on New Year's Eve. I want to spend this first one with people and things I always have. Can we go home?"

He looked at her for a long while, smiling slightly, and then got out of bed, naked and shivering, and scrooched into his sweats and socks, and said, "I think so. Let me see."

She heard him on the telephone in the next room but could not hear what he was saying. When he came back into the bedroom he was grinning widely.

"Yeah, we can go home. In fact, it's a good time for it. Hop up and get dressed and let's get the car loaded. It's snowing in Atlanta, so we'll have to take it slow down the mountain. Should be a pretty drive."

"How do you know it's snowing?"

"I talked to them at school, to tell them to get the apartment ready early. It'll all be done when we get there."

He had decided that for the first few days they would stay in the apartment at Hamilton Academy that was set aside for the headmaster.

"It's not big, but it's big enough for the two of us, and it's perfectly comfortable when all the furniture's in place. I was having it redone while I was at your folks' house, and they tell me they can move the furniture in today and even stock the kitchen. We can go right there, and then on to your folks', if you want to."

She had not been happy about that at first.... "You mean live at your school? With all those children?"

"It's on another floor entirely. You wouldn't necessarily see a single student; most of them are at home for the holidays, anyway. And besides, it's your school, too, now."

"My school...," she had said slowly. "My school..."

She had not thought of Hamilton Academy in those terms before.

"We'll decide when we get there where we're going to live," he said. "I expect Mother and Dad will have some ideas about that...."

Buckhead bloomed full and living in Crystal's mind. Of course. Somewhere in Buckhead, near the big house on Habersham Road. Why had she ever worried about that?

"Let's go, then," she said, jumping out of bed. The floor did not even seem cold to her bare feet.

"What should I wear?"

"Oh, honey, anything. Something warm. They said it hadn't gotten above freezing down there in two days."

When he locked the door to the cottage in Burnt Cove, Crystal got into the car and did not look back. She never did, all the way down the winding, treacherous road to the interstate. She would never in her life remember the snow on Burnt Mountain, though my father would speak of it often as one of the most beautiful sights he had ever seen.

It was early dark, with light snow still falling silently, when they turned off the highway below Atlanta onto the smaller one that led up to the big wrought-iron gates of Hamilton Academy. The road home, so familiar to Crystal, was a strange snowscape, another country, rather eerie. Lit houses made holes in the darkness, but it was hard for her to identify them in the blue dusk. Only the one arch over the gates, with *Hamilton Academy* chiseled on it, was familiar. Once inside the gates, the road that led up to and around the school was dark and blue and white, punctuated only by occasional streetlights, and the lit mass of the school itself seemed small and far away. My father did not pull up to it but continued on the road around it, and beyond.

"Where are you going?" my mother said, wiping at the windshield and peering out. She saw nothing but darkness. Darkness and snow.

He smiled and continued on.

The road ended at a pair of stone gateposts that had once held an elaborate wrought-iron gate. The gate was open, and the pair of iron lampposts on either side of it were dark. A wrought-iron fence stretched away on either side of it, marking off a yard that could not be seen.

He stopped.

"This is the old McClaren place," she said, looking at him in puzzlement and annoyance. "What are you doing back here? There's been nobody in this old heap since that old lunatic died; I can't remember how long it's sat empty. It's falling down."

He smiled again and tapped the horn. The world bloomed into light.

The lamps lit, soft, yellow, snow collared. The long, straight drive down to the house flowered with lights; ground lights studded its border, the overhanging great trees, into uplit statuary. Torches and flambeaus had been set along the way, flickering on the snow, dancing off the drifted limbs and the smooth white gardens beyond. At the end of the drive a great three-storied Greek Revival house stood, its flat roof a field of shining white, its twin chimneys sending blue curls of smoke up into the night. Its four white Corinthian columns were twisted with greenery and its three black iron balconies draped with more. Every window shone with light, many with candles, and the massive oak front doors were open. Each wore a great Della Robbia wreath with fruits and red ribbons. From the car Crystal could see that the house was thronged with people.

It was a beautiful house, classically beautiful, shining with health and love, looking every inch as the old man who built it had envisioned that one day it would.

Crystal opened her mouth, but no sound came. My father put his hands tenderly on either side of her face and kissed her on her open mouth. There were tears in his eyes and on his cheeks.

"Mother and Dad have spent the last few months doing all of this," he said. "It's furnished, too. It's your wedding present and your Christmas present all rolled into one. And it's your wedding reception. Don't you remember? They promised you it would be special. Welcome, my baby. Let's go home."

He opened the door on his side and people flowed out into the night, people in long gowns and tuxedos, holding glasses aloft, smiling and cheering and calling out.

These next things I know: I know that my father's heart reached out to the house in sheer joy, for he loved it always. And I know that my sister, Lily, still barely joined cells in my mother's womb, reached out to it, too, for she also loved River House, as my mother but no one else called it. Maybe not as our father did, but in her own way. Even I, so long yet to be even dreamed of, but there, in him and in her, disparate cells waiting to become me, certainly must have held out arms-to-be, for the house was for a long time my one true haven and my home.

I did not try to see my mother's face. At that moment, I quit trying at all. I could give her a honeymoon, but neither I nor anyone else could give her a home.

CHAPTER

4

By the time I was toddling at warp speed round the house, it had lost most of its look of unearthly, radiant white perfection and was no longer a castle out of a fairy tale. It was still a beautiful house; even now I know there was none lovelier in Lytton and few anywhere else that I have seen. But it was by then only and always a house. It had been much lived in, and it bore its scars nobly.

There was a chunk out of one of its columns where Lily had smacked it, demonstrating her backswing to some smitten calf or other...there were always several mooing around us. One of its first-floor French doors had been smashed when the Steinway baby grand my mother had ordered for the living room missed its point of entry and the original old lintels and panes could not be duplicated. The new window, as it was always called, was fancy enough but always looked, as my father said, like a Band-Aid stuck on a wedding cake. During a Christmas reception for the entire school, two middle schoolers had set off cherry bombs on the second-floor balcony, and though the great smears of soot could be cleaned and painted over, the surrounding stucco was left perpetually pitted, as if peppered by a thousand BB guns.

And there was no way under heaven the scuff marks and handprints on the front doorsteps and doors could be contained. Hamilton students banged in and out of the house regularly, despite stern warnings from their teachers. The boys adored my father, and he them, and most of them thought the big house where their president lived was part of the school.

This drove my mother wild. One of my first memories is of sitting at the supper table while Nellie, our family's long-suffering and indispensable maid, led a fourth grader back to campus after he had come shouting in to show my father a badly squashed toad he had found in the driveway.

"When are those little monsters going to learn that it's *our* house?" she cried. "It's not the McClaren house, like everybody in Lytton calls it, and it's not the Hamilton House or the President's Residence, not to mention the Prez, like that entire blasted school calls it. It's the Wentworth house. Can't you get that through anybody's thick head over there?"

"Probably not, by now," my father said mildly, smiling at her. "What difference does it make? We know whose it is. And in a way, it is part of the school. I sort of like that they feel that way about it."

He excused himself to go and wash the mortal remains of the toad from his hands. I looked up at my mother. I was still in the bunny-painted high chair that had been Lily's, but it could scarcely contain me. The next step would be a regular chair with a pile of books on it.

"Is this really our house?" I said.

"Thayer Wentworth," my mother snapped. "Of course it's our house. Why on earth would you think it isn't?"

I thought perhaps I was edging close to the boundary between my mother's soft side and that other side, where every hard-edged thing from annoyance to displeasure and far beyond that dwelled. I always knew I had bumped the boundary when she called me by my whole name.

"That boy said it was the school's," I said.

"What boy?" Her voice was growing crisper, and I began to plot my escape route. Out of the chair, hang a quick right through the kitchen, out the back porch and down the stairs, and deep into the half acre of manicured greenery that was our back lawn as it ran down to the river.

"That boy that comes to see Lily," I said.

My mother gave Lily, who at twelve was a pastel sketch of what my mother had become as an adult, a complacent look. She was lovely as a fledgling and, as Nellie frequently muttered, "as spoiled as sour milk." This day Lily only lowered her eyelashes, not speaking. Mother knew which boy I meant. He was mouthy and slick and his parents ran a dairy farm. He was dead meat in this house, even if he did not know it yet.

"That boy doesn't know what he is talking about, as usual," Mother said.

"Well, I thought we lived in it because we all went to the school," I said.

"Nobody in this house goes to that school but your

father, and that's because he's the president. And besides, we run that school, not the other way around. Girls can't go to it anyway. It's just for boys...."

"Lots and lots of boys," Lily murmured, a small smile calling out the lone enchanted dimple in her left cheek. I had it, too, but to me it only looked as if someone had poked a pencil in my cheek.

"*Lily*...," my mother began.

I made my escape. I had reached the back porch before I heard my mother calling after me. I put on speed and bumped into my father, who was ambling toward the kitchen drying his hands on a towel.

"Oops! Where're you going, pocket rocket?" He smiled at me.

"Mama's gone over on the other side," I said.

"Is she mad at you?" he said, still smiling but not as broadly.

"I don't know. Either me or Lily or Lily's boyfriend. The one she always says has cow dookie on his shoes..."

"Oh, that one," my father said, and sighed. "Well go on and make your exit. I'll talk to her. She may be right about Lily's swain, at that."

"Don't you like him?"

"Oh, I like him all right," my father said, not looking over his shoulder. I could hear the laughter in his voice, though.

"But you can't have cow dookie in the house, can you?"

I pattered down the steps and into high June on the river, buzzing with faraway insects and trilling with birdsong and smelling of wild honeysuckle from the river woods and cultivated blossoms from our garden, and fresh-mown green grass. I twirled around three times on my bare feet and toppled over into the cool, damp grass, head back, face tipped up to the sun, eyes closed under its gentle fist. It seemed to me at that moment that every atom in my body stretched itself up toward the sun, that my blood sang with the air and the running river, and that I would forever be as happy as I was at that moment.

"What you don't know ain't gon' to hurt you," Nellie always said.

I would have occasion to remember that later, many times.

But for that brief, indelible interval between babyhood and first grade it was absolutely enough for me to be what my father called a mini-comet, blazing around the house and garden trailing fire from my head.

From the beginning it was actually painful for me to be still for very long, and my mother gave up chasing after me and dragging me out of trees or off the small muddy cliffs down to the river and hired a young black girl—Lavonda, Nellie's niece—for the position of Thayer keeper. Lavonda was perpetually smiling and sweet tempered, adept at her given task, had the IQ of a ten-year-old and the sleek, chocolate voluptuousness of a Harlem dancer. I absolutely adored her, and, I think, she me, because our minds ran along the same vivid, flowery fairy-tale track. I loved her stories of the terrible duppies who would drop down on you out of the trees at night, and the ha'nts that could only be kept at bay by painting your front door blue, and the various wonderful things you could make out of graveyard dirt. She listened, enthralled, to my lisped accounts of the Greek and Norse myths that I so loved, which my father often read to me. My mother thought they were not fit reading for a child, but he said, "Nonsense; they'll give her all the magic she needs."

"Why does she need magic? She's got to live in the real world just like the rest of us."

"That's why she needs magic. Some people need it more than others. The real world is not going to be enough for Thayer."

He had continued to read me the shining, shifting, bloody myths, and I continued to tell them to Lavonda. On the whole she got the best of the deal. She taught her smaller siblings never to be afraid when it thundered; it was only Old Thor banging around Asgard with his hammer. On the other hand, when I painted our front door blue (as far as I could reach) it wasn't comfort and accolades that I got. My well-deserved reputation as a troublesome child was born early.

I never thought my beautiful mother disliked me. Not then and even now, not really. I know now that what she felt for me was kind of a despairing puzzlement. There was not a thread in my entire fabric that seemed to come from her, or any other woman she knew.

My sister, Lily, was Mother in miniature, and there was a deep understanding between them even when Lily was behaving her worst. Lily's small sins were smearing herself with my mother's makeup, ruining her pretty satin shoes clomping up and down the stairs in them, giggling and flirting at school chapel services, throwing tantrums because she was not allowed to wear her pretty Easter outfit to school. Things that my mother might deplore but understood in her

68

deepest heart. Lily was a wellborn and beautiful little girl. Mother had been one of those things herself, at least relatively. She only had to look over her own territory to find the words that would best chasten Lily.

"Take those off. Nobody likes a little girl who makes herself gaudy and cheap. You won't have a beau to your name if you don't stop that. I don't want to be ashamed of my pretty daughter."

But that would not have worked with me, and Mother knew it even if she did not know what would.

"Do you want everybody to think you're a wild thing with nobody to bring you up right?" she said once, when I had stripped down to my underpants and smeared my chest with red mud and was creeping through the boxwood maze dragging my father's kindling hatchet after a sniggering Lavonda.

"Who are you supposed to be now?"

"I'm Smee. He scalped people in *Peter Pan*. He didn't cut off your whole head, though, just your hair. I don't think that sounds so bad, but the way Lavonda's carrying on..."

My mother launched a long, level look at the capering Lavonda and Lavonda straightened herself into seemly erectness and stood there, a veritable statue of biddability, her enormous breasts straining at the old Atlanta Braves tee shirt she wore.

"Take her inside and wash that mud off of her, Lavonda, and put Mr. Wentworth's hatchet back where it's supposed to be. And go in through the basement. I don't want anybody from the school to see you."

"Yes'm," Lavonda said sweetly, and my mother turned

and swept back into the house, trailing a cloud of Casaque behind her. She had come a long way since the days of My Sin.

"She sho' smells good," Lavonda said.

"It comes out of a bottle," I said.

"Well, I know that. I just wish I had a bottle of that."

"I'll get you one. I know just which one it is. She's got more than one of them. You just better not let on where it came from."

"You think I'm dumb?" Lavonda sniffed. "I ain't gon' wear it here. I'm gon' wear it to 'vival tonight. J. W. Fishburne's mama makes him come every night, and I'm gon' sit right behind him and fan my perfume at him. He'll notice me then, I betcha."

It occurred to me, even in my half-naked red mud days, that if J. W. Fishburne hadn't noticed her bazonkers by now he must be blind, but I said nothing. Bathed and dressed again, I ran into my mother's bedroom and swiped a half-full bottle of Casaque and gave it to Lavonda, and she swished home that afternoon with a heart full of hope and roughly a half a year's salary in her cotton tote bag.

"I don't know where that child gets it," I overheard my mother say to my father that night. The heating register in my upstairs bedroom was directly above the one in the downstairs sitting room, and through it, for most of my childhood, I heard all manner of things that I don't suppose would have ever been said to me.

"Certainly not from me or my mother, and she's absolutely nothing like Lily. If you had a sister, maybe..."

"I have Mother," my father said, "and from what I know of her when she was little, I know exactly where she gets it."

"I simply can't imagine Caroline ever—"

"Taking off her clothes in the backyard? Chasing people with a hatchet? You'd be surprised."

"I would indeed," sniffed my mother, and that was the end of the affair.

But still, I got my share of hugs and sweet-smelling cheek kisses, and she always read me a story and tucked me into bed at night. The stories ran more to "Jack and Jill" than *Peter Pan*, but I could count on my father for literary excitement. I loved it when my mother read to me, loved it all: the one lit lamp and the shadows leaping up the walls, the silky hush of the bedclothes when she drew them closer up under my chin, the rising and falling lullaby of her voice. My mother always had a beautiful voice. Lily has it, too.

When I started first grade, in the little Lytton elementary school my mother had gone to, and her mother before her, my mother had become the legendary hostess she seemed born to be and we had parties large and small at our house almost weekly. Many were for the school: alumni and trustees and faculty and very occasionally, say at Christmas or Easter, for the entire student body. I never tired of them: house shining and smelling of flowers and furniture polish and wonderful things cooking in the kitchen, the dining room spread with beautiful things, iced and decorated and parslied, the big Rose Medallion punch bowl that my grandmother Wentworth had given Mother ringed with camellias and smelling faintly of bourbon or gin and clinking with icebergs of tiny cubes, and most of all my mother, in something floor sweeping and bare shouldered, eclipsing every other woman in her house.

Except perhaps when my grandmother and grandfather Wentworth came, as they sometimes did. My grandmother Caroline drew eyes like a living flame. She always dressed simply, though her pearly shoulders might be bare—I think now that she tried never to outshine her daughter-in-law—and her copper hair, only slightly darker than mine, was always piled on top of her small head. She frequently wore a pair of dangling amber earrings that I coveted with all my heart. They matched her eyes perfectly. They were usually her only jewelry, but they gave her the appearance of being clad in a queen's ransom of precious stones. My mother would sometimes tighten her mouth at the sight of her, and I once heard my mother whisper to my father, "Those earrings are barbaric. How she dares, at a little party for a boys' school—"

"And yours, my dear, are brushing your shoulders." He smiled at her. He must have been aware by then that his wife was searingly resentful of the mother who did not ensconce her son and his family in the heart of Buckhead, but I truly don't believe it ever bothered him. He could have done little about it, anyway.

I liked first and second grades, I remember, though it seemed strange to me that there could be another school besides Hamilton, the one that so dominated our world. My father went there every day and often on weekends. My mother's very life was circumscribed by it. My sister, who at fifteen could have stepped out of the pages of *Seventeen* magazine—that was her bible—drew virtually all her suitors from it. And I was in and out of it almost every day because I would regularly break my mother's rule and escape Lavonda and dart across the front lawn and around the road's curve into the sweet, chalky dimness of Hamilton. It was, to me, simply another and larger part of our house. Invariably a long-suffering teacher would corral me and lead me by the hand to my father's office, or even home, and I would get the Hamilton-is-out-of-bounds lecture again. It made no sense to me and I never remembered it. Hamilton Academy was where my father was. Therefore, so would I be.

He died when I was nine years old and just beginning fourth grade. His father died with him. It was a brilliant iron-blue October day and my father and grandfather had driven up into the edge of the mountains above Atlanta, not far up Burnt Mountain from Burnt Cove, where my parents had spent their honeymoon, to look at the summer camp Edgewood, on the flank of the mountain, where many Atlantans had sent their children for generations. My father had summered there and thought that it might make a good summer adjunct for the school. I don't know what they decided. On the trip home my grandfather's stately old Bentley missed the hairpin curve at the first scenic overlook and soared up and out into the blue air and into the valley below, where the suburbs of Atlanta began. Whatever their decision, Edgewood never became a part of the Hamilton school. I suppose it would have been impossible, after the accident.

It happened while I was at school, and they told me when I

came clattering into the house with an armful of pastel drawings. We had been reading *Tom Sawyer*, and my drawings were full of a chalky, heroic Tom, whom I liked, and a stunted and squinting Becky, whom I did not. I was already yelling and waving the drawings in the air for Lavonda to see, but it was not Lavonda who came out of the kitchen to meet me. It was my grandmother Caroline, customarily elegant in a jade suit.

"Grand," I shouted, "look what I—"...and stopped. Her face was blotched and swollen, and tears ran down her cheeks.

I stared, terror rising in my throat like bile.

"Come here, darling," she said in a wet, rough voice, and held out her arms. I flew into them. I dug my face as hard as I could into her soft woolen shoulder. My own tears began. Whatever it was that could so twist and smear my grandmother, it could only be beyond bearing.

I don't remember what she said to me. I couldn't seem to hear her clearly. I pulled back and stared into her face for a long time, registering the tracks the tears had made through her mascara and the soft rose blush on her cheeks. The rest of her face was bone white, and her lipstick was bitten away from her mouth so that only a ragged rim of coral remained, outlining her lips. They were as white as her face. The amber eyes were dull and red and swollen.

Suddenly I couldn't remember who she was and broke away from her and ran into the kitchen, sobbing and hiccupping. Nellie was there, sitting on the kitchen stool with her face covered by her work-gnarled black hands, but my mother was not.

"Where is my mama?" I sobbed. "Where is my daddy?"

"Oh, baby, you come here to Nellie," she said, reaching out for me, but the silver snail's track of tears down her furrowed face frightened me even more, and I turned and ran up the stairs two at a time, stumbling, weeping. My mother's bedroom door was closed, and when I hammered on it my sister's thin, high voice called out, "Go away! You can't come in here now!"

My mother cried out something to me, but by that time I was back down the stairs, dodging my grandmother, and out the door and across the front lawn running for the school as hard as I could.

I burst in through the front door and down the short hall to my father's office. I jerked the door open and stood in the doorway, gasping in great swallows of air. A man sat at my father's desk, his head down, talking on the desk telephone, but he was not my father. I did not know this man. He looked up and saw me, and his face blanched, and he rose and made as if to come around the desk toward me, but I was frightened of him, too, and turned to run back home. My grandmother's arms closed around me again. As she led me from the school I heard the man say, "We're so terribly sorry, Mrs. Wentworth." But I did not hear what she said in return. Outside, on the still, sunny lawn, a man was lowering the flag to half-staff.

"Why is he doing that?" I croaked to my grandmother. It seemed to me that if only people would stop doing strange things the day would right itself back into its proper fading after-school somnolence.

"He's doing that for your daddy and your granddaddy," she said. "To show respect for their memories."

Her voice was still trembling, but it was stronger.

"I want my daddy. I want him to come home right now. Where is he?"

She stooped down so that she was kneeling in the gravel of our driveway and put her hands on my shoulders and looked into my face. I saw as if for the first time how very much like her my father looked.

"Thayer. He isn't coming home. He and your grand-daddy died. I told you that. Their car ran off Burnt Mountain. It was very, very quick and it couldn't have hurt them at all. But your daddy can't come home anymore. You mustn't think he will."

I cried all that afternoon, lying on my bed with my flowered comforter drawn up over me and my grandmother's arms tightly around me. She pressed her face into my hair, but she said very little. Sometimes she rocked me, and sometimes she hummed into my ear. Once she sang, so softly that I could scarcely hear her, "This is the dawning of the age of Aquarius, the age of Aquarius, Aquar...ius...."

It was years before I considered what a strange song it was for my grandmother to be singing to me on the day of my father's death and how even stranger that she, who had lost both a son and a husband, could comfort me while my mother and sister clung together in their prostration and could speak to no one, could see no one but each other.

Life changed of course, after that, but not so much as it might have. My father's substantial endowment from his grandparents came to my mother, and we stayed in the beautiful old white house by the river, and Nellie and Lavonda and the grounds people stayed on with us. Once I overheard my mother saying to one of her friends who had come to make a condolence call, "At least we still have the house. That's a great comfort to me, and I know it is for the girls. I can't think how terrible it would be for them if we'd had to move."

But I wished we had moved, wished it with all my abraded heart. Our house was terrible beyond words to me without my father. Everywhere I was used to seeing him was a howling, empty space. After a while I grew actually afraid of those spaces and would not go into them. I would not watch television with my mother and Lily in the big den. He was not there, but his books were, shelves and shelves of them reaching from the floor to the ceiling, and they all seemed to me to be threatening to spill over and engulf me. I would not eat dinner in the dining room. Eventually we all took our meals at the smaller table in the breakfast room, and my mother never ceased telling me and others what a willful child I had become. I absolutely refused to even pass the door to my father's study, and soon that door was closed and never reopened.

And I was, of course, forbidden to go near the Hamilton school. The new president and his young wife were an attractive couple and lived in the private apartment at the school, and my mother was still invited to the big formal evenings. She often went, resplendent in her long dresses and her jewelry, still beautiful as ever, perhaps even more so now, with the richness and patina of widowhood clinging about her like smoke. Indeed, until I went away to college she was still the Queen Mother of the Hamilton school and no decision was made without her input. For technically, she as well as my grandmother owned Hamilton now. The school was my mother's calling and her definition. I do not know what would have become of her without its vast presence at her back, like a sheltering fortress.

Lily wore the mantle of bereaved daughter with tremendous grace, and the stream of young men from Hamilton hardly abated. But I had neither grace nor fortitude, and my behavior at home and at school crept beyond willfulness into intractability and out-and-out anger. I was perpetually furious; I couldn't have said at whom. The rage was at my father, of course, for abandoning me, but no one ever seemed to consider this, least of all me, and my tantrums and sullenness soon strained every part of life in the white house on the river.

I hid from everyone when I could, staying in my room with the door locked or in the underbrush fringing the river. I made a small house for myself there, in a hollow between the roots of a great live oak, and thatched it over with broken branches and laid an old oilcloth table covering on the ground and took a pillow and blanket into the house, and there I stayed, when I was not in my room, until someone sent Lavonda to flush me out. She was the only person in the big house who knew about my hideout; at least I think she was. No one else ever came there. When I was in my cave I felt, if still disemboweled with grief, at least secure, not called upon to interact with people who did not seem to me to remember that my father had died.

I felt comforted only by my grandmother Caroline, but after that first terrible two or three days I did not see much of her. She asked my mother once if I could come to Atlanta for a while and stay with her, but my mother said no, she needed me close by. It was Lavonda who told me this. I knew that it was a lie and a terrible one. My mother did not need me close by. She did not even want me close by. Hardly a day passed that someone at my school did not call my mother to report my transgressions. It was, if anything, worse than at home. At school hardly anyone had known my father. I set out to punish them all for that.

It was a long time before I remembered that I had not gone to his funeral. I never did remember why that was.

After perhaps half a year of those phone calls and my behavior at home, my mother took me out of school at Lytton and enrolled me in a small private boarding school a few miles south, in Newnan. It was called the Paley School, after its founder, who was not only a devout Baptist but a missionary as well. It did not bill itself as a parochial school, but upon setting foot in it you could smell the Baptist-ness rolling off it like the scent of tar from fresh pavement.

I stayed there almost three years.

It must have been a pretty dreadful place. I vaguely remember the fact that I hated it, but mired in the swamp of grief over my father I could not differentiate between the two great, sucking whirlpools of that year. It occupied a grand old house on many manicured acres, three stories of stucco and stone that had been the home of one of Newnan's first family of millionaires. There had been many in the little town and, I believe, still are. The first floor was a large reception room that once had been the "consuhvatory," as Miss

Paley, headmistress and granddaughter of the founders and so cloyingly gracious that she was loathed by all the captive girls, though much admired by their parents, always called it. The second story was classrooms, small and beautiful, with high ceilings and crown moldings and mahogany paneling. The third was a vast attic lined with narrow beds, each with a trunk at its foot, two small bedside tables, a potty-chair, and drawable curtains around it. There was no carpeting, only one great white antiseptic bathroom, and no bed had a light or a lamp beside it. We went to bed just after our dinner and an hour or so of curdled piano music courtesy of Miss Paley, and most of us stared silently at the ceiling for what seemed hours before sleep took us. Talking was forbidden. Getting out of bed except for the potty-chairs was punishable by expulsion.

I would have explored this option in my first weeks at Paley, but it would only have meant going home. My grandmother Caroline stayed in Europe or at Sea Island or in the homes of friends all over the country most of that first year, and when I came home on weekends it seemed to be a big house I had never known, where two women, a young and not so young, went about their intimate and intricate female business that had no place for me in it. Lavonda left after I went away to school, and Nellie, infirm and diminished by my father's absence, retired. In her place we had Juanita, young, just finishing high school, pretty, poised, and viperishly mean, at least to me. She did not like my sister, either, I realized at once, but she dimpled prettily at Lily and wore her outgrown clothes with a model's grace. Juanita adored my mother.

By the end of my third year at Paley I was silent, sullen, mistrustful, thin to the point of boniness, and so self-isolated that being around large groups of people was almost tantamount to drowning.

In the summer after my third year, when I was twelve, two things happened. My grandmother's lameness worsened dramatically and she moved in with us, bringing her big old Mercedes and her chauffeur, Detritus, with her. ("Don't ask," my grandmother said.)

And I went, for the first time, to camp.

CHAPTER

5

W hy on earth here?" my mother fumed to her friend
Polly Thornton, not long after Grandmother Caroline settled in on the third floor. "She could have had all the
help in the world in her own house. She could have gone into
an assisted-living place. There's one in Buckhead that looks
like Versailles. She could have bought herself a wonderful
condo. What does she want in my house?"

"Well, technically, it always was my house, you know, dear!"
my grandmother called pleasantly from the screened porch,
where she was reading on the chaise lounge. "You remember
that we gave it to Finch for his lifetime. After that, of course,
it would have come to you and the girls anyway. But I knew
you had this whole floor, and I wanted to be nearer to my
family. I don't have that much left of it, you know."

"We could easily have come to Atlanta, Mama C.," my
mother called back sweetly, grimacing at Polly.

"I was tired of all that Buckhead business, Crystal, and you would not have been happy there. I know you think you would, but believe me, it's really very enervating."

"I just mean it was a shame to sell that beautiful house," my mother said, a badly contrived lilt in her voice.

"Well, look at it this way. The sale of that beautiful house will put Thayer through college and then some. I know she was thinking about Vassar, or some place in the East. That's not cheap."

"I never heard her say a word about Vassar," my mother snapped. "Georgia State is just fine for her. I can't imagine how I'm going to get Lily through Agnes Scott."

"You're hardly poverty stricken, darling," my grandmother purred. "And she's talked to me about the East. Perhaps you just didn't hear her."

"I hear my daughter," my mother said icily, and from the porch I heard my grandmother laugh softly. I was hiding behind the thick velvet drapes that could be drawn to shelter the living room from the rest of the house. It was the best place in the house for spying.

"The hell you do," I whispered to myself, stung. I could not remember a time my mother had really heard what I was saying, although to her credit, I did not say much to her. It seemed, in that submerged and lightless year, simply too much trouble to talk to her, or almost anyone else.

I could talk to my grandmother, though. I don't remember if I always could or if it began that year, but I could and did chatter to her as easily as I had prattled to Lavonda when I was much smaller. I think it was my grandmother's eyes. Those golden-amber eyes, my father's eyes and mine, too, though not as striking on me, seemed to swallow my tumbled words like a honey pot might honey. They widened, or crinkled, and sometimes even filmed slightly with tears, but they received my words and, somehow, all of me. I idolized her. It was the way I should have felt about my mother, I knew, and I often felt a bit guilty about it. My mother knew it, too. It did not stop me from haunting my grandmother Caroline like a small, fierce spirit.

"You are going to drive her crazy," my mother said at the beginning of summer. "She doesn't want a twelve-year-old sticking to her like a burr all the time."

"Yes, she does," I said, my temper veering up crazily as it had been doing all that strange year. "You're just mad because she never talks to you."

It was the start of a real vendetta, and though I knew I could have ended it by apologizing, I refused to do so. I must have seemed to my mother that year a malevolent changeling. Sometimes even I did not know where all the anger was coming from. Lily was in her last summer session at Agnes Scott in Atlanta, and I was undeniably a bad substitute for her.

"You know what?" my grandmother said at the dinner table one evening, when the vendetta flared over the vichyssoise she had taught Juanita to make. "I think you might enjoy going to camp. I always did, and so did your father. He went to Edgewood."

"I won't go to Edgewood!" I cried, remembering that it was from there that my father had soared away from me. "I will never go there!"

84

"No, of course not. But you might like Sherwood Forest, in the North Carolina mountains. I loved it when I was your age. It's on a beautiful lake, and there are little log cabins all around it where the girls sleep, and swimming and archery and horseback riding and singing and stories around the campfire at night, and the food is really good, for camp food. You'll make friends you'll have all your life. I know I did. My treat, of course."

The image of an endless blue lake and the flight of an arrow arching from its bow bloomed in my mind, followed by one of regimented ranks of older and prettier girls in spotless shorts and blouses glaring at me down perfect noses.

"I'm not going to any camp," I muttered.

My mother looked at me and then at my grandmother, nodding her head up and down. I know now exactly what was going through my mother's mind: All summer. No money out of my pocket. Atlanta girls. Atlanta girls have Atlanta families, and they'll be people just like Mother Caroline. They'll visit us and we'll visit them. They'll have sons who will love Lily. They'll take her to Piedmont Driving Club, and me, too.

"Of course you're going to camp," she said. "It's a lovely idea. Thank your grandmother, Thayer."

I did not lift my head.

"Your father would have loved for you to go," my mother said.

I looked up at her slowly, ready for battle once more. But she had played her trump card, and she knew it.

"Yes, he would have," my grandmother said, smiling at

me. "I think it's just what he would have wanted for you this summer."

And so, in late June, suitcases crammed with regulation camp wear and my mind reeling with Camp Sherwood Forest rules, I got into the Mercedes with my mother and grandmother, and Detritus nosed the car out of our driveway and toward the Great Smoky Mountains and the rest of my life.

Sherwood Forest isn't there anymore. It closed in the early 1990s, apparently for lack of nourishment. I only learned that soon after I was married. Three of my friends and I were drinking coffee and talking about our childhoods. When the talk turned to summer camps, I felt a fish flopping in my chest but for a moment could not think why. I had buried camp deep.

"I went to Sherwood Forest in North Carolina, just south of Murphy," Eloise Costigan said. She was only a few years older than me.

"I loved it. Most of my friends went. I think we must have driven our counselors nuts. Did anybody else go there?"

The other two chimed in with their own camps, neither of them Sherwood Forest.

"What about you, Thayer?" Eloise said.

"I didn't go to camp," I said, smiling sunnily, and then a huge, sucking nausea took me and I only made it to the bathroom seconds before I threw up.

"Are you pregnant?" Eloise said.

"No," I said, striving for normalcy in a voice that wanted to wobble into tears. "But the eggs tasted funny this morning. I should have tossed them."

"There's no egg worse than a bad egg," Eloise said. "Well, anyway, I really wanted my two girls to go there, but it closed in the late eighties. By then everything was tennis camp or computer camp or Bible camp, or some 'special' thing. One of my friends' kids is going to Indian culture camp in Virginia. 'Indian' as in Hindus and saris. I'm glad I got to Sherwood Forest before everything changed. One of the neatest things about it was that there was a boys' camp right across the lake, Camp Silverlake. The boys came over for campfire two or three times a week with counselors out the kazoo, of course. But it was fun. I met my husband there. I always told him it should have been called Camp Silverback. Some of those kids were way ahead of their time. Lord, Thayer! Are you going to throw up again? You need to go to the doctor."

"I'm fine," I said, waving my hand at her. "But I think I'll go get a Coke. I don't want to taste egg all day."

The nausea didn't quite pass, and I went home early and stretched out on our bed. Flat on my back with a cold, damp cloth on my head, I decided that I might as well think about Camp Sherwood Forest again. Get it sorted out in my mind once and for all. Move past it and go on with my life. Physically I had gone past the summers I spent there, but somehow it seemed to me that when I looked back there was a chasm in my life that had swallowed those years and they simply weren't available to me.

"That's ridiculous," I said to myself. "That's most of my adolescence." I had loved Sherwood Forest with all my heart. Not at the very first...predictably, most of the other girls were indeed Atlanta girls and had known one another since birth, and my shyness turned me nearly to stone. Even the few who tried to befriend me were met with what my grandmother Caroline called my ice princess demeanor. But somewhere in that frigid first week I turned out to be, totally to my own surprise, a really good horseback rider. Accomplishment of any kind is much admired among the young. After that the walls began to crumble.

I had never been around horses much. I didn't have eight-year-old crushes on them, never, as many of my new acquaintances did, knew the names of every Kentucky Derby winner back to the first, never lobbied for a pony. I wasn't afraid of them. I just didn't think about them.

But my first time up on one of the campus's well-groomed and trained horses, I felt as if I had melted into the saddle, was all a piece with the sleek breathing, living flanks my calves and thighs gripped. I tightened my legs. The horse, a small roan mare named Lady, moved off in a smart trot. I tightened more, joy beginning to flower in my chest. Lady broke into a rocking horse canter. I threw back my head and shouted aloud, wordlessly, in ecstasy. Lady picked up her stride. I had sailed with her over the smooth riding trails for perhaps a half mile before the thudding of hooves behind me penetrated my consciousness and I turned my head, hair stinging into my face. Luanne, our equestrian counselor, was coming hard behind me on a pinto, shouting, "Hold on, Thayer! Just hold on! I can get her to stop; just hold on!"

"I don't want her to stop!" I shouted back, and Lady moved into her full gallop.

I could feel her rev up like an engine between my legs.

The forest whipped by, with occasional flying glimpses of blue from the lake, and we ran until I could feel Lady's muscles begin a fine, delicate trembling and I slowed her, and we turned around and walked back to the stables. On the way back we met two of the mounted counselors who had been pursuing us. After a good scolding for me and a rubdown and water for Lady, one of them said, "I never saw Lady move like that. Why didn't you tell us you were a rider?"

"I don't like to brag," I said sweetly. Whether or not I have ever wanted to admit it, there is more than a little of my mother in me.

That night at the campfire, two of the prettiest and snottiest of the Atlanta girls, both a little older than me, came and sat with me in the circle.

"You're the best rider I've ever seen at Sherwood, and I've been coming a long time," one of them said.

"You looked like the Winged Victory of Samothrace, or something, with your hair flying all over the place," said the other, who was known to be literary. "You're pretty anyway, but on that horse you looked really beautiful."

I ducked my head and mumbled something. That night, brushing my teeth, I examined my face closely. It had not changed; it was the face that had been looking back at me for years.

"What is 'beautiful'?" I whispered to me, mouth full of foam. "How could I be beautiful? Nobody has ever told me that before."

And then I remembered a little passage with my mother and grandmother the winter past, when I had come in out of the cold on a January weekend and taken off my cap, shaking my hair free.

"Pretty girl," my grandmother Caroline said. "You are my pretty, pretty girl."

"I don't want her spoiled," my mother had snapped, and I didn't pay much attention to my grandmother, anyway. Weren't grandmothers supposed to say things like that?

Now, though, in the cloudy, underwater camp mirror, something happened to my face. It was as if a light had been turned on behind it and my features seemed to rearrange themselves and slide into a different pattern. I didn't know if it was beautiful or simply strange, but it was different. That frightened me, and I went to bed and stared longer that night out into the star-pricked blackness visible over the line of evergreens out our windows. Whatever else I was, I was also a maybe-pretty girl who could ride a horse, as Luanne said, like greased lightning.

That one moment and that first summer at Sherwood Forest got me through the next four years at Paley and countless weekends at home. My mother was rarely in a good mood for many of those weekends; Lily had forsworn the Hamilton boys and moved on to Lytton town boys, finally settling on an almost perfectly square high school fullback named Goose Willis. Nothing about him was gooselike; he had practically no neck at all, the little he did rising stubbly from enormous shoulders. He had a handsome face, but I thought he looked like a photo from a movie magazine pasted on a square butter box. It was not, however, Goose's looks that upset my mother but his lineage. His eminently respectable mother worked as a teller at the Lytton Banking Company and went to our church, but it was widely put about that she had never married Goose's father, who had disappeared before the unfortunate gosling was even hatched.

"I won't have it," my mother said over and over to Lily.

"Then I'll run away and marry him," Lily said calmly, and just before my last summer at Sherwood Forest, when I was seventeen and a counselor myself, she did just that. If my mother thought that event was the summer of her discontent, she had another thought coming.

That was the summer I met Nick Abrams.

Sherwood Forest had given me two real ambitions, where before there had been none. The first was related to my love of the stories, myths, and legends I heard about the campfire at night. Added to the delight of the myths my father had read to me in my early childhood, the sense of sheer story became an abiding joy. I knew that somehow I would make it a part of my entire life, though I did not yet know how.

The second was to be a Sherwood Forest counselor. Counselors at Sherwood Forest who oversaw our lives for two short summer months became demigoddesses to me. They were assured, competent, affectionate, and mostly very pretty. Or at least, they were to me. They had a kind of glamour, lent them by their exalted status and the lives they led. I had by that time become a world-class eavesdropper. I listened to them shamelessly when they talked among themselves, in the dining hall at mealtime and at night after they had tucked us into our double-decker bunks and pulled up the heavy, woolen blankets. I would pull my blanket almost completely over my head, breathing in its delicious smell of damp and smoke and pine needles. Even now that smell is nectar to me. My husband teased me a great deal about my favorite scent being that of a wet blanket.

From under that blanket I heard the stories of very special lives: best friends, spend-the-night parties, boyfriends and semi-boyfriends and discarded boyfriends, dates and proms and evening dresses, whispered tittering tales of the backseats of cars and nighttime swimming pools and something mysterious and miraculous called the pill.

I thought that if I could only become a Camp Sherwood Forest counselor, that life would be mine, too. The fact that throughout my early teen years I knew practically no boys except the forbidden students at the Hamilton school meant little to me. If I became a counselor, the boys would appear. They did, after all, at Sherwood Forest: We all knew that the young male counselors from Silverlake across the lake spent many evenings with our own counselors in the recreation hall and often behind it, in the dark and silent woods surrounding the lake. If I was a counselor at Camp Sherwood Forest, there would be no one to tell me, as my mother did, that I was too immature to date and there were no boys of proper lineage in our immediate vicinity. When, the spring after my seventeenth birthday, the camp wrote asking me if I would consider being their counselor in charge of fireside evenings, I had had only four or five dates in my life and those had been an agony of shyness and social ineptitude. I finally figured my mother was right and accepted no more invitations. I got few, anyway.

But I left that summer with wings in my heart, sure that my life was about to change.

I was right about that.

At the end of my first week as fireside counselor I decided to end the evening early. I was still feeling my way through the world of story, and I had given them too much to digest. I started out with "Theseus and the Minotaur," progressed to "The Trojan Horse," and finished up with "Leda and the Swan." Hands sprang up like wildfire when I finished that one.

"But what did the swan do to that lady?" was the first question, and I could not answer it. Somehow it never had occurred to me to ask my father. I loved the myth for its grace and yearning and beauty, the lovely young nymph, the air full of fluttering pure white wings. What was truly going on had never entered my mind.

I was silent for a moment. What had I let myself in for? From across the fire, in the darkness beyond its leaping red heart, came a deep masculine voice with laughter in it.

"The swan was Zeus in disguise, and he diddled old Leda right and proper," it said. "Didn't anybody ever tell you that Zeus was a serial rapist?"

All the young campers gasped. I knew that the question was directed at me. I stared stonily in the direction of the voice, hoping my stare was as effective as my mother's. In truth I had no idea that Zeus as the swan had raped Leda. I barely knew what rape was.

The other male counselors from Silverlake, who had come over to sit in on the last of the campfire as they often did, laughed uproariously. I swept them with the Look. Tonight was the first night they had come, but I recognized most of them from previous years. I felt my face and neck flame.

"Tell her about it, Abrams!" one of them called, and another shouted, "You girls better look out for them swans. You see a single feather, you run tell your counselor. Maybe she'll have it figured out by then!"

"Bedtime," I said crisply. "Lights-out in twenty minutes. Everybody back to the cabins."

They muttered mutinously, as they always did, but they got up and headed for their cabins. I stayed behind to put out the fire, my face still burning. I had emptied the pails of water kept there for fire extinguishing and was about to stamp on the embers when a voice directly behind me said, "I'm sorry. That was a cheap shot. If any of them tell the directors, I'll probably get canned. Unless you're going to tell them?"

It was the deep voice from the other side of the campfire. I did not turn around. I did not want its owner to know that I was still blushing.

"You'd be right to do it," the voice went on, and I did turn around then.

He was all-over brown. In the dying firelight he looked a molten copper brown, from the tangled hair that flopped over his forehead, to his deep-shadowed eyes under strong brows, to his bare feet on the grass. His straight nose was peeling in strips, exposing patches of tender pink underneath, and when he smiled I could see that there was a chip out of one of his front teeth. It looked like a recent accident; somehow I could not imagine that a Silverlake counselor's parents would let him go around with a chipped tooth. He wore a white tee shirt with the Silverlake emblem on it, and he had broad, bony shoulders and big feet and a sprinkling of freckles across his cheekbones. In the dying firelight he looked half-Indian, a Plains Indian perhaps, with the slanted eyes and the all-over brown, but his accent was purely and thickly southern as sorghum syrup.

"I'm Nick Abrams," he said. "I guess you can tell I'm from Silverlake by the cool threads. Who are you?"

"I'm Thayer Wentworth," I said, feeling the heat spread up my face again. "Are you always that brown?"

"Almost always," he said. "I live on the Georgia coast. Lots of sun on the coast. Are you always that red?"

I felt the anguished shyness rise in my throat for a moment and then surprised myself by laughing.

"Almost always," I said.

We stood silent for a moment, he studying my face, I looking everywhere but at his.

Then he said, "If you're going back up to the cabins, I'll walk you."

"Thank you," I said, still not moving.

He took my hand and tugged it lightly, and I followed him out of the smoking fire pit and up the pine needle–slicked hill toward the log cabins, where the din of young girls going to bed was rising. We did not speak again until we reached the silver-weathered front door, and then he said, "See you tomorrow," and I said, "Yeah, see you."

Only then did he drop my hand.

CHAPTER

6

"Abrams, you said?" my mother asked delicately, tapping her napkin to her lips.

"It's a fine old St. Simons Island family, Crystal," my grandmother Caroline said, smiling across the wooden picnic table at my mother. It was her cool-amused smile.

"What's on St. Simons?" my mother said, studying the pallid iced tea in her sweating glass. "I've never seen anything but tourists and that silly pink hotel on St. Simons. We don't pass it on the way to Sea Island, I don't think.... Is the family in the tourist business?"

"Department stores," my grandmother said, still smiling. "Several of them along the coast. Quite substantial. This young man's grandfather was in the Driving Club with Big Finch and me."

"Abrams? The Driving Club?"

"They manage it a bit better than you do, my dear."

I watched the exchange in puzzlement.

"What's the matter with Abrams?" I asked.

"Oh, Thayer, really! You can be so abysmally dim sometimes. Abrams is a Jewish name. I was only surprised because I didn't think…people of his religion came to Sherwood Forest."

"Why not?" I persisted. "Why wouldn't they come?"

I was honestly puzzled. There had never been much prejudicial talk about Jews in Lytton, that I had heard, anyway. It was all against the blacks. I see now that it was simply that we had so many more blacks than we ever had Jews. In my childhood, Jews did far better in the cities. Not always good, God knows, but better. I don't think Lytton had any Jews in those torpid years, and I wouldn't have known them as such if it had.

"You didn't even know he was a Jew, did you?" my mother said in exasperation.

I did not reply. I had not known. The question of Nick's ethnicity had never come up. I knew about his family and his house and the island and his friends and what they did and what they dreamed of doing, even his multiple dogs. But he had never mentioned religion or church, and neither had I. By the time it might have come up we were so closely bound and nearly alike that I simply assumed we shared the matter of church, as we did almost everything else.

"You have only to look at him," Mother went on, reaching for a sugar cookie and then putting it back. "Dark all over. Those eyes and cheekbones…"

"You sure could have fooled me," my grandmother said,

stretching her tan legs out to the July sun. I stared at her. To my knowledge, nobody had ever fooled my grandmother.

"I would have said Native American, maybe, if I didn't know his family. An Iroquois, maybe, or a Cherokee..."

"Well, he seems a nice, polite boy, for all that," my mother said, her tone ending the matter, and stood up. "It's time we started home, Mother Caroline," she said. "It'll be well after dark when we get back, and I don't like driving at night...."

"Detritus does quite well at that," my grandmother said, but she, too, rose, leaning heavily on her cane. "He *is* a nice boy, Thayer. Bring him to see us when camp is over."

My mother looked sharply at her, and Grand said, "Oh, for goodness' sake, he can sleep in the garage with Detritus if it upsets you to have him in your house. He'd probably be more comfortable there, anyway."

By this time Detritus had pulled the Mercedes down to the picnic table and was handing the two women in. My mother hugged me, and Grand did, too.

"It seems a long time that you've been away," she said. "It will be good to have you home. Unless you'll be visiting your Nick at St. Simons?"

"No," I said, not looking at my mother, ensconced in the backseat fanning herself. It was mid-July and steaming... even in our green bowl of valley. "Nick and his father are going to Europe after camp. Nick's going to be an architect, and his father thinks he should see some of the buildings over there before he starts college. They'll be gone over a month."

"They're not taking his mother?" my mother asked. She said it incredulously, as if some great familial taboo was to be violated, and I knew we were not through with the subject of Nick Abrams yet. Not by a long shot.

"His mother's dead," I said briefly. "She died when he was ten. She had cancer. He lives with his father."

"My goodness, that's too bad," Mother said. She was studying her still-beautiful face in her compact mirror. "Doesn't he have any other family?"

"Two sisters," I replied. "They're both married."

"A shame to be alone in a big house like that," Mother said, as if she and I were not living the same way, or almost. "I suppose it *is* a big house?"

I remembered the photograph he had shown me, of a rambling two-story shingle house atop a dune line, staring out at an ocean.

"Yeah. But they have a lot of people around. Servants, I guess."

I did not know if you called hired people in other houses servants. We never had. The word had an old-fashioned taste on my lips, somehow Victorian.

"I imagine they must," Mother said creamily, and from the front seat Grandmother Caroline winked at me, and Detritus swung the big car up the gravel road and out of sight among the trees lining it to the camp gates.

They had come up to camp for Parents' Day, and Nick had gotten special permission to join us for lunch, since we were both counselors and his father could not come. He had kayaked back across the lake over an hour ago. Now everything was still and quiet, punctuated only by lazy birdsong and the slap of the lake against the pier pilings nearby. Only large wastebaskets full of colorful paper plates and crumpled napkins and road dust lying in still strata in the freshening late-afternoon air spoke of people in this place. I shivered, though it was still very hot. Emptiness lapped in my heart. I wished that my mother had not come. I wanted Nick. I had known somewhere deep inside that she was not going to like him, but I had had high hopes for the day anyway. How could anyone not like him?

I started up the hill toward the cabins, to assemble the girls for supper.

"Nick," I whispered, wishing him back.

From the very beginning he had struck me like a lightning bolt. It was hard not to look at him. His physical presence seemed painted on the air in luminous strokes; I would as soon have looked away from a wild animal, or living fire at my feet. No one else had ever struck me this way. Not even my mother and sister, who were widely known to be eye-stoppingly beautiful. Not even my father, who was not beautiful but, in my eyes, lit by love. I don't believe Nick Abrams appeared so indelible to anyone else, or he would have been trailed by a pack of giddy followers; it would have been a sort of human Stendhal effect. But he was not. That summer he was mostly with me.

I knew that the attraction was mutual, but I could not imagine why this brown demigod of earth and woods was interested in me. I was certain that no other boy ever had been. Toward the end of the summer I asked him why.

"Are you kidding? Don't you have a mirror? You're a knockout," he said, raising himself on one elbow. We were lying on the float at the end of the dock in the lake. We swam together almost every day, in mid-afternoon when the campers were napping or resting. He swam like a dolphin. "Like an island kid," he said. I was not a good swimmer. Horses had been my love in this place for the past five years. That I would give them up for Nick and the lake spoke volumes.

"It's my mother who's the knockout," I said, laying my arm across my face, both to shield it from the sun and so that he could not see that I was blushing. "And my sister. Everybody thinks so. Everybody at home calls them the Wentworth girls, like they were twins. They've even had their pictures in the Atlanta paper. They looked like two movie stars."

"The hell with that," he said. "Anybody can be a blonde. All you need is a bottle. Almost nobody has hair like yours, or eyes like topaz aggies...."

"My grandmother does," I said.

"Yeah, and she's a knockout, too. Puts your mother in the shade, if you don't mind me saying so. You look a lot like her. Longer and more streamlined maybe, and I don't know about her boobs because she had on that loose shirt thing the time I met her. But if hers are as good as yours..."

He let the sentence trail off and ran his fingers where my breasts spilled slightly sideways from my bathing suit top. My face felt as if it had been scalded. He knew my breasts by that time. He knew almost every square inch of me. Sometimes, when I thought about the things we had done together, I simply could not believe them. I could not believe it had been so very easy to cross that gulf between childhood and adulthood, if that was where I was now. What else do you call it? Adults had sex. Children didn't.

"What's an aggie?" I said, not caring in the least. I just liked to watch his mouth when it formed words.

"A marble. You use it to shoot with. Didn't you ever play marbles?"

"No," I said. "Did you learn at home?"

"No. I learned at my first year at Edgewood...."

And then he stopped. He had gone to Camp Edgewood on Burnt Mountain from the time he was eight until now. He was at Silverlake this summer because his friend from St. Simons, who had always come to Silverlake, had a chance to spend a summer on his uncle's dude ranch and Nick took his counselor's position here for him. Nick loved Edgewood, I knew. But he stopped talking about it when I told him about my father's death on Burnt Mountain, coming home from the camp.

"You can talk about it," I said. "I'm not going to be silly about it anymore. It must be a great place, if you like it so. My father loved it, too...." I halted, then went on. "He went there when he was a kid. Maybe you'll take me to see it, when you get back from Europe. There'll be time before school...."

"Maybe I will. We've got lots of stuff to do when I get back."

"What will we do?" I asked very faintly. The sun had lowered behind the mountain to the west of the camp so that part of the lake and the float lay in shadow. In the gloom he was all a piece of the dimness except when his white teeth flashed, the broken front one looking like a chip in a pearl. I wanted him to continue talking. I loved the flash of his smile and basked in the warmth that his skin gave off. His deep voice echoed in my very blood. I would, I thought, know his voice anywhere on earth.

"Well, you know. We've talked about it. You'll go to Agnes Scott and I'll switch from Yale to Georgia Tech. They have just as good an architecture department. We'll see each other practically every night. When we get out I'll practice in Atlanta and you can write your songs and stories, or teach them, or whatever you want to do. We'll have a house right on the Chattahoochee River; I'll design it."

"Children?" I asked dreamily, lost in the shining world that he was spinning with his lips.

"Oh yeah. Several. Lots. And, and they'll all come here to Sherwood Forest or Silverlake if that's what you want."

"They can go to Edgewood, if you want them to. Just so I don't have to. There's a lot else up there that's really beautiful, I know."

There was. There was Burnt Mountain itself, named for a long-forgotten lightning-spawned wildfire that had charred but could not kill that last towering knob of the Appalachian chain. Burnt Mountain. It had always seemed a mystical place to me, the tall green house of a hidden god.

"We'll see."

Nick leaned over me and brushed his lips lightly and softly over mine. I shuddered, partly with pleasure and partly with apprehension. If anyone saw us there would be no more meeting in the afternoons and evenings. Everyone at Sherwood Forest and Silverlake alike smiled indulgently at us, two young people so obviously in love. But they would not smile if they saw us kissing in full view of the camp, much less knew what we did at night on the top bunk of the empty log cabin closest to the water's edge.

"If anybody sees you doing that they'll kick us both out," I said. "What would you do then?"

"Marry you right off, I guess. I was planning to wait a few years, but I'd just as soon do it now. Nobody could say a word about what we do then."

"As long as we don't do it in plain view and scare the horses," I said, my chest filling with insane laughter.

He lifted my head to his face and kissed me long and hard, and the laughter bubbled into his mouth and danced on our joined breaths.

After he had paddled out of sight toward Silverlake on the opposite shore, I sat with my knees drawn up to my chest and my face up to the last of the sun, thinking about us, Nick and me. Utterly confounded, all of a sudden, that there could be us. How had this happened? I was never meant to be part of an "us"; I had always known that. I was the troublesome one, the reader, the stargazer, always scanning odd skies for even odder materializations, asker of innumerable and unanswerable questions, openly loving only my father and the house I grew up in. A cipher. A changeling. And always, essentially alone. I watched as my older sister grew up, began to flirt, to talk long and teasingly on telephones, to date first one young man and then another, then to cast her whole fervent soul into the being of a particular young man, only to withdraw it carelessly and move on to another. I had no doubt that she would always live, move, and have her being, as we said at church, in the light cast from a man. Her studies were so-so; I believe it was Grandmother Caroline's auspices that got her accepted at Agnes Scott. Men. For Lily, just men.

I thought it unnatural, insane, almost revolting. But to my mother it was obviously the accepted norm for a maiden daughter. She inundated Lily with attention, questions, advice, unguents, powders, dresses; even when she was scolding Lily for some infraction or another…staying out too late, necking in the car in the driveway, hanging up rudely on an unlucky swain…my mother's interest was obvious and all-consuming. It was territory that she knew, and she relished guiding her fledgling through it. I was thankful to the swaggering, neckless Goose that he waited almost until time for me to leave for Sherwood Forest this summer to snatch Lily up and whirl her away into eternal Goosehood. It spared me, I know, the eyes of dissatisfied motherhood turned on me in the useless determination to groom me as bride material. Once I overheard my mother say to my grandmother, "I could just kill Lily for throwing it all away on that…Cro-Magnon. Now I've got to start all over again with Thayer, and I might as well be trying to make a silk purse out of a pig's ear."

"Oh." Grandmother Caroline smiled her V-shaped smile. "I think you may be quite surprised at Thayer."

And when she found out, she was. Very surprised indeed. And outraged. Lily's defection was absolutely nothing to the devastation of my eighteenth summer. It sundered our lives; it changed the maps of our territory forever. And yet if I had known how it would end when I first began to see Nick that summer I wouldn't have changed anything I did. Anything we did. After my childhood Nick was the next thing for me. I could imagine nothing else. There could be no other.

I said as much to my grandmother Caroline, shortly before she and my mother came up for Parents' Day and met Nick. I had not talked of him at all with my mother. I knew that I would not. But I had to speak of him to someone. He spilled over and out of my heart and lips.

"I told you I met this guy named Nick Abrams, didn't I, Grand?" I said to her on one of my rare weekend visits home. Nick was in Atlanta with his father, firming up the trip to Europe. Camp felt so blasted and desolate without Nick that I simply went back to Lytton, taking a heart full of him with me.

"Yes, you did." She smiled. It was full summer and we were sitting on the screened porch. Outside, the garden burst with July. Wisteria tumbled over a live oak beside the house and cast a lavender shadow over my grandmother's face. She sat still, not speaking, waiting.

When I could not speak, could think of no way to give Nick over to her, she said, "He's very important to you, isn't he?"

I nodded mutely. I felt my eyes fill with tears of frustration. How could I make anyone understand about him?

She reached out and put her hand over mine. Hers was cool and white and soft; mine was brown and stubby and scabbed with scratches from oarlocks and rope burns. She picked it up and turned it over and kissed the callus on the inside that the weeks of handling reins had left there.

"It's a hardworking little hand," she said, smiling as she

laid it back down on my lap. "It's a woman's hand, a working woman's. I'm proud of you, Thayer. You're becoming just the young woman your father would have wanted you to be. I hope your Nick is worthy of you."

"Oh, Grand, he is!" I said, beginning to sob and not knowing why. "He's worthy of a dozen mes, of anybody!"

"Perhaps not just anybody, but he must be a fine young man for you to—"

"Love him. I do love him. He loves me, too. It may sound silly and childish, and I know Mother would say exactly that, that nobody my age can really be in love. But I am. I do. I'll never love anybody else like this again. I just can't tell Mother. I don't know if I could ever make her understand...."

My grandmother reached up and pulled my head down to her shoulder, and I pressed it against her, feeling silk and smelling the Vetiver bath soap and powder that she used. A small, snotty sob exploded from me onto her peony-printed silk and I made as if to pull away, but she held me tighter.

"I don't think you should tell your mother," she said, against my hair that was so like her own. "Not yet, anyway. Time for that later, when you've got everything worked out. I certainly believe that you're old enough to be in love, and I can see that you are. Oh, my darling, it's a glorious thing, to love, but it can bring you great pain, too. That's all I want you to promise me. That you'll remember about the pain. Otherwise, you have my deepest blessings, and I will try very hard to walk with you when the time comes that you must tell your mother. You must know that's not going to be an easy thing, no matter who your Nick is."

"I know. I know it won't. All she'd have to do is meet him. If it was anybody but Mother, I know that's all it would take. But I... How can she take me seriously when I haven't ever had a boyfriend? And now I'm in love with somebody and I'm going to marry him—"

"Well, not for a while, I hope. You both need college, no matter whether you think you do or not. I gather you've both made college plans?"

"Of course not until after college, Grand." I hiccupped. The knots in my chest that had coiled there medusa-like were loosening. Talking to Grandmother Caroline always did that for me.

"He was going to Yale architecture school, but he's transferring to Georgia Tech, and the fall quarter starts right after he gets home from Europe. I know Mother thinks I'm going to Georgia State this fall, but I'm going to try to talk her into Agnes Scott. That way we can see each other almost every day. I'm not going to live at home. I'm just not."

"You shouldn't, anyway," Grand said. "It's time you got out from under our wings. Not that we don't love you, but we need to start letting you go. I'll talk to Crystal about it. I'm sure if I pay your tuition there's not a lot she can say about it."

"Grand, you don't have to—"

"Shhhh. Yes, I do. This is one thing I have always wanted to do. This is one thing in my life I will do. I'd have loved to see you at Smith or Wellesley, but Agnes Scott will do nicely. I was never going to let you go to Georgia State."

I rested against her, breathing quietly, smelling wisteria and Vetiver.

"I wish you'd been my mother," I said.

I felt rather than heard her laugh.

"And you'd have just had to find somebody else to run to when things got...puzzling. It's almost never your mother, darling. Almost never. Mothers are givers of roots, seldom wings."

And when my mother came home from her hairdresser's I was able to hug her and smile and say, "Yes, I just had a free weekend and wanted to see y'all....Yes, I'm really enjoying it. I got a counselor's medal in campfire and riding."

"Yes, and just look at your hands," my mother said, pulling one of them close to her face. She needed glasses, I knew, but only wore them when she was alone. "They look like a field hand's. Run up to my bedroom and get me some of that Dior lotion; it's in the pink bottle...."

Later, lying in bed lotioned and pin-curled, I stared into the milky darkness over the tree line where soon the moon would pour through. I smiled in the dark. It would work out. It was going to work out. Grand said it would.

Grand knew.

On our last day together at Sherwood Forest, Nick and I sat together on the steps of the big red boathouse, where all the Sherwood Forest canoes and kayaks and small sailboats were kept. He wore tan chinos and a white oxford-cloth shirt and had a dark blue summer-weight blazer slung over his arm. I had never seen him in anything but Silverlake shorts and shirts...or, on a few occasions, nothing. His thick copper-brown hair was slicked back and showed wet comb tracks, and he was clean shaven, as he said, to baby-butt pinkness. Usually he was stubbled by the time I saw him. He was grown-up that day, a young man I did not know. I kept cutting my eyes at him to see if this was the same Nick who laughed and danced with me and teased me and kissed me and in the dark arms of the top bunk of the empty cabin did other things to me, things that I had not known existed, that could ignite flesh to near fire, stop breath, explode deep inside me with stabbing sweetness. I could never really believe we did those things. I? I who never even had held a man's hand except my father's? When Nick had kissed me for the first time, the night after the day we met, I had pulled my head away a little uncertainly, and he had let me go and said, "I'm sorry. Didn't mean to rush things," and I said, "No, it's just that I've never known where you put your noses. I could never figure out what people did with them."

"I'll show you," he said, laughing, and I saw at once.

After the kisses there was no question of what would follow. It was I who urged it, pulling him so hard against me that I could feel his body heat through my shirt, whimpering, tugging at his clothes. I, who had felt scalded and a little sick when anyone spoke of "going all the way," was the one who pulled him down onto me, wriggling my hips snakelike until my shorts and panties were off, thrusting myself up to receive him.

"Are you sure? Are you?" he whispered against my face.

"Oh, God, yes!" I cried.

When it was over and I lay in his arms shaking like an

ague victim, he said, "I would never do this if I wasn't going to marry you. You know that, don't you?"

"Yes," I sobbed. "I know." And I did know, from that first night down to this last day.

I did not say this now. I had said it last night, over and over again lying in his arms on the rough camp blanket on the top bunk, said it fiercely as he had kissed my face and neck softly and repeatedly, cried it out as he rocked me softly, faster and faster, until we could not speak at all, only cry out. After that, I simply lay in his arms and cried. He did not try to stop me. I think he cried a little, too.

"The last time," I sobbed, finally.

"Only for here. The next time and the next and the next after that and so on will be even better. I'll have been to Paree, where they know about these things. I'll show you things you never dreamed of. Probably that I didn't, either."

He laughed softly and rolled off me, and stood up and walked into the darkness behind the bunk. I could not see him; the near full moon had crested the lake, but not this hill, and he walked in darkness. I knew he had gotten up to dispose of the used condom. I felt a small surge of revulsion; I hated this side of sex. Practical, mechanical, messy, pedestrian. None of the things I associated with Nick. But he had been adamant from the beginning.

"You think I like 'em? No guy likes 'em. They make the whole thing...something else. But I'll never make love to you without one. I know guys who do it all the time, and it's the most selfish thing they could possibly do. It puts the whole thing on the girl. I'll stop using the damned things the night we decide to get pregnant, and not before."

I had my head on my knees today. I could see him, but only a little. We were waiting at the boathouse for the big tom-tom over at Silverlake to boom out over the water, his friend Charlie's sign that Nick's father had arrived to pick him up. They would drive down to Atlanta tonight and stay over at an airport hotel and leave very early for London and their voyage of discovery. Nick was packed up and signed out. He was leaving a week early; Charlie would take his place for the remaining week. I would not go until camp ended, another eight days for me. I did not know how I would stand them.

"I wish we had one more night in the top bunk," I said into the hair that hung over my face.

"You wish! I wish we could do it right now, right here on this step, with both camps lined up on each side cheering us. Do it until the sun set and everybody had to go in to supper—"

"Oh, stop! I can't stand this," I whispered.

"It's just a month, babycakes. One little month, and then I'll come find you at Agnes Scott and you can sign out for a chamber concert at the auditorium and I can take you to Piedmont Park or somewhere...."

I began to cry in earnest.

"Don't," he said. "Wait a minute."

He stood up and fished something out of his pocket. He sat back down and said, "Stick out your feet."

"My feet?"

"Just stick 'em out."

I did, both feet, clad in white lace-up sneakers with rubber toes.

He picked them up, one after another, and with the red felt-tip pen he had had in his pocket wrote *Just* on my left shoe and *wait* on the right.

"You can explain it or not." He grinned. "I wouldn't. Drive your mother crazy. Probably lock you in the barn."

I sat up and he pulled me against him and rested his chin on my hair. I thought he could feel my heart pounding, but if he did, he did not mention it. We sat so for perhaps two or three minutes, rocking slightly to the slap of the water inside the boathouse, feeling the sun slide away from our faces and down toward the west. I wished that my life could end just then, just like that.

Across the lake the big tom-tom spoke. It seemed to roll across to us on its own thunder. Then it boomed again.

Nick kissed me on the top of my head, then lifted my face in his hand and kissed me again, long and soft and searchingly, on my mouth. I could feel it tremble and distort under his.

"Don't," he whispered into my mouth. "Don't, or I can't do this."

"I'm okay," I said, trying for perkiness. "As long as you don't go doing this to those French girls..."

"Fat chance," he said, scrambling to his feet.

We stood on the step, looking at each other, saying nothing. Then he kissed me swiftly on the cheek and ran down the steps to the red kayak beached on the sand. He was in it and had pushed off strongly before he looked back at me. I stood watching him, my hand lifted, not waving, just standing. Watching.

"Just wait!" he called from far out, his hands cupped around his mouth. "Just wait!"

I watched him until he was a red dot and then nothing at all, and then I looked down at my Magic Markered toes and sat down on crossed legs to wait.

CHAPTER

7

During my last week at Camp Sherwood Forest a murderous wave of heat coiled up from the south and buried everything in its path in a gagging miasma. Our mountain valley had seldom felt anything like it. Grass burnt brown; leaves wilted and curled; the surrounding evergreens were not stirred by so much as a breath of fresh air; the sky was lost in a dirty white, shimmering haze. It was hardly possible to continue outdoor activities; the horses foundered and the campers threw up after softball and hiking. Even swimming and sailing were like bathing in tepid bathwater. Some of the campers ended up in the infirmary, lying white and still under wet cloths on their foreheads, and many of the younger ones were taken home early. We suspended campfires for the time being; even after dark the heat sucked the life from us. The small television in the dining hall said that the area had reached 108 degrees and there was no sign of abatement. The directors decided to close camp a few days early and called parents to come and get their prostrate offspring before Sherwood Forest could be sued.... For what I could not imagine. A heat wave?

Even I felt it, sunk as I was in the misery of Nick's absence. The same nausea that dogged most of us pooled at the bottom of my tongue, making eating, even drinking water unpleasant, as the ice machines had given up. The cooks in the dining hall set out cold salads and sandwiches for meals. Attendance was down by at least a half by the time the first parents rolled in to collect their stricken young. I heard several of them remark that it was no cooler at home. This was usually followed by a sigh that I thought might have been translated "but at least we'll all die together."

My grandmother sent Detritus up for me in the Mercedes, but she did not accompany him. She and my mother, I knew, were down at Grand's house at Sea Island.

"You stretch out there in the back and I turn up the air," Detritus said sternly when I slumped into the car. "You don't look so pert to me. Yo' grandmother comin' back on the train tonight, but yo' mama gon' stay on for a little. She say for you to stay in the house and don't go runnin' around town till she get back. Yo' grandmother got one of them window air conditioners for every bedroom, and it feel real good. I ain't never seen no heat like this in all my born days."

I nodded and closed my eyes and let the blast of stale, chilled car air wash over me. It felt like pure heaven. After a while I pulled the old tartan car rug up over me and drifted off to sleep, the tires droning in my ears. It was a sound I could remember from childhood; I associated it with my father and the driving trips we took. I slept, not stirring, until the motor noise stopped abruptly and I heard the thunk of the emergency brake being pulled up.

"Are we here?"

"Yassum, we home. You go on in the house. Your grandmother say Juanita gon' give you some supper and stay with you till she get home. I gon' pick her up at Brookwood Station about ten."

It was still hot in the big white house, but not so suffocating with all the fans on. I almost tiptoed through the empty, darkened rooms. It felt utterly alien to come into this house with no one in evidence, with all the rooms dark and breath held, with no sound at all. I crept down the center hall into the kitchen, where I had seen a light under the door, but heard nothing. When I opened it, Juanita sat at the kitchen table, a fan trained on her, reading a movie magazine. Her hair was pinned up on her head and she wore one of Lily's old flowered sundresses. She looked, I thought, ten times better than I did.

"I got you some cold chicken and salad in the refrigerator," she said. Juanita was not much on hellos or good-byes. "You go on up and I'll bring it to you. I got you in Miss Lily's room. The air conditioner is on."

"What's wrong with my room?"

"Your mama got some stuff piled up in there. We was gon' to take it out before you came home, but you come so early..."

Her tone rang with the grievance of my early homecoming.

Still faintly sick and feeling as if I had done Juanita a discourtesy, I crept up the stairs and went into my sister's room and crawled straight into the bed without turning on the lights. In a minute, I thought. In a minute I'll get up and unpack and all that stuff....

When I woke I looked into white sunlight on the rose-papered walls that were not my own and for a moment could not think where I was.

"Welcome to the world, sunshine," said my grandmother's musical voice, and I turned my head and saw her sitting in Lily's slipper chair beside the bed, with a laden tray on the footstool beside her. The smell of coffee curled into my nostrils and I swallowed thickly. I knew that I could not drink the coffee, nor, for that matter, eat the eggs and bacon on the plate on the tray.

"Can I have some water?" I croaked. My throat was dry as far down as I could feel it.

She poured from a carafe, ice clinking into the glass, and I took it and gulped it down in one long swallow. For a moment it threatened to come straight back up, and then it settled, and the delicious coolness in my mouth and throat made me close my eyes in pure joy.

"Oh, boy," I said, smiling at her. "I've been thirsty for cold water for at least a week."

She kissed me on the cheek and pushed a straggle of hair off my forehead.

"I heard it was as hot as sin up there in that valley," she said. "You're pale as a little ghost. I'm keeping you inside for a while. We'll read and watch TV and we can start to get your clothes ready. You've only got a month or so before classes start, don't you?"

"Yes," I said, thinking that fall and Agnes Scott seemed as far away as the millennium and that Nick would be back before then. I stretched and smiled.

"I'm glad to see you, Grand," I said. "When is Mother coming back?"

"In a few days. She ran into some people she and your father knew from Hamilton, a student's parents, I think. They live on the island, and they've asked her to stay awhile with them. Doesn't your friend Nick live somewhere down there? I wouldn't be surprised if she ran into his father. Everybody knows everybody on the coast."

"Nick's in Europe with his father, looking at architecture," I said. It was delicious to speak of Nick, to use his name, in front of people. "He'll be back in about a month. He's starting at Georgia Tech."

She gave me another hug.

"Things are going well with you two, aren't they? That's a happy thing. Is he going to be the one, my dear?"

"Oh yes. Yes, he is. It's not too soon, Grand. I'm not too young. I know Mother thinks I am, but... I know this. I just know."

"Well, who better than you, darling?" she said. "He's going to keep in touch from Europe, of course?"

"Oh yes. Every day. He'll write almost every day, and he'll call— Do you know if there's been a call yet?"

"No, but I've just come home, and he'll think you're still at camp, won't he? Give him time to get his feet on the ground. And eat your breakfast. I'm going to get Juanita to help me move you into your own room. Lily's is lovely, but it's hardly you, is it?"

Lily's room was literally a bower. Roses climbed, rioted everywhere, from her bedspread to the curtains and rugs and slipper chairs. My mother loved roses. Her firstborn daughter had little choice in the matter. Fortunately, Lily loved them, too. She was a rose girl from her fair, flushed cheeks to her small pink toes. My room was serviceable blue chambray and blue-striped curtains. My rugs were dark, close-knit blue, as sturdy as iron. Mothers learn a lot with their first daughters, I think. And from the beginning, I had no hint of roses about me.

"Wild red honeysuckle," my father had said once, when I asked him. I thought honeysuckle was better than roses any day. I still do.

I poked at my breakfast while my grandmother and Juanita carried my things across the hall to my room. I felt bone-less, limp, bled of energy. It was not hot in the room with the air-conditioning on, but perhaps the fact that I knew that outside was still a motionless swamp of heat was sapping my body. And, of course, Nick not being here. Without Nick I felt as if half my breath was gone.

Presently I pulled out some faded blue shorts and found a tee shirt in Lily's drawer. It had roses on it, of course, but it was loose and cool, hardly touching my body. I went out into the hall and started downstairs and met the still, thick heat at the top of them. My head whirled sickly, and I clutched the stair rail and sank down on the step with my eyes closed, waiting for the world to settle.

"What's wrong, Thayer?" I heard my grandmother say from behind me, worry in her voice.

I shook my head. "I think maybe it's still the heat," I said foggily. "It's really hot in here without the air-conditioning. I don't think I ever felt it like this before."

"It's not that hot," she said. "I hope you're not coming down with something. Stay there; I'm going to get you a cold washcloth."

"Grand..."

"Stay," she said.

The washcloth felt good, and the dizziness passed. I went on down the stairs and into the kitchen, thinking to snag a cold soda and go down to the riverbank, to check out my small fortress there. I had not thought of it for a long time, but today it seemed welcoming, almost pulling me there.

"I'm going down to the river for a little while," I said to Juanita, who was stirring something in a blue pottery bowl. "Tell Grand I'll be back before lunch."

"You better not stay out there too long," Juanita said. "The weatherman said it was going to be one-o-six today. You look pretty peaked to me."

"Back atcha," I said in mild irritation. "Oh, by the way, have there been any phone calls?"

"Yes, none of 'em for you. The man's gon' come fix the ceiling fan in the hall, and your mama called and said she'd be home tomorrow afternoon...."

I thought of my mother, crisp and cool as a melon in something linen, probably sea green, and her gilt hair pulled back as she always wore it in hot weather. I could not imagine that one drop of sweat had been permitted to stand on her forehead or in the hollow of her throat, much less under the arms of her linen dress. She was the only woman I had ever known on whom linen did not wrinkle. This irritated me even more and I went out the back porch door and let the screen door slam. This always drove my mother wild.

I walked across the long lawn down toward the trees that fringed the river. The grass was spiky and brown under my bare feet, and the earth was actually hot. Above me the sky was high and white and so heat hazed that the sun looked like an orb dropped into milk. No wind stirred the drooping trees. No birds sang. No dogs barked. No lawn mowers buzzed. By the time I reached my little house, still ringed with boughs, in the roots of the big live oak, my head was throbbing with heat and my heart was pounding high in my throat. I leaned down to duck into the little enclosure and felt the world spin wildly again.

When I woke up, Detritus was bending over me, trying to pull me erect, and my soda was pooling on the dry earth beside me. My grandmother was kneeling on my other side, wiping at my face with a damp cloth.

"We're going to get you right back to bed, darling, and then I'm going to call the doctor. See if you can stand up now."

"No, Grand, it's just that it's so hot…," I began, and vomited on the earth in front of me.

"You'll have to carry her, Detritus," my grandmother said. "I'm going ahead to call the doctor."

He did, as easily as if I had been a bag of feathers.

"Grand, please don't call the doctor, I'll just rest awhile, and then...!" I called to her retreating back.

She and Juanita tucked me into my bed with the window unit grinding out cool air, and I did feel better. My room closed its arms around me, and I felt lulled and far away, as I had sometimes when I was sick as a child and knew that I was being cared for and nothing remained for me to do but lie still on piled pillows. Usually it was my father who sat at my bedside, at night, anyway, and his deep, cool voice seemed to lift me up on waves. Now it was my grandmother's.

"Dr. Neely says it's probably heat; he says he's got half of Lytton down with it. But he said for you to rest today and drink lots of fluids, and for us to call him in the morning if you're not better. He feels you will be."

I closed my eyes and then opened them.

"Has... have there been any phone calls?"

She looked at me steadily for a long minute and said, "No. But you know I'll tell you if there are. Let it go for a little while, darling. He hasn't had time yet."

She brought me iced tea and a couple of aspirin, and I settled back on my pillows and closed my eyes again.

"Do you want the radio?" she said, and I nodded. In a moment the mannerly strains of an old song that I knew my father used to like floated into the darkened room.

"I found my April dream... in Portugal with you...."

"Lisbon Antigua."

Lisbon, I thought, sliding into sleep. We could go to Lisbon.... Maybe you'll go this time, and you can take me back another time.

Anywhere you want, Thay. Anywhere you say, Nick whispered. I heard the door close softly as my grandmother went out of my room and I turned over in my bed and into Nick's arms. I don't believe I dreamed, but when I woke again I thought for a moment that I was on the top bunk of the cabin at Sherwood Forest and Nick was still sleeping beside me.

I sat up abruptly when my hand reached out and touched, not his warm skin, but a pile of books and magazines. I looked around in confusion and distress and saw my grandmother again, sitting beside my bed. No bunk. No cabin. No Nick. She looked as if she had been there a long time. The entire room was dim and she reached over and switched on my little bedside lamp and smiled at me.

"What time is it?" I mumbled, my voice clogged in my throat.

"After six. You've slept all afternoon. How do you feel?"

"Okay," I said thickly. "Sleepy, but I don't feel sick. I was sick, wasn't I?"

"Indeed you were. Do you remember throwing up and fainting in your little tree house?"

"I...guess so," I said. I could remember, but it was like remembering a dream.

She was silent a little while, not looking at me but at the evening light lowering outside my drawn curtains. Then she turned her head back to me and said, "Sweetie, are you having your period? That can make you pretty sick sometimes, especially when it's hot."

"My period? No."

"Can you remember when you had your last one?"

I couldn't. I remembered no cramping, no bleeding, no awkward explanations to Nick. What was she talking about?

"No," I said doubtfully.

She took a deep breath and let it out in a long sigh.

"I don't like to pry, darling, but have you been ... intimate with Nick?"

"I ... I guess so. ..."

"For very long?"

I began to see where this was going. My heart slowed to huge shuddering thuds and my eyes blurred.

"I guess ... since right at the first," I whispered. "But Grand, we always used ... I mean he used, you know, those things. ..."

I could not say "condoms" to my grandmother.

She leaned over and put her hands on either side of my face and looked into my eyes. My eyes, so like hers, so like my father's ...

"My darling, they don't always work. Not always."

"But that would mean ... I mean, do you think I could be ..."

I could not say "pregnant," either.

She still cupped my face but did not speak.

"But that would mean a baby!"

"Yes, it would," she said. Tears stood in her eyes.

I felt nothing but a sort of white shock buzzing in all my veins. There was nothing at all real about any of this. We were acting in some sort of play, an old, sweet one, like *Our Town*. Grandmother and granddaughter in a lamp-lit room, talking about ...

"I didn't know babies made you sick," I said stupidly.

She sighed and leaned back in the chair and covered my hand with hers. She closed her eyes and then opened them and said, "We must talk a little about what you want to do, before your mother comes home," she said. "Of course it's entirely possible that it's not that at all, but we have to decide some things now, before we tell your mother. There'll be many plans to make, and the choices should be yours."

"Plans?" I said, and a wild joy bloomed inside me. It felt sweeter than anything I had ever felt before, or tasted. "We'll get married now instead of waiting, Grand! We were always going to get married. We were always going to have children. We'll just do it now instead of after college. He can go on to Tech, and I can..."

She was shaking her head, back and forth. Tears spilled out of her eyes now and ran down her cheeks.

"Thayer, you are not eighteen yet. It'll be a while till you are. Your mother isn't just going to let you run off and get married in two or three months or so, or whenever Nick gets back. And do you really think you could begin right now to take care of a baby? You must realize that if this is true your whole life will change. The main thing is to decide if you want to keep this baby—"

"Of course I do! What else would I do with it? Even if we don't get married yet, Nick will love it...."

My voice was rising and my heart was pounding so that I could not get my breath. I knew without being able to see it that my face was red and furious and corrugated.

"Darling, your mother—"

"Don't tell my mother! Don't you dare tell my mother!"
I was almost screaming.

She pulled my face back into her shoulder. It felt the same: warm, safe. She still wore Vetiver.

"This will work out, sweetheart. I promise you that. But your mother will have to know. Of course she will. I'll talk to her first. But your mother will have to know."

"But what if it's not true? Then we would have told her and it wouldn't be true at all, and it would be just awful...."

"Well, the first thing you'll have to do is find out."

"Can't you do that? Can't you help me do ... whatever ..."

"No. Not for this. This has to be your mother. But I can tell her for you. Tell her first. I think that might help a little. And you might be surprised. She might understand far better than you think she will."

"No," I said, beginning to tremble hard. "She won't."

I spent that night and the next day in a maelstrom of emotions, so vivid and conflicting that I could almost see them, like swirls of violently colored water heaved up by a great whirlpool: simple disbelief that such a thing could happen to me, fear of my mother's outrage and my own ineptitude as any sort of a parent, a joy so fraught with tenderness at the idea of Nick's and my baby that it made me weep. The heat outside had not abated and the nausea was back, crawling and lingering at my throat. Grandmother and I scarcely spoke of the day before, but once when I leaped for the telephone and almost fainted on the floor she said wearily and tenderly, "It won't be him until the day after tomorrow, darling. You weren't supposed to be home from camp until then.

Give yourself a break. I think it would be best if you didn't talk to him until after we know one way or another, anyway. I'm going to give you half a sleeping pill, and then when your mother comes in tonight I'll have that talk with her. I expect that even if she doesn't much like it she'll understand."

I simply shook my head, unable to fathom that my grandmother really believed that my mother would understand. Not when the mere name Abrams had seemed to burn her lips. But, in fact, she did. Or at least, she did not seem to be angry.

She was sitting beside my bed the next morning in the same chair Grand had been sitting in, drinking coffee and staring out my window into the heat-shabby treetops. I was right about the linen and the hair, only this morning it was a peach shirt and white slacks and her hair was tied back with a scarf of the same peach. She was tanned to honey gold, and when I made a small sound and she turned her head toward me the blue-violet of her eyes was startling in the shade-drawn gloom.

"Well, Thayer," she said, and sighed. But she did not frown. She simply looked at me, rather, I thought, as if she had never seen me before.

"Mama...," I began, and then, to my disgust and horror, began to cry. And then threw up on the bedspread.

I continued to cry, nearly strangling on my own sobs, while she whisked away the bedspread and brought a towel and a wet washcloth for me and called downstairs for Juanita.

"Not Juanita!" I hiccupped. "Grand! Can't you call Grand?"

"Don't be silly, Punkin," she said crisply, but her touch

with the washcloth on my face was gentle. "This is what Juanita was hired for. Besides, your grandmother is at her doctor's appointment. I know all about it. Your grandmother and I talked last night."

Punkin had been my father's nickname for me when I was small. I had never heard my mother use it before. I stared at her, sniveling. After Juanita had gone with the soiled bedspread, careful not to look me in the eye, my mother said, "Now. The first thing to do is to find out what's what. It could easily be something else, you know."

"It isn't something else," I whispered. "I know it isn't. But Mama, it's all right! It is! We wanted children; when Nick gets home—"

"Shhhh."

She laid her finger over my lips. "There's plenty of time to talk about what comes next after we've seen the doctor. That's number one. We'll go from there."

I said nothing. I could not have asked for a better reaction, at least not from my mother, but none of this rang right, felt real. The feeling of being in a play intensified. But this time not *Our Town*.

"I'm going to have Juanita bring you up a tray," she said, rising. "I want you to try and at least eat some toast. Then jump in the shower. We have an appointment at three this afternoon to see the doctor."

"Not Dr. Neely!"

"No, of course not. This man is in Atlanta, and he's supposed to be the best. Several of my friends' daughters have used him, and I understand he's the ob-gyn for Buckhead."

She kissed me briefly and went out of the room. Her trail was not Vetiver but un Jardin sur le Nil. Even I knew how much that cost. I suddenly remembered the day long ago when I had stolen a bottle of my mother's Casaque for Lavonda. I smiled with my salt-sticky lips. We'd both come a way since then.

I stayed in my room until it was time to go and see the patron saint of Buckhead maternity. Even walking from the house to the car was misery; the white corona of the sun seemed to lean closer each day. Detritus was sitting in the driver's seat of my grandmother's Mercedes, staring straight ahead. I could hear the car's air-conditioning from the side-walk. Detritus wore his peaked chauffeur's cap, though not his livery. My grandmother forbade the livery; it had been my grandfather who had liked it. I wondered if the cap was in honor of a trip into Atlanta or as a tribute to incipient young motherhood. On the whole, I decided on Atlanta. No one but me seemed too thrilled about the motherhood thing. Oh, but Nick . . . Nick would be. I could see the smile that slitted the dark eyes and curved his mouth.

"Oh, Nick, please!" I whispered, getting into the back-seat beside my mother. "This is about you as well as me. I can't do this without you. . . ."

"You look very pretty." My mother smiled. "Maybe I'll take you to tea at the Frances Virginia Tea Room after this appointment." I looked back at her. Tearoom? Was this then simply another trip into Atlanta for my mother? Could she not see that this was the rest of my life?

"That would be nice," I said faintly. I had scrubbed color

back into my face and brushed my hair into the waterfall of red curls it fell into on its best days and added pink lipstick and put on a flowered sundress from Lily's closet. I owned no such dresses. I could not have said why I had done all this. But deep inside I knew I was doing it for my baby. Nick's and mine. He would want to know that he had a pretty mother, wouldn't he?

"She" did not enter my mind.

We did not speak for the rest of the trip. The frigid air was like settling into a deep, cold river, and I had goose bumps on my bare arms. My mother noticed and draped the car rug around me. The motor droned and the air-conditioning shushed and I fell asleep on my mother's shoulder. When I awoke, my mother was shaking me gently and we had stopped.

The Mercedes stood in the driveway of a huge, ornate Victorian house on a street of similar houses. It was no street I knew: It was littered and shabby and the close-crowded houses all had peeling paint and shingles askew, and most of the small front gardens were littered with broken toys. Everything outside the car was bled white with heat. You could actually see it coiling in a sluggish haze above the pitted pavement.

"Mama?" I said. Surely it was not into this Charles Addams house we were going.

"I know. It looks like a slum, doesn't it? It was Dr. Condon's family home back when this was the fanciest part of Atlanta, if you can imagine that it ever was. He keeps it to honor his father. He was a doctor, too, and practiced here. It might hurt any other's doctor's image, but Dr. Condon doesn't have to worry about that. He turns patients away."

"But not us..."

"His son went to Hamilton. He knows who we are," my mother said. She got out of the car, slumping a little under the fist of the sun.

I followed her, dazed from my thick sleep and reeling on my untrustworthy legs. She supported me up the smartly painted steps, lined with vivid pots of flowers that did not seem to feel the sun. Perhaps, I thought, they were artificial. Behind us, Detritus sat at parade rest in the Mercedes, looking straight ahead. He kept his hat on.

My mother laughed, a small, silvery giggle.

"He's not used to having to sit out in front of houses like this," she said. "He's going to let everybody know it."

I didn't blame him. The effect of the big, perfectly manicured house in the surrounding decay was eerie. I did not want to take my maybe baby into this house.

"Come on," my mother said, taking my elbow. "You'll see when you get inside. Martha Coursey told me they give you sherry and biscuits, or Cokes, if you'd rather."

She opened the door and I followed her into the dark, varnished cave of the front hall. It smelled of furniture polish and fresh flowers and antiseptic. We went into a room just off to the right, and I saw what she meant. This had obviously been a drawing room in the grand manner, chandeliered and Aubussoned, and little had changed except the small windowed cage in which a pretty young woman in glasses was typing something. She looked up and smiled. There was no one else in the office.

"Mrs. Wentworth? Please have a seat. Doctor will be with

you in just a moment. May I offer you something cool to drink? That heat is murder."

My mother smiled and shook her head, and I did, too. I could have gotten nothing past the lump in my throat.

"Actually, it's my daughter who has the appointment," my mother said. "Miss Thayer Wentworth."

The pretty girl smiled brilliantly at me and said, "I'll just tell Doctor that you're here."

"If he's such a hotshot, where are all his patients?" I said, hardly lowering my voice.

My mother frowned delicately at me. Forty-odd years of her little frowns had not left a mark in the porcelain of her brow.

"He was kind enough to stay late for us," she said. "He usually closes at two."

A mahogany door beside the typist's cage opened and a tall man in a spotless white coat came into the room. He wore gray slacks and a blue oxford cloth shirt and a striped tie, and his dark hair was frosted becomingly at his temples. He had a stethoscope around his neck and horn-rimmed glasses over mild blue eyes, and when he smiled his teeth seemed to fill his face, blinding white. I thought he looked like a shark.

"Mrs. Wentworth? Miss Wentworth? I'm Dr. Forrest Condon. Please come into my office. Martha Coursey has told me all about you. I believe we have the Hamilton school in common, don't we?"

"We do indeed." My mother smiled. I said nothing. It was bad enough that this was a doctor's appointment. A social occasion was infinitely worse.

"Well, now, what can I do for you?" He smiled, looking at both of us. He knew, though. I knew that he did.

"My daughter has missed a period or two and we just thought we should check," my mother said. She might have been saying, "I bid two spades," to the smiling man.

"Yes. Well," the shark said. "We can certainly do that. If you'll just sit up here on this table, my dear, we'll check you out in no time. Is...ah...the prospective father with you?"

"No," my mother said. "Yes," I said over her. "Or at least he will be. He's in Europe now, but he'll be home in a couple of weeks."

"And is he aware—"

"No," my mother said, and again, over her, I said, "It's a surprise."

"A happy surprise." The doctor grinned fiercely and then said, "I'd really like to offer both of you something cool to drink. It's punishing hot out there. Let me just go tell Becky...."

"I'll come with you," Mother said, and followed him out of the room. "Do you want something, Thayer?" she called over her shoulder.

"No."

She shut the door behind her and I sat back on the crackling white paper and waited for her to tell him whatever she thought she should tell him. The office was very cool, and again I shut my eyes.

Whatever it was, the telling of it did not take long. They came back into the room, both smiling, and the doctor said to me, "My dear, have you ever had a pelvic exam?"

I shook my head mutely.

"Well, they're not the most fun in the world, but I'll try to be very gentle. I'll ask your mother to wait outside, and then we'll see where we are. First, though, I want to give you a little IV."

He gestured to a clear pack of liquid hanging from a stand beside the table.

I sat up in fright.

"IV?"

"It's just saline fluid, my dear. You are seriously dehydrated; look at the skin of your arm."

He picked up a fold of it and pinched it gently. It stayed there in a little pucker for a long instant before it sank back into the smoothness of my arm.

"Your symptoms could just be a matter of dehydration. It's not uncommon. And if you should be pregnant, the last thing you and your baby need is dehydration. It won't hurt, I promise."

I looked wildly at my mother. She nodded, smiling.

"You've been way too hot way too long," she said. "You'll feel much better after this."

I nodded and turned my head away from the needle approaching in the doctor's hand. First a cold sting of alcohol, and then the cold and much sharper bite of the needle, and then nothing.

"There. That wasn't so bad, was it?" Dr. Condon said around his teeth.

I shook my head. "No, it wasn't."

And the next thing I knew I was lying on the papered

table with a sharp pain between my legs and an even sharper one deep in my belly, packed from my vagina to my knees with sterile cotton pads. In the wastebasket beside the table there were more pads, some of them bloodstained. The doctor was not in the room. The overhead lights had been turned off and my mother sat beside me, holding my hand.

"Mama," I said, starting to cry weakly. "Mama..."

"Hush, darling," she whispered, and there were tear tracks on her perfect cheeks. "You'll be all right now. Honey, there was a baby, very tiny, and very badly...malformed. Dr. Condon had no choice but to take it. You could not have carried it; it could not have been born. So much better now, darling..."

I began to cry in earnest, wrenching sobs, deep ones. They hurt my stomach, but I could not stop.

"Mama, no...no, Mama..."

"Shush, Thayer, you must not cry. You have some delicate stitches and we need to keep you quiet and still. The doctor was called to the hospital, but his assistant is going to give you something for the pain and clean you up a bit, and then we'll go home, and you can have a nice, long, cool sleep. I know it must hurt, but it won't for long. It was really next to nothing...."

"What will Nick say?" I almost screamed. "We killed his baby! What will he say?"

"Perhaps we'll never know," my mother said softly, or that's what I thought she said, but just then the nurse came in with a hypodermic of painkiller and a package of large napkins for me to wear and some yellow pills in a vial.

I began to slide away again, on the pain medication. I remember that Detritus came in and carried me out in his arms and put me into the backseat, where a clean pillow and a blanket waited, and I did not really wake up again until late into that night.

I woke moaning with pain and felt the soft, cool hand of my grandmother and heard her voice, like music and cool water.

"It's time for another pill, sweetheart," she said. "I'm taking the overnight. I'll be right here with you."

"Grand...there was a baby...."

"I know, darling. I know. I'm so terribly sorry. I know you don't want to hear it now, but you'll have other babies, you and your Nick. Now lie back down and close your eyes. We'll get through this. We always do."

I lay back, sinking into cool linen, still holding her hand.

"I want Nick...."

"He'll probably call tomorrow. It's the day for it. We'll track him down. Don't worry about that."

"Grand, he'd want to know...."

"Of course he would. And he will. I've got my sources. Don't think I haven't."

I let myself slide back into sleep. Grand would fix it. Grand had her sources. Of course she did.

But he did not call the next day, and no letter came from somewhere in Europe, and by the time the great, devouring infection took me that night I knew somehow that he would not.

And he did not. Not during the long days when I was

nearly delirious in the darkened room and my mother and grandmother and a white-capped nurse flitted ghostlike around me, and not in the weeks when I was better and could sit in a chair and eat a little, and not even in the days after that, when I could finally walk and climb stairs and even walk down to the river, leaning hard on Grand.

I never asked but once.

"Did he ever...," I said to Grand one morning as we sat on the screened porch and felt the cooler breath of early September kiss our cheeks.

"No, darling, he never did. I am so sorry."

"I'm not," I said levelly.

That evening I went to my closet and scrounged far into the back of it and pulled out the sneakers I had worn at camp, the ones on whose toes Nick had written *Just* and *wait*. I took them down to the river in the twilight and threw them in. They eddied for a moment and then whirled away on the brown river water. I watched them out of sight.

But still, for a long time, I waited.

CHAPTER

8

It is called, variously, Sewanee, the University of the South, the Mountain. But those whose hearts and minds it has truly captured—and there are many—often call it simply the Domain. There is a stone arch at its entrance, on the flat top of its green mountain in southern Tennessee, and on it the words *The Domain* are carved clearly and deeply, so that when you roll under it you know by its instruction, as well as by the folk-art beauty of the campus and its buildings, that you are entering a place of unworldly, living magic. I know that I felt a tiny shudder of that when Detritus and my mother and grandmother drove me up the mountain to its summit on that day in late September. And I know that that was what my grandmother intended me to feel.

By the middle of the month I was physically well enough to start packing my clothes for Agnes Scott, but I had not yet done it. I had spent a lot of time reading in my cool, dim room or on the screened porch, and I had slept a great deal, great, white, dreamless drifts of it. I read with avidity things that I would never have considered before: Winston Churchill's two volumes on World War II; a chronicle of the French Revolution that fairly reeked of curdled blood on hot paving stones, called *Paris in the Terror*; *Swann's Way,* which even my word-bedazzled father had declared the most boring novel in the English language; the collected poetry of Robert Service. I spent a few faultless blue days down in my little retreat by the river, hoping to recapture some of the sense of perfect peace and safety I had felt there when I was small, but I usually simply ended up sleeping and woke not to safety but to tears.

I cried enormously in those first days. I would cry my way into sleep, yearning for its dark relief, and awoke with tears still wet on my cheeks. I sobbed in the long, still afternoons as the shadows of September lengthened on the lawn. In the middle of a conversation with my mother or Grand I would feel my eyes fill and my mouth contort and would stumble from the room and up the stairs to my bedroom. Sometimes I could not, for a moment, even remember what I was crying about, except that my body felt as if I had thrown up my viscera and it had been replaced with cold, echoing pain. I remember thinking that surely you could die of such pain but knowing still that people didn't and wishing that I could. The crying was never cathartic, only terrifying and ultimately embarrassing. I seldom in my life had cried. I think it was the embarrassment that finally stopped the overflowing well.

The tears must have, finally, been maddening to those around me, but my mother and certainly my grandmother never sighed or muttered, "For goodness' sake, stop that crying." Grand did not weep with me; she had at times, but now she simply sat close and held my hand or touched my hair, her face a blanched mask of pain. My mother cried, though. Often I would look at her and see tears tracking down her faultless cheeks, and sometimes she hugged me hard and said, "So sorry, baby. So sorry," and I would feel her tears in my hair. Her tears brought me unease and confusion instead of surcease, but still, no matter where we traveled afterwards, she and I, I would always remember that in the worst pain of my life my mother cried for me.

When the crying stopped, it was if a great whirlpool, perhaps made of my tears, had sucked the past summer and everything in it deep into its lightless maw. It seemed a summer that had never happened; I could consciously remember little of it. A great, heavy stillness set in and nothing seemed to penetrate it. My mother was fussing about getting ready for college and finally began simply to pack some of my clothes. I no more noticed the packed suitcases sitting in my room than I noticed the furniture there, or the columns on the portico of our house. I could not seem to get my mind around the fact that Agnes Scott College, sitting in its prissy little urban enclave in Decatur, Georgia, was waiting to receive me. Past the day I was living in there seemed nothing at all.

It was my grandmother who broke the spell. I still do not know if she meant to or not. We were sitting on the screened porch in the late afternoon, and in the lowering green dimness my grandmother was reading one of my college catalogs.

Better her than me, I remember thinking, turning the pages of *Man and Superman,* which meant nothing to me at all.

"There's a freshman course at Scott called Southern Folklore and Magic," she said. "You'd like that, don't you think?"

The cool, freighted blood sliding through my veins turned suddenly to fire. I felt as if I had swallowed molten lead.

"No!" I screamed. "I would not like it! I would hate it! There is no magic! There was never any magic! Magic is a lie you tell little kids to make them stop crying! I will not take that damned course and I will not go to Agnes Scott! Nobody can make me!"

She was silent for a moment and then said, "Of course they can't make you. I would not permit anyone to make you go anywhere to college that you did not want to go. That would be a futile and dangerous thing. So what do you think you want to do now? Is there somewhere else that sounds good to you?"

"I want to get out of this house! That's all! I have to get out of this house!"

Only then did I realize that it was entirely true. I did have to go. I had known that far down inside me since the day I came back from the bloodstained Victorian house in Atlanta. I stopped shouting and looked at my clenched hands. I did not know what to do even in the next instant.

After what seemed a long time, with only the sound of my grandmother's creaking rocking chair breaking the silence, she said, "I think I know what you should do. I think I know just where you should go. It's a very special place. It's a college, but not like any other college I know about. I agree with you, you do need to get out of this house; I would love to see you go there. It's in another state, on the top of a mountain. Quite far away."

She stopped, waiting, I know, for me to reply, to say, What is this place?

But I did not.

"I'll go there," I said. "That's what I want to do. I want to go to college in another state on top of a mountain. I want to go as soon as I can; I want to go this fall. Can you make that happen?"

"Yes," she said. "I probably can. But don't you want to hear a little about it? Its name is—"

"I don't want to hear its name!" I cried. "I just want to go. Does it all have to be so hard?"

"Not in the least," she said, ringing the little bell that would bring Juanita to her. "Consider it done. Give me a hand here and I'll go get the ball rolling."

"Mother..."

"Will be delighted," she said, and took my hand, and I pulled her out of her rocking chair and together we set off on the journey that would bring me, two weeks later, into the Domain.

The University of the South in Sewanee, Tennessee, crowns the summit of its mountain like a mortarboard or a forage cap, or perhaps a bishop's mitre, apt similes all. It was founded just after the Civil War expressly to serve the southern diocese of the Episcopal Church in the Christian education of its young gentlemen. It was modeled hopefully after the venerable Anglican churches of England and held together in its early hardscrabble years by many recently unemployed Confederate officers. Many southern bishops blessed it, and not a few came to teach there. Several still do. Widows of Confederate officers and Episcopal clergymen were its first housemothers. It became the indulgent little joke early on that in Sewanee's case, the holy trinity was God the Father, God the Son, and Gen. Robert E. Lee.

God the Father and God the Son are still manifestly present in the mellow gray dimness of its chapel and seminary, and General Lee's portrait, flanked by draped Confederate flags and crossed dress sabers, still hangs in Commons. The education presided over by these eminences is unalterably classical liberal arts, and generally first-rate in spite of it, and many undergraduates now are drawn from all over the country and even the world. Very few now come to be molded by God and Gen. Robert E. Lee, for life and service in the vanished world of the Christian Gentleman's South; in fact, a great many new students come up the Mountain for the first time prepared to jeer. If I had known a thing in the world about the school I would have undoubtedly been one of them.

But in the course of my years there I learned the primary truth of the Domain. Most of those who remain are reluctant to leave. And the young who enter laughing and stay to graduate almost always go out into the world off the Mountain taking with them the swish of academic gowns and a set of values stained at least a bit by that old chivalry. There is enormous power in those old gray stones, cloistered away up on the Mountain. I used to think that the last sound many new graduates heard as they rolled out through the Domain's stone arch was the triumphant laughter of long-dead bishops and generals.

The sheer, dreaming old beauty on the Mountain is the snare, of course. Those who do not need it often do not stay. A high percentage of freshmen and sophomores do not return. Some flunk out, but many simply bolt back to the rich, comforting stench of the world. Those who do stay somehow find that they need bells in their ears, and plainsong, and countless angels dancing always on the heads of pins.

And, oh, the mossy old stones and the flying dark gowns and the ranked pennons in the chapel looking for all the world like medieval banners, and the slow turn of the seasons in the great hardwood forest, and the mists of autumn and the white snowfall of spring dogwoods; the entire world spread out at one's feet from the flank of the Steep, and the drunkenness of poetry and mathematics and the illicit flow of good bourbon and the night music of concerts and dances through new green leaves, and the delicately bawdy laughter of young girls and the sheen of their flesh and hair, and the trembling awareness of the cold dew and dawn breaking on hangovers after you have talked all night and sung many songs and perhaps made out by the lake on the Steep. These things are golden barbs in the flesh and will hold long after you have left the Domain. Sewanee is eccentric and elitist and chauvinistic and innocent and arrogant and very, very particular, and it holds its own like a great gray raptor.

It has held a deep-laid part of me for all the years since I left it. How could it not? It has been my future, as well as my past.

*　　*　　*

If I said that I was happy in the Domain, I would not be telling the truth. I know that I thought that I was, but for more than three of those four years what I felt was a kind of sweet abstracted comfort, a feeling of well-being that I perceived but did not quite feel. The campus was inordinately beautiful; there was charm in all its seasons. I never ceased noticing that beauty, even if it did not pierce me through, as it well might have before that summer.

How lucky I am to be here, I would think, drifting across campus on a stained-glass fall afternoon, or in a powdery little winter snowfall. And it was true. It would have been awful to have to look at strip malls, exhaust-clogged freeways, the rows of barracks-like housing that haunted so many campuses. I would probably smile as I thought it; once my roommate, a diminutive dumpling of an economics major from New Jersey, said that I reminded her of a character in a bad romantic movie, drifting down University Avenue wrapped in a tan trench coat, my hair flying in a bitter little wind, smiling a goofy secret little smile. I tried to replace the goofy smile with an expression of alert interest, but I did not often succeed. Even I could sometimes feel the corners of my mouth tugging up. But it was mere contentment; I did not think there was any exaltation left in me. That had swirled into the whirlpool that had taken Nick and Sherwood Forest and the sheer delight of being young. It did not seem to matter on the Mountain.

Vice-Chancellor Martinson was a friend of my grandmother's; he had been best man in her wedding to my grandfather, and she had been on the Mountain many times.

"I always wished women had been allowed to go there when I was college age," she said. "I wanted Finch to go. But then you came along, and I found the perfect candidate. I only wish I'd thought of it sooner. We could have visited; you could have gone into your freshman year knowing the college. I think it might have made you very happy."

"I love it just the same," I said. "It's made me happy, Grand."

"Has it, darling? I know it's been satisfying for you. . . ."

She let it trail off, and I did not reply. Satisfying. Yes, of course. The Mountain had given me all the warmth my heart could hold. My grades were good. I loved my English major and thought my professors empathetic and gifted. Some became quite good friends, in a seemly, facultyish way, and even Dr. and Mrs. Martinson had me to dinner a few times, a fact that did not endear me to my classmates, even if it was only a sweet nod to my grandmother. And when Laureen, my New Jersey dumpling roommate, asked crossly why I never dated, I was able to say, "I do date. I've gone to every prom; I went to all the concerts this winter; just last week I went to the movies with—"

"Oh, you know what I mean," she snapped. "If I looked like you I'd have dated every single male on this mountain by now!"

"There's still time," I replied a bit sharply. I did date. I just had not felt any real connection with my dates. My mother was always asking me why I didn't bring some of my friends home to visit, and I knew she meant young men. My grandmother did not ask, but sometimes she studied

147

me with a slight puzzled frown when my mother launched another bring-a-boy-to-dinner campaign. I took to staying more weekends at school so as not to have to force a reply. Once I said in exasperation, "Did you send me to Sewanee just to get a husband?"

"Well, of course not, what a thing to say," she replied indignantly.

"In a pig's ass," I said under my breath.

And so on the Mountain, well into my fourth year, I continued my dreamtime walkabout, almost sleepy with comfort, nearly submerged in content.

At the beginning of my last winter quarter, I discovered that I was a quarter short of my English requirements. I could not understand how this had happened; I was, after all, an English major and thought that I had scrupulously kept up with my course requirements. That I could determine there was not an English course on the Mountain that I had not taken. My professors and even the vice-chancellor joined the paper chase, but to no avail. Six months before graduation I lacked the credits to graduate. Undoubtedly, everyone said, it was a clerical error of some sort, but no cleric came forward and the gaping hole in my required courses shone out, as Nellie used to say, "like a crevasse in new snow."

"There's not a new English course that would be suitable for you until next fall," Vice-Chancellor Martinson said. "Maybe we could find you one somewhere off the Mountain that could work for you; I'll call around this afternoon...."

"No, wait," my faculty advisor, a sweet brown wren of a woman whose knowledge was vast and vital, despite looking as though she could produce nothing but pies, said suddenly. "Doesn't Dr. O'Neill's class on Irish literature and folklore start this quarter?"

"Irish folklore?" I said doubtfully. Of what possible use to me would leprechauns and rainbows and barrels of gold be?

"It would work for your major," Miss Gerber said. "And who knows? You might actually enjoy it. I would. I'll call and see if he's got a space for you."

She came back into the room smiling.

"One space," she said. "A student dropped out yesterday. He said if it didn't suit you to hang on, there would undoubtedly be more classes later."

"Probably many more," I groused. Irish folklore indeed. And then I thought, My father would have loved Irish folklore.

And I nodded. "Fine. Irish folklore it is. Who is this Professor O'Neill? Irish, no doubt?"

"As Paddy's pig," Dr. Martinson said, grinning. "He's a great antidote to all the Anglican effluvia dripping off the walls."

And so the next morning I dashed out into a driving winter rain, late and unable to find my umbrella, and skidded, leaving a puddle with every step, into the classroom where Dr. Aengus O'Neill was dispensing Irish folklore. I sank into a vacant chair on the end of the front row, hoping to be as invisible as possible. I knew it was not working when everyone in the class turned to stare at my soaked raincoat and the red locks of hair plastered to my face. Some of them giggled. The tall man with his back to me, holding an open book and intoning something in an Irish brogue so thick as to seem a parody, did not turn around.

"'I am of Ireland,'" he said into the overheated air of the classroom. "'And the Holy Land of Ireland, /And time runs on,' cried she. /'Come out of charity...'"

And he turned, looking at me out of the bluest eyes I had ever seen, the blue of the heart of a coal fire. His black hair hung in sort of a comma over one of them, and high on his cheekbones there was a peppering of black freckles. He walked over to me and took my wet face in his hands.

"'Come dance with me in Ireland.'"

His eyes locked on mine and I could feel his breath stirring the damp hair on my forehead.

I began to cry.

Five months later, just into June on the Mountain, I married him in a small outdoor ceremony on the lip of the Steep. We might have married at home, in River House, but my mother did not like Aengus and did not approve of the marriage. We might have married in the chapel, but Aengus did not approve of Anglicans, thinking them bloodless and drowned in ritual. My mother did not attend, but my grandmother did. I did not care about my mother. Grand and Aengus were all I needed on my wedding day, and for many days after.

CHAPTER

9

A ngus?" my mother said with a small, contrived frown on her still-perfect brow. "Like the cows?"

Aengus smiled at her, the quick, quirky grin that lit his dark face like a lamp. I had never met anyone who could resist that smile, but my mother did not smile back.

"I wouldn't be surprised," he said. "I grew up with more cows than people."

"And that would be...where?" my mother said, as if his accent could have come from any other place on the earth than where it did.

"That would be Connacht, in the west country of Ireland," Aengus said. "There are fine towns and cities there now, but we didn't live in one. We lived on a farm in country so backward that many of us still called it Cruachain. Beautiful it is, but there are no homes of such refinement as this."

He nodded his black head around the porch of River

House, where we were sitting, he and I and Mother and Grand.

"Hmmmmph," my mother muttered. I heard the tiniest of snickers from Grand. Aengus's smile widened. I closed my eyes.

I had brought him home to Lytton to meet Mother and Grand at the end of winter quarter. By then Aengus and I were together. I hoped it might be for always. It was hard to tell what Aengus thought, about this, anyway. I never knew anyone who lived so totally in the moment. If I prodded him to think ahead, to make plans for the future, he would laugh and say, " 'Sufficient unto the day the evil thereof,' " or some other aphorism that meant "Don't push me." In this, if not in other ways, he was rather like a child. When I pointed this out to him once, he said, " 'Backward, turn backward, O Time in thy flight. Make me a child again, just for tonight.' " Aengus was big on aphorisms.

"Why do you want to be a child?" I said. "What were you like as a child?"

"Very much like I am now," he said.

I thought this might be true. I could almost see him, a grave, dark boy totally absorbed in whatever he was doing, his black head cocked to one side, his lips pursed in a soundless whistle. And then the head raised and the quick white grin. I had seen him so many times. I had also seen him come out of a deep, still study and snatch me up and whirl me around, or burst into a fragment of hideous song that he swore was an authentic Irish folk tune, or do a swift intricate shuffle, also purported to be *the* original Irish Jig. It was a part of the magic that was Aengus. For Aengus did have magic. I think that when I discovered him I also rediscovered magic.

Grand felt it, too. She adored Aengus, as he did her. But sometimes her eyes were thoughtful as she regarded him, and once she said to me, "Don't let him go too far into the Irish thing. Don't let him take you there with him."

"Grand, it's one of the things I love most about him," I protested. "It's who he is."

"No," Grand said. "It's *what* he is. He doesn't know who he is yet. You're a strong and resilient woman at heart, Thayer. He'll depend on you to tell him who he is. Otherwise he'll be gone in a puff of sea mist and moonbeams and you'll never know him. Keep him in the world with you."

"I don't know what you're talking about."

"I hope you never do."

At first, even after the day that he cupped my face in his hands and I cried, I would have little to do with him. I told myself that his pure exuberance, his passion, was off-putting, almost unseemly. He spun such lilting and dazzling stories of gods and poets and heroes and horsemen and rainbows that his class crackled with them like wildfire. They were unlike anything I had ever heard, in a classroom or out. My father had loved the myths of the Norsemen and the Greeks, but he had told me none about the beautiful wild, murderous Celts who rode out of the north adorned in golden torques and took the heads of those they slew in battle and carried them on their saddles. Aengus himself admitted that though

153

the Celtic empire covered a great deal more territory than Ireland, it was there, in his homeland, that he preferred to chronicle them.

"You can find all you like about them in their other haunts. The library's got it all. But it's Ireland where they bloomed like stinking roses. More than two million people still speak Gaelic.

"And my God, what a spectacle they must have been, charging into battle in their chariots! They fought naked, and they whipped themselves into a wild bloodlust; the Romans called it furor, the Germans *Wut.* Their swords were masterpieces of carving; one of them, the Caladbolg, passed on down to King Arthur, who called it Caliburnus, or Excalibur. Yeah, the same one. And the songs and myths! Today I'm going to read you 'The Tale of Bulls of Cooley.' For the weekend I want a paper on the Celtic beliefs about death; use the *Book of Leinster* for background. I've got enough Xeroxed copies if you share. You'll hand them in on Monday."

Someone would groan, and Aengus would flash the white grin and say, "What better have you got to do of a weekend up here on this goddamn mountaintop?"

Aengus was like a lightning bolt that clove the quiet Mountain. Students followed him everywhere. Some of the faculty did, too. I came to think later that it was partly because I did not that he singled me out. In truth, he frightened me. I felt instinctively that his brush-fire energy could crack the carapace of my content like an eggshell. I skipped his class the next few days but realized that I would have to go back or lose my credits and I could not graduate without them.

The day that I went back he asked me, when class was over, if he could walk me back to my dormitory. By the time we got there I was laughing so hard that I did not realize, for a moment, where we were.

We sat down on a stone bench outside my dormitory and he said, "Now that wasn't so bad, was it?"

"What wasn't so bad?"

"Spending ten minutes in my presence outside the class-room."

"Why on earth would that be bad?"

"You tell me, Miss Thayer Wentworth. She of the mahogany hair and eyes like amber. Do you have a fly in your eye, Miss Thayer Wentworth? Do you have a middle name?"

"Antonia," I said gloomily.

"Are you kidding? It was my mother's name! Antonia Maeve Murphy O'Neill! My grandfather first fell in love with an Antonia before he married my grandma, and so my mother got stuck with the name of Granddad's old flame. How did you come by it?"

"My father fell in love with Willa Cather."

He laughed again.

"Literature will do you in every time," he said.

"Literature or the teachers thereof," I said, looking up at him from the corners of my eyes.

"I shan't do you in, I promise," he said. "Do you? Now that's another matter entirely."

"Dr. O'Neill! Aengus! If you think that's funny..."

"I apologize," he said ruefully. "Entirely inappropriate."

He fell silent beside me on the bench.

"Actually...," I said. "When did you have in mind?"

He stood up and wriggled a small leather book out of the hip pocket of his tight-fitting jeans. I watched him in the long shadows of the late winter afternoon. It was not cold; winter sometimes allows you a breath from long-dead summer on the Mountain. He had on a blue oxford-cloth shirt with the sleeves rolled midway up his arms; like his face, they were tanned dark and peppered slightly with black freckles. His hands were long and well shaped. Aengus always had beautiful hands. I wondered how they would feel on my flesh and felt my face scald. I looked down so that he would not see the blush.

He thumbed through the little book.

"Teaching tonight and tomorrow night," he said. "I seem to have Friday night free, though. Does that work for you?"

"It works fine," I whispered. I could not seem to get any breath behind my words.

"Friday it is, then," he said, swinging me up from the bench and giving me a light kiss on my flaming cheek. He grinned, whether at my hot skin or at the sheer audacity of arranging an assignation on the steps of a girls' dormitory I do not know. He touched the comma of dark hair over his eye and swung off into the rapidly falling dusk toward the English department. I stood in green shadow for a long moment, every inch of me seeming to quiver as if he had already touched me. Midway up the stairs my legs buckled and I sat down hard. I buried my face in my hands and laughed helplessly. I think I cried a little, too. So this was what it was to want a man. I had loved what Nick and I had done together, but this was entirely new and uncharted territory.

I could scarcely look at Aengus in class the next day, nor the day after. He did not look at me, either. He concluded the class with another of Yeats's poems. It ended:

O hiding hair and dewy eyes,
I am no more with life and death.
My heart upon his warm heart lies,
My breath is mixed into his breath.

Still he did not look at me, but I knew that he had read the poem for me. When I left my room that night to meet him at the end of the Steep, I was trembling so hard all over that my roommate said, "Are you coming down with something? You don't look so hot."

"I'm pretty sure I'm coming down with something," I said, and ran from the room so that she could not see me laughing.

"Or somebody," I added aloud, letting the door swing shut behind me and giving myself to the high January night wind.

The Mountain was a font of winds. Tonight's seemed to howl and swirl and bite from all directions at once. When I reached the lip of the Steep there was no one there, but the wind was a living presence, seeming to roar straight up from the valley. It almost lifted me from my feet.

"We can't do this!" I cried into its teeth.

"No question," Aengus said from behind me, wrapping his arms around me. The wind could not sway me, pressed hard against him, but I knew that if we broke apart it would have us both on the ground.

"Don't you have a room or something?" I shouted.

"I do, in the home of an iron widow with all the virtues stamped on her face and a sitting room beside the front door. It smells of cat pee and canned English peas. We may go there later, but I want this first time to be on the side of a mountain with all the stars in heaven above us. Come on; I know a place...."

I'll just bet you do, I thought, but I let him pull me along to the edge of the Steep and into a small, dense grove of birch trees. It glowed in the dark like a little citadel. Inside the grove there was a floor of emerald moss scalloped with ferns, and on the moss lay a rose-flowered quilt and a hamper with the necks of two bottles poking out of its lid.

"The widow's grandmother's prized Leicestershire quilt," he said. "When she lies under it again, she won't know where the little tickle came from. And two bottles of champagne. Not bad stuff. Not great, but pretty good for a teacher's salary...."

The wind could not reach us here, and there was a cold, fresh silence like you sometimes hear among winter trees. He sat down on the quilt and reached for the hamper.

"A little nip, for before?" he said.

"No," I whispered, almost choking on my own audacity. "For after."

I sank to my knees and held my arms out to him and he came into them, murmuring something under his breath that I thought to be Celtic. He never did tell me what he was saying. For a long space of time there was only dark fire, and the earth under my hips and the fierce fullness and rocking, and the cries, soft and then louder, and the great slamming explosion, and then only our breathing again, fast and hard, and the old, sly laughter of the wind.

After a much longer time we did drink some of the champagne, but we did not finish the first bottle, and Aengus left it and the unopened second one at the foot of the largest birch "for whatever gods tend this grove. By rights I should be burning an offering. But I've nothing precious enough to leave here."

"Nor do I," I said, "but I wish I did."

"And I'll be asking about the one who took that precious thing one day, but whoever he is, he doesn't matter this night," Aengus said softly.

After a long time, I said, "No. He doesn't."

Student-faculty relationships are frowned upon on the Mountain, but Aengus was so charmingly correct about ours that little was said. He knew how, among other things, to be perfectly discreet and intimate at the same time. Oddly, I never learned a great deal about him before he came to America. His parents were both dead. He promised to take me back to Ireland one day. In the meantime, my family was, he said, all we needed.

They soon turned out to be more.

The second time we visited my mother and Grand in Lytton, it was mid-April and by then Aengus and I knew that we would marry at the end of the spring quarter. Grand was delighted.

My mother was patently not. My sister, Lily, was back home without Goose for the first of what would be many times, her face puffed with tears and her underlip far out with injury at whatever misdeed Goose had perpetrated upon her. During all Aengus's and my talk of a June wedding, my mother looked pointedly at Lily and then at me.

"I wouldn't be so quick to jump into it if I were you, Thayer," she said. "Not many marriages turn out the way you expect them to."

Lily burst into tears and fled, and Aengus grinned his wolf's grin at my mother.

"We expect nothing from ours, Mrs. Wentworth, except that it will make us both very happy," he said. It was rather sweet. Even if I hadn't known him well I would have been captivated by it. I think Grand was; she laughed softly. Mother was not.

"I suppose you'll have it in that chapel," she said. "It's a pretty enough little place, but it looks like Church of Rome to me."

I stared at my mother. I had never heard her say "Church of Rome" before. I still don't think she ever had, or has since.

"More like Church of England," Aengus said. "But no. It will be an outdoor wedding. There's a little grove of silver birch trees on the lip of the Steep; it's a place that means a lot to us." He slewed me a wink.

"Under a tree," my mother snapped. "How like Thayer. So will your canon or priest or whatever do the honors?"

"No, a friend of mine from Ireland. She's just come over to work in Washington. She's ordained. She said she'd love to do it."

"Ordained in what? Not one of those newfangled tree-worshiping sects, I hope?"

"Oh no. It's a very old and respected religion. You'll see. It should be a very . . . gentle ceremony."

My mother did not answer. She got up and followed Lily to the kitchen, from whence we could hear fresh sobs. My grandmother sighed.

"You might as well be married on elephants with fireworks," she said. "She isn't going to approve, no matter what. But she'll behave at the wedding. I promise you that."

Just then my mother called to Aengus from inside the house, and he got up and excused himself and went off to find her.

"Now what?" I said, exhaling a long breath.

"Who knows?" Grand said. "But she sounded pleasant enough. She'd like him if she let herself. It's almost impossible not to."

"Is it that he's Irish?" I said. "Or a schoolteacher? Or both? If not him, what on earth did she want for me?"

"The incoming president of the Piedmont Driving Club," Grand said lazily, and we both laughed.

I'm glad I have that moment. I did not laugh often with Grand again.

My mother and Aengus came back out onto the porch. She was carrying fresh iced tea and smiling winsomely. He was carrying a plate of cookies and looking as though he had swallowed something large.

On the way back to Sewanee I begged him to tell me why she had called him into the kitchen.

"Nothing much."

"'Nothing' crap, Aengus! She was grinning like a Cheshire cat and you looked like you'd swallowed a bug."

"Nothing much, Thay, okay?"

"Okay, but you're going to have to tell me sometime."

"I will. Sometime."

He told me that night, after we had gotten back to the Domain and ordered a pizza and carried it up the widow's immaculate stairs to his room. The widow was at choir practice, which made the excursion easier. We'd stay, I knew, until after she went to bed and then I would tiptoe downstairs in my socks. She knew we were there; she always did, but it seemed all right unless she actually saw us.

"I think it's the actual sight of our sin-raddled bodies creeping upstairs bent on more sin that would do her in," Aengus said. "This way, if we ever get caught at it, she can tell the choir she had no idea."

We had just finished the pizza and were sprawled on his bed watching Jay Leno when Aengus told me.

"Thayer," he said, pulling me into his shoulder. "Listen. Your mother told me about Nick Abrams tonight. She told me about . . . the baby, and having to have it . . . you know . . ."

I stiffened against him and drew in a great, trembling breath.

"I can't believe she did that," I whispered on the breath that came out. "I absolutely cannot believe she would do that! I was going to tell you! It just...Aengus, it just didn't seem important! I never even think about it now!"

He went still. Too still. And then he said, "You never think about not ever having any children?"

I jerked away from him and twisted around on the bed until I could see his face. I was panting so hard I could hardly get my breath. There were tears on his face as he looked back at me. I had never seen tears on Aengus's face before.

"What are you talking about?"

After a long while he dropped his head onto my shoulder. Against it, he said, "You didn't know, did you?"

"Know what? Aengus, my God..."

"Thayer, you had a bad infection after the...operation. It got into your...tubes. You can't have children. I had no idea on earth you didn't know about it."

"Did you think I would know a thing like that and not tell you?"

I was on my feet and screaming. Literally screaming. Could this be true? This awful thing, could my mother know it and not tell me? This thing that would smash my life, alter it completely and forever, and the life of anyone I loved...

Aengus stood up and pulled me to him and put his hand over my mouth. My tears ran down over his hands; I could feel them dropping onto his forearms, my blouse.

"It isn't true," I wept into his shoulder. "She was telling you a lie! She just doesn't want us to get married...."

"It's true, baby. She showed me your doctor's report. Just happened to have it lying around, I guess...."

I sagged until he picked me up and put me back on the bed and held me, rocking me, kissing me, kissing the sides of my face and hair, until I had cried myself out. The sky outside was graying when I finally stopped. The sleepy twitter of a dawn bird drifted in through the window screen.

"I want you to go to sleep, now," he said. "I've got an early class, but I want you to snuggle in under the covers and sleep. I'll be back after class and we'll go get some breakfast."

"The widow..."

"Fuck the widow," Aengus said. "Thay, listen. I know it has to be a huge, awful thing for you, but we'll get through it. We will. Don't worry about me. I never really wanted children, to tell you the truth. I want to be your child, as well as...everything else."

Incredibly, I laughed, a watery, hiccupping laugh.

"As long as you stay grown-up about...other things," I said.

"Always," he said, reaching for me. "Always."

I told my grandmother about my mother's betrayal on the phone and she was as angry as I had ever heard her, but she promised she would be at my wedding and would keep my mother away.

And she did. On the soft Saturday afternoon when we married in the little grove of silver birches on the Steep, the entire faculty was there, and most of the student body, and my grandmother and Detritus, too. But not my mother. The mist from the valley swirled almost to the very lip of the Steep, and we all looked as if we were rising out of it, grown out of the mist as if from some magic medium. Aengus's friend from Washington was radiant and tender, and read a lovely service from a small black leather book that I assumed was a Bible. She was full of reverence for the day and the earth and the trees and the sky and us and our union, and I remember that from somewhere in the crowd small silvery bells rang.

After the wedding, when almost everyone had gone, I saw that she had left her Bible on the small twig table we had used for an altar, and I picked it up and gave it to Aengus. When I looked down on it, the gold letters on it said, not *Holy Bible*, but *The Book of Shadows*.

After all these years, and until my last one, I will always love knowing that I was married under a tree on a mountain by a witch.

CHAPTER

10

On the first morning of our honeymoon we slept late. It was nearing noon when we woke fully, and for a long time we simply lay entwined and still, tangled in Grand's silky sheets.

"Porthault," I said lazily. "At least one-thousand thread count. What a way to start a honeymoon."

"I don't know about thread counts," Aengus said. "All I know about sheets is that the widow's are made of something you could strike a match on. Well, you know."

"The higher the thread count the more expensive the sheets. Look, you can almost see through these. Fine French linen."

"Well, then," he said comfortably. "It's almost lunchtime. Do you want to get some lunch at the Beach Club, or would you rather..."

We were in Grand's big old house on the beach on Sea

Island, Georgia. Besides the residential homes that ran the length of the island, set in groves of live oaks and palms facing the sea, there was only the fabled old Cloister hotel on Sea Island. I loved the Cloister. Every time we visited Grand's house, we took some of our meals there, eating huge breakfasts and listening at dinner to the string trio. I loved the spectacular Spanish room, with its towering stained-glass windows and cages of singing birds. There were graham crackers and milk set out for you in the entrance lobby at bedtime, and the vast green lawns were carpet smooth, bordered with blooming flowers and overhung by ancient, twisted live oaks scarved in Spanish moss that sometimes touched the grass. There were stables, sailing, outdoor Plantation Suppers, cycling, skeet shooting, tennis, deep-sea fishing, two ocean-side pools, and numerous small patios tucked away for alfresco dining. The Cloister always seemed an enchanted kingdom to me. Grand's house was almost as good.

It rose two stories of stucco above its emerald seaside lawn. In her second-floor bedroom we were in the treetops; you could touch the Spanish moss from her balcony. A hedge of roses along the shorefront opened to the path down to the beach, and someone had set up an umbrella table and little wrought-iron chairs on the highest shelf on the beach. The low dunes ran down to wet, hard-packed beach and then into the water, slow and gentle and dark green, toy waves ruffling on the sand. Pelicans and gulls rode the thermals over the water, but we saw no people. Most of them, I thought, would be at lunch, or perhaps swimming in the pools that lay behind the dunes. We had had a midnight swim in Grand's.

My hair still smelled of chlorine and sulfur. I could not imagine that it did not gag Aengus, but he buried his face deep in it and said it had an exotic kind of beachy smell. Grand's bedroom was papered in a soft peach satin-stripe wallpaper, and in the glow from that and the flare of the June sun off the balcony his face, dark stubbled as it was, was lit like an excited child's.

"I'm not hungry right now," I said. "I guess maybe I'd rather..."

He was reaching for me when the bedside telephone rang. He hesitated.

"Should I answer it?" he said. "Nobody but your folks knows we're here, do they?"

"I don't think so. You better answer it, though. I asked for a hair appointment; maybe that's them...."

He picked it up and said hello. His face went still and he lay propped on one elbow for a long time, listening. I turned over and looked at him curiously. He looked back at me and then said, "All right. Thank you. We'll be ready."

He hung up the phone slowly, but he did not speak. Sudden anxiety knifed me.

"Aengus..."

He shook his head. Tears filmed his eyes.

"Aengus..."

"Thayer, your grandmother died. She died very suddenly, early this morning. She hadn't even gotten up yet. Juanita took her breakfast up and found her. They think maybe a stroke. Your mother is sending a car for us; it's picking us up at two. We should be home by eight or nine tonight—"

"No, Aengus!" I cried. "She was okay yesterday! You remember how we laughed when she said she didn't think Detritus had ever driven twenty miles without her before.... You remember, don't you?"

"Baby—"

"I don't believe you!" I shrieked. "Mother's just being mean! You know she's been trying to spoil this wedding—"

"Thayer!" he said, shaking me a little with both hands. "We don't have time for this right now. We have to get up and get going. The car's going to be here in less than an hour."

I sat staring at his face. It was sleep creased and had paled; the sun had moved off the balcony and didn't fall over us now. The peach-striped wallpaper was dull and ordinary looking; it might have adorned the walls of any chain motel. The satiny sheets looked gray. Our clothes lay in a pile in the middle of the Mexican tiled floor; they did not look film-noir erotic but simply careless and sloppy. I began to cry.

"I want Grand," I sobbed into my hands. "I want my grandmother."

"They need us at home, darling," he said, getting out of bed and pulling me gently behind him. "Your mother wants us to be in on the planning, whatever that means. You know your grandmother would want you to do that. Lily and what's-his-name are already there."

"I do not want Goose...in the same house with my grandmother's..."

I could not say "body" and cried harder, but I got up and stumbled after Aengus into the bathroom and stood in the shower while he adjusted it to spray warm, sulfurous water over me. The soap he handed me smelled of Vetiver, Grand's scent, and I could not lift my hand holding it. It was he who soaped me gently all over and lifted the spray to rinse me off and then folded a huge, soft terry towel around me.

"I'll bring you some underclothes and put out some things for you," he said. "And I'll put the bags outside on the veranda. I'll call when we're under way, so they'll know. I know how much you loved her, baby. So let's do this for her, okay?"

I do not remember a longer ride in my life. The car, a big Chrysler driven by a taciturn woman named Mrs. Moore, had tinted gray windows and air-conditioning turned to sub-arctic. I shivered, but when she turned it off I ran sweat, so we went back to frigid. The flat South Georgia landscape, mainly peach orchards and peanuts and soybean fields, fled by all of a dun color. By Valdosta I had stopped crying, and I fell asleep on Aengus's shoulder somewhere near Macon and did not wake until the car slowed and stopped and I looked up to see the front of River House blazing with light. I felt a smile start and then remembered who was not in it anymore.

"I can't go in there," I said, beginning to cry again, but then the front door opened and my mother and sister came out onto the portico, and I could see that there were other people in the house behind them.

"Do it for Grand," Aengus whispered, and I got out of the car and stumbled up the walk and portico steps and let them sweep me into their arms. My mother's face was blanched and swollen and Lily was sobbing outright, but I did not cry any more that night, and I don't remember that I ever cried again for Grand.

I broke free from my mother and sister and dodged through the crowd, not responding to their murmurs of condolence. I did not know them. I noticed as I went by that the dining room table was laden with platters and trays and the big silver candelabras that Grand had given Mother held white, lit candles. What was my mother thinking? A party, when Grand had died this very morning in this house? I jerked open the door to Grand's room, thinking only that I had to, *must*, see her, that to do so would somehow mean that none of this dreadfulness was true. Surely she would put down her book and smile and say, "Hi, darling," as she so often did and hold out her arms. Surely her touch, and her fragrant, after-bath smell, would cancel out the terrible day and we could laugh about it. Surely no one would remember it afterwards. Surely. Surely. . . .

She was not in her room. Her four-poster rice bed, the one she had brought from Charleston, was made up with her ivory damask linens and shell-pale satin comforter, and only one small lamp burned. Her beautiful old mahogany bedroom furniture shone faintly in the dim room. There was a huge vase of white calla lilies on her desk. I was opening the door to her bathroom when my mother came in. I spun around.

"Where is she?" I cried. "Where is Grand?"

My mother came and put her arms around me again. Aengus stood behind her. He had tear tracks on his dark face.

"Darling, she's at Magnusen's. She . . . wanted cremation. I'm sure you knew that. We'll keep her urn in the beautiful little room they have for that at St. Philip's. She most emphatically did not want a funeral, so I thought we'd just have some of her close Atlanta friends tonight. I'm glad so many of them could come; it was such short notice—"

"I'm sure Grand wouldn't have wanted to inconvenience you," I said. "Maybe she'll apologize. Puff ashes all over you."

"Thayer—"

"I'll stay with her for a little while, Mrs. Wentworth," Aengus said, moving in to slide me from my mother's arms. "It was an awful shock for her, especially today—"

"Oh, that's right," Mother said. "It's your honeymoon, isn't it? And you were at Grand's house. That's really too bad, but Thayer must come down and speak to her grandmother's friends. Lily is already there. Everyone will wonder—"

"I don't give a happy rat's ass what they wonder!" I shouted. "I'm not going down there and moo around about what a wonderful woman she was, and how much I'll miss her. If they don't know that by now they don't need me to tell them—"

"Thayer!"

"Please, Mrs. Wentworth. Mom," Aengus said. "Just give us a few minutes. We'll be down soon."

"Fine," Mother said in her clipped angry-in-public voice. "If Thayer can manage it, of course."

She left, closing the door with a little bang, and Aengus put his chin on my head and said, "What a bi—witch she can be," into my hair. "You think you can go down?"

I shook my head no into his shoulder.

"I'm going to stay here," I said. "I'm going to sleep here. I hope you'll stay with me, but if you don't want to—"

"Don't be an ass, baby," he said. "Wherever you are, I am.

You need to eat something, though. I'll go get you a plate and say a few words around for both of us. I won't be long."

I don't think he was, but by the time he returned with one of Grand's Haviland plates full of party sandwiches and cheese straws I was sunk into Grand's bed, fast asleep in a cloud of Vetiver. He slid into bed beside me and I turned into his arms, but I did not wake. We both slept, that night, with Grand's arms around us.

My mother sent Juanita to wake us early.

"Miss Crystal got some stuff she want to go over with you," she said. "She and your sister and Goose are on the porch. There's coffee out there."

Alternately yawning and sniffling, I went down the stairs and out to the screened porch. Aengus stayed behind to shave, said Goose would probably kill him with a hoe handle if he saw the state of his stubble. By the time he joined us, his cheeks fresh shining, we were finishing our second cups of coffee. For the last few moments no one had spoken.

When Aengus had settled beside me into the long porch sofa, my mother said, "Well. This won't take long. I know you two want to get back to your honeymoon, and it's all so simple I believe we can just talk it out. Your grandmother"— and she looked around at Lily and me—"has some specific bequests to you that I thought I would tell you about. You can verify them against her will, of course, but I don't think there'll be a reading until a bit later."

She waited, looking at us, and we both nodded. I did not want anything from Grand. I only wanted Grand. But apparently this doling out was going to happen anyway.

"Lily, Grand left you and Goose"—did anyone else notice the slight flaring of my mother's nostrils at the name?—"a trust fund for each child you might have and five hundred thousand dollars."

Lily gasped with what looked to be surprised pleasure; Goose looked taciturnly displeased, but since his brows met over his nose anyway it was hard to tell.

"The rest of her estate, except for bequests to her charities, comes to me. You girls will inherit it one day, of course. She has left Detritus the Mercedes and a good sum. He will continue to drive for me." (This never happened; Detritus and the Mercedes took off the next day and did not return to Lytton. I learned much later that he had a car service with a nice small fleet and was prospering like the green bay tree.)

My mother swept her eyes toward me.

"Thayer, your grandmother has left you a house."

She did not go on, and finally I said, "What house? I didn't know Grand had another house."

"Neither did anyone else, apparently," my mother said repressively. "But she did, and it is now yours. And Aengus's, of course."

He nodded affably at her.

I did not say anything else and she went on.

"It is a stone house on Bell's Ferry Road, out near the Chattahoochee. It has three bedrooms and three baths, and is furnished with pieces from your grandmother's Buckhead house. It is quite a nice house. The neighborhood is considered very good. All the houses were vacation homes once, I believe, because of the nearness to the river. She has apparently had it cleaned once a month since she moved to Lytton, and all you would need to do is move in. If you should want the house, of course. I know your plans were to remain in Sewanee. In that case I would be delighted to take it off your hands for a very generous sum. There is a letter she left for you, too."

She fell silent. I could think of nothing to say. Aengus said, "Did she tell you about the house, Mrs. Wentworth? You seem to know a lot about it."

"No," she said levelly, studying, not him or me, but the sweating iced-tea pitcher. "I went up yesterday afternoon and looked at it."

He and I were both silent, simply looking at her.

"I wanted to make sure that your inheritance was commensurate with the others, of course, Thayer," she said. "I was prepared to augment it a bit if it wasn't. A house, you know, is not quite the same thing as...financial inheritance."

"And was it?" Aengus asked interestedly. "Commensurate?"

"I believe so. It isn't exactly grand, but it's really quite lovely...for what it is, of course."

"Of course," he said. And suddenly it occurred to me that Grand's mystery house must be a really wonderful house in a faultless location, for it was obvious that my mother was furious to the core of her being that the house had come to me and not to her. A house in northside Atlanta...wasn't it what she had yearned for since the beginning of her marriage?

"You said there was a letter...."

She picked the envelope up from the coffee table and handed it to me. She did not move from her chair. No one else stirred, either. Obviously, I was meant to share the letter.

I got up.

"I think I'll read it on the way," I said to Aengus, and he got up and followed me off the porch.

"On the way where?" my mother called back after me. Her voice was edged like broken glass.

"To see my new house!" I called back.

No one spoke until after we had gotten into Aengus's car and turned out of the driveway toward Atlanta. If they had I would have heard them.

On the outskirts of Atlanta I finally opened Grand's letter. At the sight of her graceful Palmer handwriting I felt my throat and eyes flood again with tears, but I was determined not to smudge Grand's words, so I shook my head hard and read aloud to Aengus:

My dear Thayer,

I hope it will be some years before you read this, because I hope I will be allowed a good long time with you yet. But if not, know that you were born in my heart and have stayed there all this time.

I am leaving to you a house that I have always loved dearly, although for one reason or another we never used it much, especially after your dad was born. Big Finch always loved the old colony on Burnt Mountain, and I came to love the house at Sea Island. But this one would have been the vacation home of my dearest dreams.

All the oldest houses on the river were initially vacation places for Buckheaders, although now that the city has spread out so, it encompasses all of the land on both sides of the river, almost to the western edge of Cobb County. Now your house is just one more house on a street of city houses, but I think it is still special and always will be.

I used to visit at least once a month. I don't think your parents ever knew that. I don't even think your dad knew about the house. He was always a Burnt Mountain boy. The home owners on Bell's Ferry at the river have always had the good sense to leave the river forest largely intact, so it is rather like living in an enchanted forest beside what might be, if you catch it on a good day without shrieking rafters or floating garbage, an enchanted river. I think the river there is at its most beautiful; it is not navigable there or anywhere below because of the rapids, and the white water is spectacular. I have always loved the old iron bridge, though by the time you get there they may well have replaced it with something square and modern and spiky. When we were children, the bravest of us used to dive from that bridge. I do not recommend it.

You have always been my Ondine, because you loved the river behind your parents' house so much. I always wanted a water sprite to live in this one. I know you will have already made plans for your future, you and Aengus, but pamper your old granny and give the house a try. It's the sort of house you can build your life around, not merely a house to accommodate a life. Will you do that?

I've loved you best of all, dearest Thayer. You should know that someone did.

Love always, Grand

I rode the rest of the way into the city, to where we turned off in the middle of Buckhead on Bell's Ferry Road, with my face buried in my hands. I did not cry. I merely let my internal movie of Grand run: the times when I was very small and she would take my hand and let me toddle down to the water behind our house and sometimes splash with me in the shallows; curling into her warm lap on a cooling summer night on the porch glider, listening sleepily to her and my grandfather Big Finch talking with my parents and breathing deeply of her perfume; showing her my first long dress and hearing her delighted words that made me feel I was truly beautiful, at least on that night; her arms hard around me after the searing pain of the baby and defection of Nick; her words on meeting Aengus: "Don't let him go too far into the Irish thing. Don't let him take you there with him."

I lifted my head and looked at him. I still did not know what she meant.

"Almost there." Aengus smiled at me. "Almost home."

"How do you know it will be?"

"I don't know. I just do."

I had been down Bell's Ferry Road before, I think, but

I did not remember much about it except for the great river forest that was cloven in two by the Chattahoochee River. I remembered no houses. But now here they were, tucked back into glades hewn out of towering hardwoods and pine. Most were older, with mature shrubbery and gardens. Sunlight slanted in through the treetops, picking out a gabled roof here, a summerhouse there. There was considerable traffic, but this end of Bell's Ferry seemed to generate a green silence. When we slowed at a mailbox to read the numbers, I could hear the deep laughter of the river.

"Here we are," Aengus said, turning into a driveway. "Holy Saints!"

He stopped and I looked up at the house and began to cry.

"Oh, Aengus," I sobbed. "Oh, Aengus!"

It was not that my grandmother's house was grand or even elegant; it was just that there was not an inch of it that did not look like something out of a child's fairy tale... Hans Christian Andersen, not Grimm's. It rose out of the center of a circular glade, sunlight falling on it as if trained like a spotlight. The grass in the glade was almost pure emerald, and the trees around and above it were lacy with new green, leaning close as lovers. The house itself was three stories of river stone, with bayed casement windows on each floor and a wide carved door set into a portico. The roof was old slates, warm grand fawn and green where moss clung to them. All the trim and the shutters and doors were painted French blue.

"It's a Normandy house," I said when I could get my breath. "Normandy in a forest on the river. It's pure magic!"

"So does it look like home?" Aengus laughed. I could see

the house reflected in his blue eyes. On that day, Aengus's eyes were full of home.

I ran up the flagstone walkway and put the old key into the bronze lock and the big blue door swung open. Even before it closed behind us, I believed in my heart that I was then and forever home.

CHAPTER

11

From the Bell's Ferry house we went, not back to Lytton, but on to the Mountain and the Domain. There seemed to me nothing to go back to Lytton to. Lily and Goose had not yet gone back to their home in a small town south of Lytton but would soon. It was a dreary little house with no trees around it, in a sun-smitten suburb called Summer Garden. There was not a flower in it, nor a garden.

"A nice little starter house," my mother said of it. I feared secretly that Lily would both start and finish there. Goose had worked up to manager of the local supermarket; his one marketable skill had been football, for which there was little call in the small-town South after high school.

"Should've stood up for the draft when they first asked me," he would say, settling in on the sofa with a beer and the TV remote. "They get pissed off if you don't take 'em up right off the bat."

181

We were meant to assume, I think, that he meant the NFL, but Aengus always insisted that he was referring to a team of draft horses. He said it aloud to Goose once, alas, and so we did not, as Goose would put it, hang out much with them. I missed my sister. Sometimes we met in Atlanta for lunch, but not often.

I thought that they would be leaving Lytton today as soon as Lily felt they could decently do so. Then there would be only my mother there. That fact seemed somehow skewed and wrong to me. For the first time I realized that for a long time I had thought of River House as Grand's house.

Before we left Bell's Ferry Road, Aengus had asked me if I'd like to go back down to Sea Island.

"We've technically got six more days," he said. "I hate to do you out of a honeymoon. It seems like a bad omen."

"I couldn't go cavort around on a honeymoon with Grand just dead," I said. "Let's just go back to school and see what we need to do next. I'd say we ought to go straight to work, but...now there's the house."

"Now there's the house," he echoed.

"I think I have to live in it, Aengus."

"Of course we're going to live in it," he said. "I could never have given you anything like that. It'll be a wonderful life. I can teach at any one of the Atlanta colleges and you could have your choice of kindergartens. Or maybe just write your stories, if you want to. It's a dream come true. I always knew you'd bring me my dreams."

"It may not be as easy as all that," I said. "You can't just walk into a school and say, 'I want to teach here.' Neither can I, for that matter."

"Wanna bet?" He smiled. And at that moment, drunk on my stone house with blue doors and the whitewater river below it, I wouldn't have bet against Aengus for anything in the world.

Our life on the Mountain was in order. We had rented a top-floor apartment in a house in the village where we would live for the first few months, while we decided what sort of life we wanted to make in the Domain. His classes on the Irish Celts had blossomed into a full series of mythologies among the world's literatures, though none of them laid hold of him like the Celts did.

"It's because they ran around naked and lopped off everybody's heads," I said. "I know you. You'd be naked as a jaybird all the time if you could get away with it, and boy, would you love to lop heads!"

"Starting with Goose's, had he a neck, but alas," Aengus said, "he has none. No, the main reason I love the Celts is that they figured out how to live forever. They didn't have to grow old. They didn't have to die."

"Why aren't there more of them, then?"

"Well, it was a little tricky." He grinned. "There's supposed to be an old land called Tir Na Nog. You lived forever there. Only Celts allowed, I'm guessing. I don't know how you got there. Nothing I've read about them has mentioned it, except one book, and that was in passing. I'm determined to find out, though."

So Aengus was well set to continue in the Domain, and I had landed a part-time job working with kindergartners in a small private school just off campus. Our apartment windows overlooked the chapel and across to the Steep, and when we looked out we saw what we had seen for years: flying academic gowns open over blue jeans and tee shirts; gray stone; green treetops; cars and the occasional motorcycle; every sort of flower that bloomed in the southern mountains. My kindergarten classroom opened into the chapel close, and Aengus, who had the run of the English department now, saw nothing out his various windows that did not charm the eye. I could have wished for nothing more, wished to live no other place but with Aengus in the Domain.

But now there was the house...my house...and I would live my life in it. Of that there was no question. Aengus had none, either.

We only slept three nights in our apartment on the Mountain. It only took Aengus that long to talk with Vice-Chancellor Martinson, make a few phone calls to people he knew who might be suitable for his post, collect his belongings from hither and yon about the campus, load up his old Volvo station wagon, and park the car the last night with its nose pointing down the Mountain toward Atlanta. On that last night we made love once more in the little circle of birches on the Steep, as well as in the alien sheets of our newly rented bed, and the next morning before seven we were passing under the stone arch that read *The Domain,* this time going away.

"Will you miss it?" I said, tears thick in my throat.

"Of course I'll miss it. It gave me the best things I'll ever have in my life. But I'm taking them with me."

I said no more, tipping my head back to look at the last letters as we left them behind, and then turned my eyes forward, toward the road down the mountain toward Atlanta. I did not look back.

It was a long time before I was on the Mountain again. That mountain, anyway.

We drove straight to the house on Bell's Ferry Road. I had not gone back to Lytton to collect any more of my things. Lily had said she would bring them up before she and Goose left for home; she wanted to see the house anyway. She said she figured it must be the house to end all houses, since Mother would not discuss it.

"She got a bundle from Grand," Lily said discontentedly. "She could buy herself any house she wanted. I don't know why she's so bent out of shape about that one."

"Because she couldn't buy this one," I said, knowing I was right but not happy in the knowing. There would always be a rift between my mother and me; I knew that, too. Partly perhaps because I had so failed some of her expectations and so exceeded others. Lily had derailed herself off my mother's track earlier on, by marrying Goose. Mother had been spared a son-in-law named Abrams, but I, too, jumped off the track, and into the arms of an Irish O'Neill, and had been married to him by a witch to boot. Mother wasn't long in picking that up. Of it she would only say, "Well, of course, you're not legally married. Everybody knows that. Perhaps you don't care, but I have taken my share of persecution because of it."

"What do you suppose people do?" I said. "Leave broomsticks on the front porch?"

"We really should give her a black cat," Aengus said.

When we reached the Bell's Ferry house from Sewanee, Aengus pulled the Volvo up next to the front steps on the circular drive and we unpacked it and set our worldly possessions on the small portico. Its pillars were slender and painted Norman blue to match the other woodwork, and there were two stone benches flanking the door. Terra-cotta pots of ivy sat beside each. Grand had had someone hang ferns on either side of the door. The afternoon light filtered through the latticed roof and the overhanging trees gave the entrance a subaqueous feeling, as though we were entering an underwater chamber. When the big door swung open, Aengus picked me up and carried me over the threshold into our new house.

Inside, every room glowed with greenish summer light. It pooled in from banks of high windows set over the large, wide bayed ones in the two front rooms. At the back of the house French doors opened onto a broad stone veranda with faded sail red awnings over it, and trellises thick with blooming roses at each end. They were small, old-fashioned, and intensely scarlet. Later I learned they were called Paul Scarlets, and knew in my heart that Grand had had something to do with that. An extra touch of enchantment, to supplement all the others. The whole house spoke of Grand. It did not disturb me. We spoke in one tongue, Grand and I.

The large living room was stucco, with a wall of the outside stone that held a huge fireplace. The ceiling was beamed and the windows cut deep in the stucco. The one at the end of the house held a padded seat. I remembered much of the furniture from Grand's house, the long, faded brocade sofa and the striped velvet love seat, the deep, high-backed chintz wing chairs beside the fireplace, the low Oriental coffee table and the delicate Chinese side chairs that flanked it. The high, curly old secretary that had been Grand's mother's sat beside the door, and on the other side the little mahogany table where, she had always said, General Washington played chess with General Lafayette on his way to the battle of Monmouth. The huge, gilt-framed paintings in the room, interiors and land- and seascapes, had come, I knew, from Europe, and were said to be "good." I forgot who said that... probably my mother. And they were good. To me they were glorious. They shone like jewels in the green light.

The room across the hall from it was obviously the library, its wall-to-wall shelving crammed untidily with books. There was another fireplace, deep armchairs beside it, and an immense library table.

"I'm going to get at those books and put them in order," Aengus said, but I liked them as they were, threatening to spill out and engulf whoever did not value them. I thought that they would have eaten my mother alive, and grinned at the thought. I don't think my mother's reading extended much past the *Ladies' Home Journal* and *Vogue*.

Up the old polished stairs three bedrooms and bathrooms

invited repose; I could not seem to pick the one I wanted for ours. The last flight led up to an enormous room, the length and width of the entire house, again beamed and stuccoed and floored in glowing old heart pine. There was a big old Kirman in the middle of the floor, faded almost to pale gold and pewter and shell colors, and open bookshelves divided the room at one end. Through its opening you could see that it made a small, beamed room with windows on all sides, looking straight out into the trees. Over them, and over the roofs of three or four other houses, I could see the river, sun fire struck from its white rapids.

"That's where I am going to write," Aengus said.

"That's where I'm going to...do whatever I do," I said, looking into the little room with joy. "You'll have to share. And we're sleeping in this end of it."

"Absolutely. And everything else, too. Want to give the rug a try?" he said.

I am not at all ashamed to say that we did.

"Not bad for a first-house fuck," he said sleepily into my hair as we lay in the waning sun on the Kirman.

"Might be even better with a bed," I said, absently rubbing the carpet abrasions on my hip.

"Always bitching. Can't even appreciate a great lay in a great house."

"Can, too," I said. "I just meant—"

I never did remember what I meant. At that moment there was a loud crash from downstairs—the kitchen, I thought—followed by the tinkling of glass and an angry, indistinct expletive in a woman's voice. Aengus and I looked at each other, scrambled up adjusting our clothes, and ran downstairs.

We reached the bottom step just as a small woman came into the foyer, leading a struggling little boy by the arm. In her other arm a basketball was cradled. We all stopped and looked at one another.

"Oh, Lord," the woman said in a clipped eastern voice. Her face was flushed red and her short blond hair flew all over her head as if it had been electrified.

"At least you're not patrician and blue haired and eighty years old. I'm Carol Partridge from next door and this is my son Bummer, who just took out your kitchen window with a basketball. I am *so* sorry, but not nearly as sorry as Bummer is going to be."

The little boy began to cry.

I began to laugh.

"I never liked that window anyway," I said. She stared at me and then began to laugh, too. So did Aengus. Bummer did not laugh, but he gave me a watery, hopeful smile.

While I swept up the broken glass Carol Partridge held the dustpan, promising to pay for the damage and admiring the house in a nonstop patter-fire of words. Mostly I laughed. I liked her instantly. Aengus had taken little Bummer, still hiccupping, out onto the veranda, and when we joined them with a pitcher of iced tea and cookies Bummer looked up at his mother, his great hazel eyes shining, and said, "Mama, Aengus knows a goat that farts 'The Star-Spangled Banner'!"

"That goat must be better than the rest of us, then," Carol said, laughter welling up in her throat. "I can't even sing it."

189

I fixed Aengus with a long look, and he shrugged and held up his hands: "Well, what can you do?"

We all laughed.

It was the start of a lot of laughter shared with Carol Partridge.

We sat on the veranda watching the long shadows of our trees fall over the velvety lawn. Carol told us a little about herself: born in New Haven; met her husband, Walter, at Yale; divorced him four years before when he had run off with the daughter of a major Midwestern industrialist and married both her and her father's hubcap empire; lived now in the house where he had grown up. (His family had known the Wentworths and his father had been a friend of my father in grammar school; both she and Walter had known and loved Grand and wondered who her house would go to.) Carol had two older sons, Chris, twelve, and Benjamin, ten, in addition to Bummer (Buxton, but who would call a child that?). The boys all loved river rafting; perhaps Aengus and I...?

"Aengus could go on my raft!" shouted Bummer, who had obviously taken a great fancy to Aengus. A farting goat, after all...

"'Mr. O'Neill,' Bummer, not 'Aengus.' I've told you," Carol said.

"Actually, it's 'Dr.,'" Aengus said, and then added hastily as Bummer's eyes widened in terror, "but I'm not the kind that gives shots. I'm a doctor of storytelling. I tell about myths and legends and dead people who did wonderful things."

"Like what?" Bummer breathed, his eyes enormous.

"Like turning people into swans. Or cutting off their enemies' heads and carrying them in their saddlebags."

"Aengus!" I said sharply.

But Bummer's eyes held only fascination. "Cool," he said.

"All my sons are bloodthirsty hooligans," Carol Partridge
said. "The kids on this side of the river have their own gang.
I think they call themselves the Jets or the Sharks or something equally bucolic. I expect to see the police any day now."

"Just on this side of the river?" Aengus asked with interest.

"Oh yes. The other side is far too chic and refined to put
up with that sort of stuff. Their kids are practically perfect. I
kid you not. Little zombies is what I think. But they do have
good manners. Better than their parents, by a long shot."

"I gather you aren't fond of the parents. What are they
called?" I asked.

"Besides shits? 'Scuse me; I have a bad mouth. They're
called Woodies. They live in a subdivision . . . only they'd kill
you for calling it that . . . called Riverwood. Fairly new, hid-
eously overpriced, houses like bad copies of Versailles, *way*
too much money. Nobody drives anything less than a Mercedes, including the perfect children. They've managed to
start their own perfect school, K through 12, kids have to
live there to attend, and even their own camp, up on Burnt
Mountain. God, if any of them are your best friends I'll cut
my own tongue out—"

"Not likely," Aengus said. "All our friends are left-wing
sanitation workers and ladies of the evening."

She laughed again. "Except you, I think. I think you teach."

"Right. Most recently at Sewanee. I'm looking now. Know any schools that need a frightener of small children?"

"I bet somebody around here does. I'll look," Carol said. "And Thayer? Do you teach, too?"

"Sort of," I said. "Only kindergarten level, though."

"Oh, God, one of the teachers at Bummer's kindergarten just left. I mean the one he was in two years ago. I'll bet they'd love to have you! I know just who to call—"

"I don't want you to go to any trouble," I said. "I haven't even thought much about it."

"No trouble. Are you kidding? They'd kill to get Mrs. Wentworth's granddaughter on the faculty. Everybody knew and loved her. Oh, I didn't even tell you how sorry I was—"

"Thank you. We are, too. But I feel like we'll always have her, what with the house and all—"

"Then so will we. Well, come on, Bummer. We've done enough damage for one day. I ought to make you pay for that window out of your allowance."

"I don't get an allowance, Mama," he said. "But I want to stay. I want to hear some more about the goat—"

"Come on now, or Dr. O'Neill will turn you into a goat," Carol said. "Thanks for putting up with us. When you get settled I'd love it if you'd come to dinner."

She towed her son out of sight around the house, and Aengus and I sat grinning at each other.

"I like her," I said.

"Me, too," said Aengus. "She's very...real. Oh, look, they forgot the basketball."

"I'll run and catch them," I said.

"Don't bother. I have the feeling we've by no means seen the last of Bummer."

"I hope not," I said, still smiling. "He's just the kind of little boy I'd..."

I let it trail off.

Aengus reached over from his chair and squeezed my hand.

CHAPTER

12

On the Tuesday morning after our first night in the Bell's Ferry Road house, Aengus took a phone call in the library and came into the kitchen where I was making breakfast, grinning hugely.

"Don't call them; they'll call you," he said.

"What?"

"I just got a call from the president of Coltrane College. You know, the little one over at Oxford? The good one?"

"Well, of course I know Coltrane. Grand's sister went there, Aunt Courtney. I never knew her really, though she was my great-aunt. But Grand talked about Coltrane a lot. It's supposed to be kind of a little gem of a liberal arts place, isn't it?"

"Correct. Well, thanks to Grand's sister, or her sister's family, or somebody, I just got asked to interview for the chairmanship of the English department. Seems that whoever it was called the college painted a pretty glowing portrait of me. I'd love to thank whoever's responsible, but I have a feeling she's dead. He said we'd discuss who the caller was at the interview."

"It's something you're interested in, then?"

"My God, of course. Head of the department? It's only about half an hour's drive from here. I could be home for dinner every night. Not to mention that the salary is, shall we say, attractive? Well, to an academic, anyway."

"Oh, Aengus!" I cried, hugging him hard. "I'm so happy for you! All of this...this stuff: the house, this call...it just seems as though it's meant to be, doesn't it? I wonder where Coltrane got our number."

"Oh, I'm sure they called Sewanee to check me out. Probably from there. Listen, you want some champagne with that omelet? I've got a bottle of Mumm's around here someplace."

"I put it in the refrigerator last night. Just like I knew we'd be wanting it. Oh yes, let's do!"

We sat on the veranda and drank the silky, frothing Mumm's and never did get around to the omelet. I raised my first glass to him and said, "Congratulations, Your Headship."

He put his glass down. "No. Seriously. Don't congratulate me yet. I haven't got it yet. Say 'Good luck' or 'Way to go,' but don't say 'Congratulations.'"

He looked serious and a little agitated.

I put my glass down, too. "But you will get it. I don't have any doubt of that."

"No. Maybe. Probably. But to assume it before it happens is to...sort of curse it."

"Aengus..."

He held one hand up. "Okay. So it's stupid. Just don't do it anyway."

"Well, then...way to go," I said lamely. He couldn't possibly believe such a childish superstition; he dealt in superstitions every day. They only amused and energized him.

I did not know what to say next but felt vaguely that I should pursue this. I was saved by the telephone bell.

"I'll get it," I said, and went in and picked up the kitchen telephone. It was Carol Partridge. Somehow her rapid-fire New England honk brought normalcy back to the world.

"Can you come to dinner Saturday night?" she said. In the background I could hear rock music thumping and blaring.

"Love to," I said. "Can I bring anything?"

She said something I could not hear, and I said, "I'm sorry?"

"Benjamin, turn off that stuff!" she yelled. "I'm on the phone."

There was a mumbled reply and the music blared on.

"...because I said so!" she yelled, and the music stopped.

"God," she breathed. "It's only midmorning and I'm ready to call Juvie and tell them to come get them....No, you can't bring a thing. I'm making gazpacho. Found some gorgeous tomatoes at the farmer's market. Only they'll probably be as hard as rocks and I'll end up using canned. I'm glad you can come. I promise to have tamed the savage beasts by then."

"Not on our account, I hope," I said. "Aengus has been knee-deep in kids for the last ten years, and I like little boys."

"I'll check with you on that again after Saturday," she said, and I hung up, laughing.

It was a good week. Aengus had his interview on Thursday and was indeed offered the chairmanship of the Coltrane English department and did indeed accept it.

"Now you can say congratulations," he said that evening, producing another bottle of cold Mumm's. I congratulated him and more; after we had finished the champagne we simply rolled over in our bed, which I had indeed put on the third floor, where it floated in all that sunny and/or starry space like a barge, and went to sleep.

Family by family our new neighbors dropped by, with flowers or pots of soup or freshly baked sweets, and we found them all agreeable. Most of them were older, than me, anyway, but many were Aengus's age, with a sprinkling of seniors. All of them had children, whether or not they were in residence on Bell's Ferry, and all of them had the same half-mystic, almost fierce feeling about the river and the forest. All of them had the same feeling about the Woodies across the river, too.

"Barbarians at our gate," a gray-thatched older man with a stiff brush mustache said. "Come thundering up this road like an invading army. Drive chariots if they could. Never say hello, never even wave. One of them ran over the Hendersons' corgi a month or so ago and didn't even stop. Several of us called the police, but of course they all look alike and drive the same things...Jaguars, BMWs, Hummers...and they'd never admit it anyway. There's a back way out of here that could get them up to the freeway, but they'd have to slow

197

down. So Bell's is their own personal speedway. I've clocked them at ninety and over."

We couldn't argue with that. In the short week we'd been in the house, we'd seen strings of speeding luxury cars and heard growling engines but never seen a wave or heard a honk. So far it did not bother me. Riverwood might have been in another country entirely.

On Saturday we worked in our overburgeoning garden most of the day, cutting back Grand's towering camellia bushes and weeding the flowering borders. They were spectacular; I had no idea what many of them were. Aengus was no help.

"If it's not four-leaf clovers or roses of Killarney I can't help you," he said. He was sweaty and disheveled, with smears of dirt on his face and thorn scratches on his arms. I could see that Aengus was going to be no gardener. In truth, I wasn't wild about it, either. Score one for my mother's genes, I thought; she loathed gardening. We had always had a gardener.

"I wonder what gardeners go for in this neighborhood," I said.

"More than I make," Aengus said, savagely swatting a mosquito. "I could maybe curse one into taking us on, though."

We stopped for a while and sat under the shade of the portico lattice, drinking lemonade. The late afternoon was green and still.

"That's the second time in a couple of days you've said

something about cursing," I said. "You're not buying into your own myths, are you?"

"No, but don't I wish," he said. "Make things a lot simpler. Think of all the things you'd never have to do if you could curse somebody into doing them for you."

"What do you do that you don't want to do?" I said, honestly curious. I would have said our life so far was full to the brim of sweetness.

"Oh, nothing, really," he said, smiling at me. "Not about us anyway. Well, gardening, maybe. Tying my shoelaces. Driving in five o'clock Buckhead traffic. Getting old..."

I laughed. He did not.

"Are you serious? You're only thirty-three. You have the body of... well, I won't say it out loud, but it ain't bad."

"I found a gray hair yesterday."

"For God's sake, Aengus, I have gray hairs. I've had them since I was a teenager."

I peered closely at his temple, and he moved his head away. I saw no gray, only the lustrous crow black I had always seen.

"I don't see it, but if it bothers you, just yank it out when you get dressed for Carol's dinner party. Speaking of which..."

"Yeah. You want the first shower? I've got to polish my shoes."

It was about six thirty when we walked through our hedge into Carol's backyard. It was much the same as ours; there were flower borders and masses of mature shrubbery, and a veranda that ran the length of the house, as ours did. But the grass was uncut and the borders had not been planted for spring and the paint on the veranda railing was peeling in spots. The house was a yellow Dutch Colonial, badly in need of re-yellowing. The backyard was littered with the stigmata of children: a basketball hoop nailed on a tree, two bicycles lying on their sides at the edge of the driveway, a small red wagon with scarred paint and one wheel missing. An oval pool took up half the yard, full of detritus and floating water toys. Still, it was a nice house and a nice yard and Carol was, after all, a single mother with three active boys. Suddenly I liked Carol Partridge even more for her backyard. Obviously, to her the important things were the ones inside the house, not outside it.

"Faith and begorra," Aengus said mildly.

"Can it," I said. "It's how the other three-fourths of the world live."

Carol let us in the back door. She wore a flowered sundress that displayed her nicely shaped and tanned arms and shoulders, and there were gold hoops in her ears. She smiled and gave us both hugs. But her fine blond hair was exploding around her head like a dandelion again, and two hectic red spots burned on her cheeks. Moreover, I could have sworn that her eyes were puffed and red from crying.

"Is this a bad time?" I said.

"Absolutely not," she said over her shoulder, taking an armful of yellow lilies I had cut for her and plunging them into a pitcher that sat on the counter.

"These will be perfect on the table. Everything I own

seems to be yellow. No, it's just a little hectic around here. The boys' father dropped in unexpectedly for a little visit and that always rouses the rabble. I didn't even know he was in town."

"If you need to be with him...," I began, and she shook her head vehemently.

"He's the last person on earth we need to be with. Besides, he's gone. Probably on the way back to the airport right now. It's just...hard on the boys, the older ones especially...when he flies in and out like this. Of course they want him to stay, and that's not going to happen, or they want to go with him, and that's not going to happen, either. You-all are the best antidote I could have right now. Come in and let me get you a drink."

We went, not back out onto the veranda but into the front room that served, I supposed, as the living room. It was immaculate and filled with air and light; the tall windows were open and the furniture gleamed with polish and scented the air with lemon. It was somehow a pure room; there were few bibelots around on the polished surfaces and no plants or flowers except an exploding bower of white hydrangeas that sat in the fireplace, so huge and perfect that they were obviously fake.

Carol saw my glance and grinned ruefully. "Faux, of course. I'll bet I'm the only house on Bell's Ferry Road with fake flowers in my house. Chris and Benjamin and Bummer gave them to me for my birthday. I made a huge fuss over them and put them in here where living feet seldom fall."

"I think they look lovely," I said. Somehow, they did. "It's a beautiful house. I've always loved Dutch Colonial."

"It is indeed," Aengus said. "Although coming from one who grew up in a peat hut with a straw roof—"

"Oh, shut up," Carol and I said together, and we all laughed. The night was suddenly good.

We had, surprisingly, mint juleps. They tasted wonderful.

"The secret is to make your own simple syrup," Carol said, only she said "shimple" and I realized she'd had a couple before we arrived. "Mint's out of my garden, too. Isn't it funny? You can't kill mint even where nothing else will grow."

She fixed us another and got up to see to dinner. I offered to help, but she said there was really nothing left to do. As we raised our second drinks, Bummer came into the room.

"Hey, Aengus! I mean Dr. O'Neill," he said in a froggy voice that somehow went with the chipmunk teeth and the yellow hair, now slicked to his head and showing comb tracks.

"Hey, Mrs. O'Neill."

"Hello, Bummer," I said, smiling. He had pink cheeks dotted with tawny freckles; I would have liked to pinch them lightly.

"Hallo, Bummer. *Cén chaoi a bhfuil tú?*" Aengus said.

Bummer looked at him suspiciously. Aengus laughed.

"It's Gaelic," he said. "It's a very old language that they spoke in Ireland and Scotland and so on. It's Celtic language. You remember me telling you about the Celts the other day?"

"Those guys that cut off people's heads? Is that what they said?"

"Well, not exactly when they cut people's heads off." Aengus grinned. "'*Cén chaoi a bhfuil tú?*' means 'How are you?'"

"Well, I'm pretty good except I have a boil on my—"

"Bummer!" Carol exclaimed, coming back into the room. "Enough about the boil. Go call your brothers; dinner's ready."

"Okay, but I don't think they'll come. They're still mad about having to go to camp."

"Oh, God," Carol sighed, gesturing for us to follow her into the dining room. We sat down at her table, set with yellow flowered pottery and with my lilies resplendent in a blue bowl in the center.

"Chalk up another one for dear old Dad. I almost had them talked into going to camp somewhere this summer; I don't know if I can handle all three of them just running loose, and he comes along and says he thinks camp is for fags, and so of course the rebellion has been mounted. They'll go, of course, because I'll cut off their allowance if they don't, but now it's going to be such a damn battle, and it just didn't have to be."

"I'd like to go to camp," Bummer said. He began to sing, "The Cabbal King with the big old ring fell in love with the dusty maid..." He ran up the stairs after his brothers and out of sight.

"'The Cannibal King with the big nose ring,'" I said, laughing. "He 'fell in love with a dusky maid,' and so forth.... It's a classic camp song. I sang it at my camp."

"Is it ever. That damned bus from Riverwood goes by at dawn every morning with all the little Woodies on it singing about the Cannibal King at the tops of their lungs. I'd like to shoot out the tires."

Bummer came back in, followed by two older boys. They walked straight and stiffly, and they were neatly dressed in clean jeans and striped long-sleeved oxford shirts, but you could tell they would rather be anyplace on earth than that dining room. They were handsome boys, both dark haired and dark eyed with mellow swimming pool tans, but their brows were drawn into straight lines and their mouths were pressed thin lipped and shut, without looking at any of us as they dropped into their chairs.

"Chris, Benjamin," Carol said tightly. "Please say hello to Mrs. O'Neill, our next-door neighbor."

The oldest, who was seated next to me, turned slowly in his seat and looked at me. Or rather, leered at me. His eyes raked me all over, up and down, lingering on my breasts under a white cotton tank, and he licked his lips slowly. Then the wet lips curled up in a smile that seemed to scrape my underwear off beneath my clothes. It should have been a young boy's parody of lust, but it wasn't; on this boy it looked disturbing and corrupt. I felt myself flush. Across the table from me I saw Aengus make a small movement in his chair.

"Next door's lookin' pretty fine," the boy drawled.

"This is her husband, Dr. O'Neill," Carol said, her voice like ice.

The boy did not take his eyes off me. "Are you really married to that old geezer?" he said. "What a waste."

"Chris!" Carol cried.

Aengus was out of his seat and around the table in an eyeblink. The boy turned his face to him, startled, and Aengus took both his shoulders in his hands and leaned close to his face and spat out a long string of words; they sounded guttural and dangerous, rather like a snake hissing. I knew he was speaking Gaelic. When he stopped the boy sat still for a moment and then jumped to his feet. His face was pale under the tan and his eyes were wide with fright. He turned and ran out of the dining room, followed by his brother Benjamin. No one spoke. Aengus walked back to the table and sat down. Bummer began to cry.

It took a long time to get it sorted out. Carol was appalled and apologetic for her son; she was near tears. Bummer nestled in her shoulder and cried quietly. Aengus apologized, too, but it was fairly obvious that he did not mean it. There was no question of dinner. I finally kissed Carol on the cheek and said, "Bring dinner to our house tomorrow night and let's start fresh. There was no harm done. I can't imagine what Aengus—"

"I've never seen Chris behave like that before," Carol said dully. "I don't know what I'm going to do with him. He's not a bad boy, but sometimes after his father—"

"I'll even make dessert," Aengus said, kissing Carol Partridge on the cheek. "How about humble pie?"

"Done deal," she said, managing a weary smile. "Dinner will keep. It was only gazpacho and eggplant parmigiana."

"Can't wait," said Aengus, who loathed eggplant more than he did war or famine.

Outside in the cool darkness, walking through our backyard, I said to Aengus, "What did you say to him? Was it a curse? It sounded like one!"

"Nah," he said. "Just Yeats. You know, 'The Lake Isle of Innisfree'?"

" 'I will arise and go now, and go to Innisfree,/And a small cabin build there, of clay and wattles made;/Nine bean rows will I have there, a hive for the honey bee,/And live alone in the bee-loud glade.' "

I began to laugh.

"I wonder how he's going to feel when he grows up and finds out that he was cursed by William Butler Yeats."

"Very badly, I hope," Aengus said. "Nobody looks at my wife like that. Not even a snot-nosed twelve-year-old."

CHAPTER

13

Aengus did not like his new job. I was surprised and somehow frightened. I had never seen him discontented or unhappy before. Annoyed, yes; angry, certainly. But never this dull, diminished apathy.

He himself could not really explain it.

"It's just that almost all I do now is supervise. Just... supervise.... I didn't realize how hard it would be to give up the direct contact with...oh, mythology. Stories. The sense of the Celts as real, brave, bloodthirsty, stinking *men*."

"But you can still read about them, can't you? I mean, there can't be many people who know as much about them as you do. Can't you just sort of...be with them in your head?"

"No. I guess I can't. I never even thought about it before, but what I really need is to be giving them to people. Making them come alive in other people's minds."

"Can't you teach just one course? Surely they'd agree

to that. They know what your specialty is. They must have liked it or they wouldn't have hired you."

"I guess I could. Next quarter, maybe. This is just a summer program. I'll suggest it. It just doesn't seem that Coltrane is a very... mythic place. Life is real; life is earnest."

"How about some kind of private tutorial thing?" I said. "Maybe here, at night?"

"Yeah. Maybe."

He did not seem to want to pursue it, so I didn't. But his unhappiness lodged itself in my soul, and its shadow went before me everywhere I went in this new green river world. Even the house seemed darker, as it did on cloudy days.

I told Carol Partridge about it one day when we were down at the river watching Bummer swim. The river just above the old iron bridge was shallow and sun dappled at its edges, and fairly gentle. Out in its middle it ran deep and straight toward the falls below the bridge, but these shallows were made for swimming or, rather, for thrashing and dabbling. Upriver there were a few other children minnowing about in it, just as Bummer was, all watched by tanned women in shorts and halters. I wondered if anybody on Bell's Ferry worked. I would begin teaching in the fall at a new charter primary school nearby, and I knew that Carol spent a couple mornings a week working at the Junior League consignment clothing shop. I also knew that it was volunteer work. Walter Partridge had paid pretty dearly for the privilege of pursuing young women. Carol and the boys lived well, if not lavishly.

The day was rich with sun and the clean fishy smell of

wild-running water. Sun sparkled off the whorls of the river and lit Carol's tousled hair to white-gold. Bummer's wet-seal body glistened all over. I felt the sun deeply on the top of my head; the smell of sun-heated hair was thick in my nostrils, and my shoulders were just before burning. Wild honeysuckle starred the darker woods; its heartbreaking fragrance rode to us on the little river wind. Deep, swift joy bubbled up in me, as it does sometimes when you are a child. I still could hardly believe that this world had been given to me. I closed my eyes and smiled, and felt my cheeks stretch under the bite of the sun. I would have to go in soon.

Not yet, though.

"Aengus isn't happy with his job," I said to Carol, my eyes still closed. That way I wouldn't have to see the day dull with my words.

"Why on earth not?" Carol said. "It sounded perfect for him to me. Coltrane is an awfully good school."

"He mostly supervises," I said. "There's no time to teach. I didn't realize he was so plugged into all that Celtic mythology stuff, but it's really painful for him not to...live it, I guess. It's as though he's lost his tribe, or something."

"He's head of the department," she said. "Surely they'll let him teach at least one class on whatever he wants."

"I thought so, too. It didn't seem to cheer him up. I've never seen him quite like this."

We were quiet for a while, and then she said almost dreamily, "I have an idea."

"Shoot."

"Bell's Ferry has this block party thing every summer,

around Midsummer Night. I know it sounds awful, but it's sort of fun to get everybody together. Mostly people just drink and eat hors d'oeuvres, but there's always some kind of entertainment. We've had our kids' bands so many times we're about to throw up, and once or twice we've had some kind of dance thing, but we're all getting tired of the kind of stuff we can do without having to pay for it. It's at my house this year—lucky me—and I've been putting off even trying to think about entertainment. But what if Aengus would come and tell some of those old legends and myths, or whatever he'd like to do? He'd be a sensation! I'm sure he's charmed every single soul he's ever met...."

She looked at me expectantly. My heart sank. There was no way I was going to ask Aengus if he'd come be the entertainment for Carol's block party.

"Oh, Carol, I don't know....He's pretty private about that sort of thing...," I began.

"Nonsense! It's an inspiration. I'm going to call him right now. Is he home?"

I knew that he was, it being Saturday. I imagined that he'd be on the veranda reading the *New York Times*. I almost lied about it, then sighed.

"Yeah. He's home. But really, I don't think..."

She got up and trotted up the bank a few paces to where she'd left her purse and her cell phone. She didn't come back for quite a while. I sat and watched the river play with itself and smiled at Bummer. If Aengus didn't want to do it, he would tell Carol. No harm done.

But he did. She came scrambling back down the bank grinning.

"He'd love to. He said something about the summer solstice and the Beltane Fires and…I don't remember the rest, but he sounded really enthusiastic about it. Maybe I won't have to get everybody so drunk."

"Well…good. I'm glad. You must be a sorceress."

"I whined." She laughed.

"Are you really going to do it?" I asked Aengus when I got home. He was eating a sandwich and reading Jonathan Carroll.

"Oh yes," he said, smiling. "I'd love to do it. This is the time of year for most of the big fire festivals. I think I can do the Celts proud."

"Without cutting off any heads?"

"Not unless I absolutely have to."

"Will you need anything special?"

"Not really. I can build what I need. I may borrow her odious kids' band, though."

Later that afternoon he went down into the basement and would not let me come with him. I thought I heard him banging around with wood and metal, but he would not tell me what he had been doing when he came back up, and forbade me to go into the basement until after the big event.

"Rats," I said. "Just the thing I wanted most to do."

"I want it to be a surprise for you, too."

On Midsummer Night we got to Carol's house about seven. Since it only involved walking through a hedge, I'd had time for a long soak in the tub and a nap, and felt cool and festive in floaty, flowered cotton voile, ready for an out-door party on a summer night. Aengus had been shut up in his den all afternoon. I could hear him talking and some-times chanting but paid it no mind. He often did both, almost absently, as you would whistle through your teeth.

"Where's that thing you've been working on all week?" I said.

"Took it over there this afternoon. Carol promised nobody would peep at it."

Carol's backyard was beautiful in the last of the slanting light. There were small white lights strung in some of the big oaks, and she had lined the grassy area in front of the pool with pots of flowers and other plants, so that it seemed a kind of dance floor. Beyond it, beside the pool, long tables were set up with candles flickering on them and platters of pick-up food, and bottles of wine. One of them served as a bar, laden with bottles and glasses. Apparently everyone's children came to this block party; the lawn and pool were full of them, laughing and shouting and acknowledging the adults with curt, mulish nods. Everyone wore summer fin-ery and laughed and thronged the bar table. Music thumped from somewhere, rock 'n' roll, but better than any of these kids' bands, recorded, undoubtedly. We stopped at the lawn's edge and looked, silently. It struck me how very beautiful even the most ordinary suburban yard is on a summer night, the lapping surges of green and the fresh smells of new-mown grass and blooming flowers, the tender gold light deepen-ing toward dark blue, the sweet, heady feeling of dark fall-ing down over you. Anything could happen on a southern summer night. Magic could come; mystery could live. I felt tears stinging my eyes.

"I wonder if I should have brought something," I said, mainly to break the silence.

"You brought the entertainment," Aengus said. "Who could ask for more?"

"Who indeed?" I said, and we walked into the party.

A good party can literally drown you; it is what I love and hate most about them, depending on my mood. This one swallowed us instantly and whole. We sank into a living mass of convivial humanity and did not really come up until after full dark. I know that someone or other kept my glass and plate full and everyone spoke warmly and interestedly about Aengus and me and our lives, and I know that I ate and drank and laughed and answered and felt warmly connected to these people who would be our nearest, if not dearest, for a long time. I got separated from Aengus early on but did not worry about it; I had seen him work a crowd before. But as the dark outside the circle of light grew dense, I began to wonder about him. Wasn't he supposed to do some entertaining?

I was just about to excuse myself from the bristly mustached man I had met before and go in search of Aengus, when a drum boomed once and echoed into the night. Silence fell.

"Listen up, y'all!" Carol Partridge called out. We all turned toward her voice. She stood at the head of her driveway with an overhead spot trained on her. Beside her sat a three-legged stool and a big portable metal fire pit. The pit was full of crossed twigs and limbs piled atop charcoal.

"It's time to entertain you-all, and you'll be happy to know that I didn't bribe any of our kids' bands or hire a mambo instructor."

There was laughter and clapping.

"I did better than that," she continued. "Tonight I'm proud to present to you our new neighbor Dr. Aengus O'Neill. I can never tell anyone what I had to do to get him to agree, but he's going to tell you some of his very special, spine-chilling, heartrending Celtic myths and legends, for which he is justly famous on three continents. I guarantee you will never forget them."

There was more applause and cheering. Carol took a lighter from the pocket of her dress and knelt and touched it to the fire pit, and flames leaped into the darkness, showering sparks. As they settled, Aengus walked out of her garage and came and sat down on the stool. He was wearing white pants and a dark blue tee shirt, and the firelight danced on his sharp-planed face and lit his blue eyes nearly to phosphorescence. He leaned a wheel-thing against the stool and smiled and said, "Oscar Wilde said that we Irish are too poetical to be poets; we are a nation of brilliant failures. But we are the greatest talkers since the Greeks."

His brogue, rising out of the night and the fire, was almost as alien as Greek; there was a small murmur from the crowd.

"And so," he went on, "I am going to talk."

And he did. Into the firelight he spun the stories of his beloved Celts; some I had heard, but many were new to me.

"Out the Kilronan/Kilmurvey Road, beside the holy well

at the Church of the Four Beautiful Persons, called also the Ceathair Aluinn...," he began.

He slid directly into the *Táin Bó Cúailnge* (The cattle raid of Cooley). Next he told of the wanderings of Oisin, the ancient Celtic pagan hero who met with Saint Patrick to defend the old pagan order against this new Christendom.

And on and on. Kings, warriors, hermits, ghosts, druids, holy mountains, the waves of the Irish sea, madmen, saints... there was nothing for an hour in the summer-sweet air of Carol Partridge's backyard but the tapestry of Aengus's Celts, nearer and realer to us by then than the partygoers standing beside us.

He finished up with the tale of Hazelwood, a peninsula of Lough Gill between Annagh Bay and Half Moon Bay, where Yeats had imagined that the wandering Aengus, the ancient Celtic master of love and the god of youth, beauty, and poetry, had finally grown old.

He stopped. There was no sound. Then, one by one, people began to clap, and then to whistle and cheer. The din went on for fully two minutes. Through it, Aengus smiled.

"Now," he said, "I'm going to end up with a celebration of the midsummer fire festivals that flourished wherever the Celt lit his torch. The most portentous of these festivals took place at mid-summer, when the sun, which the fire celebrates, both is at its highest and begins diminishing. To pay allegiance to the sun was to invite its blessings, without which people could not survive. Many people carried lit torches abroad in the night; many built bonfires and leaped over them, or danced about them. The Celts took it a bit further. Often they built a gigantic hollow man of wicker, filled it with human enemies and miscreants, lit it, and burned them alive. I shall not do that tonight. I seem to lack wicker."

There was a hushed whisper of laughter from the crowd. It was distinctly nervous and died out almost immediately.

"But," Aengus went on in a stronger voice, "I will give you the Celtic custom of the burning wheel."

He reached down and picked up the thing he had been working on all week, which he had secreted in Carol's garage. He held it aloft. It was about the size of a bicycle wheel and seemed to be fashioned of strong, thin limbs bent into a circle, wrapped with smaller vines and straw.

"By rights it should be ignited by a fire made by rubbing together two pieces of wood, preferably the oak, sacred to the druids. I will make do with the fire we already have. Watch the wheel carefully. If it burns strongly as it is rolled downhill until it comes to rest and continues to burn, all here will be blessed with growth and prosperity, as shall their crops and the beasts. If it goes out before it gets downhill…make an appointment with your doctors and take your cats and dogs to the vet. Behold now the need-fire of the Celt, the Fire of Heaven!"

In total silence we watched as Aengus skinned his tee shirt off over his head. Lit only by the dying flames in Carol's fire pit, his body was dark and coiled with muscle, gleaming with sweat or some sort of oil…I had no idea which. Around his neck a golden sort of neck plate gleamed. A Celtic torque; he had told me about them. I could not have spoken even if I had had breath, which seemed to have gone out of me. This dark, firelit figure before me was nobody or nothing I had ever seen before. The suburban backyard around me had morphed into any wild place at any time on the earth. I could hear little breathing; I supposed everybody's breath was held, as mine was.

Slowly he swung the wheel up and into the fire pit. After a moment it burst into flame.

"*Teintean!*" he cried, and swung the flaming wheel under-handed, straight down Carol Partridge's driveway.

No one made a sound as the flaming disk rolled steadily down the middle of the long driveway. Aengus ran beside it, his white-clad legs pumping steadily, the gold torque blazing in the flickering light. He ran quietly. The wheel made no noise except a faint *hushhhhhh*. Occasionally its fire leaped high and crackled. At the bottom, out on the dark street, it tipped over, bounced a bit, and lay still, flaming higher into the night. Aengus stood beside it, one arm raised high, fist closed. It was by far the most surrealistic thing I had ever seen, a circle of fire blazing below me, a tall, half-naked man with a collar of gold standing beside it, arm raised, face lifted up to the dark sky. Just at that moment the half-moon of mid-summer broke free from the sheltering oaks and poured its white light down on the wheel and man. As if given a signal, the crowd burst into a single roar.

By fire and moonlight Aengus lowered his arm and turned his face to us.

"Blessed be," he said.

By the time he had stamped the flaming wheel out and

come back up to the stool and pulled his shirt back on, they were still cheering.... Someone snapped the outside lights back on and Aengus stood in the driveway, nodding agreeably to the people hugging him and pounding on his back and shouting into his ear. He looked now like nothing more than my husband being congratulated by an agreeable crowd of people. I walked off, out of the light, to a spot under the nearest oak canopy and leaned against the trunk and tried to breathe deeply and normally. I was so dizzy that I felt that I might faint.

"Holy shit," someone beside me said in a quavering voice, and I turned to see Carol leaning against the other side of the trunk. She was breathing heavily, too.

"What is it that you have married?" she said.

"Before God, I don't know," I whispered. I looked back at him, still surrounded. "But I think I'm going to be a little afraid to get in bed with him after this."

"Afraid?" Carol laughed. "I think you'll have to beat off half the women on this street."

"Are you serious?"

"Serious? Without his shirt? In that gold necklace thing he had on? Jesus! I'd jump on him myself if I didn't like you so much."

"That's a torque," I said foolishly. "The Celts wore them into battle. They fought naked except for that."

"Oh, God, please! I'll never think of Aengus any other way but that. I'll bet half the men here are thinking maybe they'll surprise their wives some night soon by popping into bed naked, with one of those torque things on. Can you even imagine?"

I could. Carol and I collapsed together in each other's arms, laughing almost hysterically.

Much later, as Aengus and I walked home through Carol's hedge under a high-risen moon, I said, "You can't possibly have any idea how you looked."

"Yeah, I can," he said, grinning. Energy like electricity still swarmed off him. "I practiced in front of the mirror."

"Aengus…"

"There's no use doing a thing unless you mean to do it well," he said.

CHAPTER

14

I had thought we'd sleep late after Carol's party, but when I rolled over at first light Aengus was gone. The pajama bottoms in which he sometimes (but not often) slept were crumpled in a ball on the Kirman, and I did not hear him in the bathroom. Yawning, I looked at the bedside clock. Six thirty? I sat up. Could he be sick?

I pattered barefoot down the stairs; he was not in the kitchen.

"Aengus?" I called, my voice thick with sleep.

"Out here."

I found him on the lawn just beyond the veranda. He had on a pair of denim cutoffs but no shirt or shoes. I remembered his body last night, both in the firelight and later in bed, and shivered slightly. In both, Aengus had literally burned with exuberance and passion. I could remember no night quite like it.

Afterwards, as we lay in the moonlight, I had said so.

He reached over and took my hand, and said to me: "O I'd make a bed for you/In Labysheedy,/in the twilight hour/with evening falling slow/and what a pleasure it would be/to have our limbs entwine/wrestling/while the moths are coming down."

I turned my face into the hollow of his neck.

"That's beautiful."

"Is it not, now?" The brogue was thick. "Nuala Ni Dhomhnaill. She calls it 'The Silken Bed.'"

"I'll think about that now, whenever we..."

"I always do," he said.

This morning he was sitting on the grass planing a long, slender piece of wood. It looked to be sword shaped.

"What on earth are you doing?" I asked.

"Making a sword."

Far up on Peachtree Road to the east, the bells of St. Philip's rang, shivering down to us on the clear, still air. Early-morning service.

"A fine thing to be doing on the Sabbath," I said.

He did not stop.

"It will be a blessed sword, then."

"If I may be permitted to ask, who's going to get whapped with it?"

"Woodies?" Aengus said, smiling. "No. Nobody, really. There are just so many Celtic myths that call for swords, I thought I'd make me one to order."

"You planning to be the hit of everybody's party?" I said, walking over to hug him. His skin was warm and smooth.

"No, but it just felt so good to *be* one last night. It was like living another life. Awfully real. I'm going to see if Coltrane will let our classes do some reenactments. If anything could bring mythology alive, that could...."

"Aengus...," I began, then stopped. I seemed to hear Grand's voice, faint and very far away: Don't let him go too far into the Irish thing. Don't let him take you there with him.

"What?"

"You want pancakes for breakfast?"

We were scarcely half through breakfast when the veranda door swung open and Carol Partridge came into the breakfast room. She was in faded, oversized pajamas that had to have been her ex-husband's, violently striped in maroon and gold, and she was fairly dancing on her bare feet. Her yellow hair was in its accustomed exuberant explosion; perhaps, I thought, that was its accustomed style after all. Her sleep-crumpled face was stretched into a jack-o'-lantern grin, and she was singsonging, in a voice that sounded much like Bummer's froggy one, "I know a secret! I know a secret!"

"Have you come to prevail on me to pick up bottle tops or foot the bill for psychiatric care for the whole street? After last night...," Aengus began.

She threw her arms around him and buried her face in his dark hair. "I came to crawl in bed with you and your gold necklace, but I see I'm too late, so I'll settle for telling you a wonderful secret, but you've got to promise you didn't hear it from me."

"Actually, that was Thayer's necklace, but I'll pop it on

anytime for you." Aengus grinned, hugging her. "What's your secret, pajama girl?"

She looked at herself ruefully and shook her head. "I forget," she said. "I really do. Can you spare a cup of coffee? I haven't even plugged mine in yet."

I poured a cup and set it in front of her at the table. She was shimmering with her news, almost as Aengus had been last night. Lord, was there no one at all phlegmatic on Bell's Ferry Road?

"Well," she said, draining her cup. "I just happened to be talking to Mayor Carmichael last night, and *he* said—"

"The mayor was there?" Aengus said. "God, I could have at least kept my shirt on—"

"Shut up, Aengus. He's that white-haired guy with the little thatch mustache; you talked to him half the night, Thayer. Mayor Gibson Carmichael. Lives in that brick Colonial right on the river across from me—"

"Oh, him!" I said. "For some reason I thought he was a pharmacist—"

"Anyway, he's going to call you today, Aengus, and ask you to be on some hotsy-totsy advisory panel he's putting together for the Olympics next summer. You *did* know they were going to be here, didn't you?"

"I guess I did," Aengus said, frowning a little. "What kind of panel did he mean? I can't imagine he wants me to run around the Olympics with my shirt off and Thayer's necklace on—"

"I don't know, you idiot. Something about representing the creative, artistic side of the city; I guess there'll be other people on it doing other things. The point is, he's going to call you today and ask you. He said last night that you beat some fool singing 'Dixie' and accompanying himself on the harmonica all to hell."

"Well, I do know a goat that farts the—"

"Oh, get serious! I thought you'd be pleased—"

"He is!" I cried. "Oh, Carol, of course he is! Oh, Aengus, it's just what you were wishing for...."

He looked at Carol, then at me.

"Well, it could be, at that. Gee. You know, it really might turn into something—"

"Shut up!" Carol and I cried together.

He laughed.

"Champagne," Carole said. "There should be champagne. Do you have any—"

"No!" Aengus roared. She looked at him quizzically.

"He thinks to celebrate a thing before it's formally been offered is to curse it," I said. "Wait till hizzoner calls and then we drink champagne. Probably lots of it. It really is wonderful, isn't it?"

"Better than. Good enough to get me off the hook for that damned party for the next five years. Got to go, thanks for the coffee, yay, Aengus!"

She was gone back through the hedge before we could get our breaths.

We tried to act as if nothing had happened, and we did it badly. The telephone did not ring until late that afternoon. Aengus ambled to pick it up so slowly that I was drawing a breath to scream at him.

"Just what Carol said," he said mildly, coming back out onto the veranda. "It's just a committee to educate international visitors about what resources Atlanta has to offer different groups. There might be some traveling. I don't really understand quite what it's about yet. But I don't think I'm going to do it."

"My God, why? It's a great honor!"

"Because the chairman is, and I quote, 'Jim (Call Me Big Jim) Mabry.' He's given untold millions to various city concerns, and there's talk that he might well be the next governor, or maybe a senator."

"So?"

"He lives in Riverwood. I'm not going," Aengus said again mulishly.

"Oh yes, you are!" I cried. "You can stand it for one night. There's no telling what this could do for you."

The matter was more or less settled for us on the following Wednesday, when the *Atlanta Journal-Constitution* ran a photograph of Aengus over a cutline that read: "Noted local mythologist Aengus O'Neill to sit on Mayor's Olympics Panel." The photo was of Aengus standing before the fire, almost a silhouette, without his shirt, wearing my gold necklace and holding a clenched fist aloft. His eyes were closed and his face was rapt, unsmiling; he looked like a pagan war god.

"Or an escaped lunatic trying to evade capture," Aengus spat when he saw the picture. "Who the hell took that picture? I didn't see any press there that night."

He stalked toward the telephone. I sat regarding the picture. It was a beautiful image to me, but I could see that without its context, without all the firelit magic that had gone before, it could look…strange, perhaps. A little over-the-top, especially crammed in between an article about an offshore oil rig spill and a Campus Crusade for Christ dinner at Georgia Tech. Oh, God, now Aengus was really going to want to cancel it.

He came back into the den and slumped heavily into his chair.

"Bummer," he said thinly. "Bummer took it, and was so proud of it he gave it to the mayor, who was apparently quite taken with it himself. A next-door neighbor to whom the mayor is an old family friend is a fine thing, is it not? Carol was almost speechless. She just saw it herself."

"Aengus, you're not going to refuse to do it?"

"How can I?" he snarled. "Carol's already been all over Bummer. Not that it's an 'unflattering photo,' you understand, just that he didn't ask my permission to show it to the mayor. She says he's been in his room crying for the last fifteen minutes. How can I add to that? Christ, I wish I *had* cursed the lot of them when I had the chance.…"

"Maybe nobody much will notice it—"

"A half-naked guy in somebody's backyard wearing his wife's necklace? You're right, who the hell would notice that?"

A great many people apparently did. Most of them called us. They were people who had been at the party, or friends from Sewanee or Coltrane, a few of my friends. All were congratulatory or at least affectionately humorous, but Aengus took the phone off the hook just after dinner.

"They've all been great calls, Aengus," I said, chiding him mildly.

"Well, I wanted to put a stop to them before your mother weighed in." He sighed. "I ain't up to that tonight."

Suddenly we were both laughing, laughing so hard that we could not talk, clutching each other, almost rolling from our chairs onto the floor. We laughed for a long time. Then we went upstairs to bed and made love. We laughed during that, too.

My mother did indeed weigh in, just before eight o'clock the next morning, via my sister, Lily.

"Thayer?" she said hesitantly, and before I could even reply I began to laugh again. Presently she did, too. We laughed as hard and long as Aengus and I had the evening before, and I was still gasping when I finally got out, "Well, tell me. Don't keep me in suspense."

"Oh, Jesus, Thay, she said...she said...," and Lily was off again. Finally she chortled, "She said she'd never be able to hold her head up in town anymore, that everybody knew that gold neck-plate thing had been hers before she gave it to you, that Daddy gave it to her for an anniversary gift—"

I shrieked with renewed laughter. "He did not! Grand gave me that necklace; she brought it back from Crete—"

"I know it!" Lily howled, and we laughed some more.

It was a good five minutes before we could collect ourselves enough to wind up our conversation. I was still giggling when I went back in to Aengus.

"Your mother," he said, not looking up from the *New York Times.*

"My sister about my mother," I said.

"Tell me later. I've got a feeling I'm going to need another good laugh before this thing is over."

That was on Thursday morning. That afternoon Mayor Carmichael called and said that he hoped I would be agreeable to coming along with Aengus to the meeting the next night.

"Big Jim wants to meet all the committee's womenfolks. Says the way to get a committee in action is to include the womenfolks. Hidden assets, he calls all of you. I'm sorry, Mrs. O'Neill, but if you could just put up with this for a couple of hours I think that'll be the end of it, for you anyway. I've made it plain to Jim that I was *not* asking anyone's wife to sit on this committee—"

"Of course, Mr. Mayor," I said. "I've never seen Riverwood. It'll be interesting."

"It probably ain't worth crossin' the river for, but thank you," he said, and hung up.

"Guess what," I said to Aengus, who was again planing his sword on the veranda. He looked up, one eyebrow raised.

"I'm going to the big party across the river with you. Big Jim wants to meet all us wives."

"I'll just bet he does, the old porker," Aengus said, but the good humor was back in his voice. I was glad for that.

On Friday evening we drove across the old iron bridge and into Riverwood. The old river forest was just as lush and green here as it was on our side of the Chattahoochee, but there was not nearly so much of it. What there was, was a lot of grass. Undulant, endless, velvety, perfectly manicured grass. It seemed to sweep up out of the river and out of sight over the first rolling hill of Riverwood, pierced only occasionally by an immaculate ribbon of driveway. At the end of each driveway was a House. There was no way one would use a small *h* on these Houses; "t'wouldn't," as Grand might say, "be proper." I stared mutely as we rolled along looking for the street number. I saw a Versailles, a Monticello, a Petra, and a Taj Mahal. I saw Jaguars, huge Mercedes and BMW touring cars, Rolls-Royces, Bentleys. I saw a Brooklyn Botanic Garden's worth of perfectly tended blooms. Only behind all this did I see the trees of the river forest. They seemed to cower behind the homes of Riverwood in shame. Fury tightened in my throat.

"I'm not getting out of this car," I muttered between clenched teeth.

"Too bad." Aengus grinned. "Also too late. Here we are and we've been spotted. There seems to be a reception committee. Welcome, my dear, to the Parthenon."

My mouth opened. I could not seem to close it. It *was* the Parthenon, or at least a smaller copy of it, from the great frieze of nobly reclining Greeks to the eight monolithic columns atop the shallow steps. Yellow and red tulips bloomed in marble basins at its feet and pruned, phallic junipers rose behind it. Before it stood, poised on the circular white driveway, one perfect silver Rolls-Royce. Behind the car stood an honest-to-God liveried butler (unless, Aengus whispered, he, too, was marble) and a woman in a one-shouldered black silk sheath and stiletto heels. She was gesturing toward the huge double front doors, and a shrinking couple, the woman in what I thought of as the Atlanta woman's casual summer night out uniform, linen slacks and sleeveless top, such as I wore, cowered before her.

"Oh, dearest God," I whispered.

"Make that 'gods,'" Aengus whispered back.

We got out of the Volvo and went to meet Artemis, or whoever the hell she was. I felt laughter shiver like jelly in my throat. Aengus's shoulders were shaking lightly.

"Don't you *dare!*" I hissed furiously into his ear.

"Hello, sweeties, I'm Precious Mabry," the woman caroled, extending both hands. "Now, I know you've got to be our famous mythologist, Dr. O'Neill, because I saw that *gorgeous* picture of you in the paper. My goodness! What a pity you wore a shirt tonight. And you are, of course, Mrs. O'Neill."

Aengus goggled stupidly at her and took her outstretched hands. She leaned up and gave him a peck on the cheek. A wave of something primal and floral perfume smote me. She turned to me.

"I'm Thayer O'Neill," I said. "You're nice to include us wives, Mrs. Mabry."

She gave us both an enormous smile. It seemed to stretch into her jet-black lacquered hair and tangle with her diamond hoop earrings. Suddenly I felt like a smudged and tattered child deep in alien adult territory. I actually caught myself standing on one foot, hiding my other flat sandal behind it.

"Well, aren't you the pretty thing." She glistened at me. "Dr. O'Neill, I'll introduce you around, but you, my dear, I'm saving for Big Jim."

She tugged us both across the porch and down the steps

toward the garden. This turned out to be a vast clipped maze of boxwood and cypress, with symmetrical ranks of tulips bordering it and a gazebo in the middle. In the gazebo a knot of people surrounded the biggest man I have ever seen. He was at least six feet, seven inches, and nearly as round as he was tall. His chins and face and bald head were red almost to vermilion, with sun and perhaps general temperament, for he was laughing, a laugh that boomed out and, I thought, must surely reach the river. He was, he must be, Big Jim Mabry.

Without turning his head away from the crowd he reached a gigantic arm out for me, and Precious Mabry pushed me into it. The arm nearly crushed me, Aengus reached for me, and Big Jim turned to look at him, then at me.

"Dr. Aengus O'Neill," he bellowed, his great moon face radiating cheer. "Know you anywhere, even with your clothes on. And this must be your missus. Or maybe your daughter? Don't matter; she's a right armful, isn't she?"

I saw blank white anger start on Aengus's face and said loudly, "Wife, of course, Mr. Mabry. Thayer O'Neill. It's a remarkable house and garden. I'm so glad for a chance to see it."

"Well, now, you come on in and I'll show you the rest of it," he boomed. "Got a pretty little doohickey behind the pool, think my wife calls it a fancy."

"Folly, Jim," Precious Mabry said. Her voice was not glittering now. I tried gently to pull away from Big Jim, but he only tightened his grip and widened his smile at Aengus.

"Get one like this, you gotta hold on to her, don't you, son?"

Before Aengus could open his mouth, a woman's slow, sweet voice spoke beside me.

"My dear, I'm Helena Carmichael," the owner of the voice said. She was slender and suntanned and her dark hair was pulled simply back, showing tiny diamond clips and a graceful neck. "I missed meeting you the other night, but Gibby told me about you. We knew your grandmother, and we're so glad to have you in the neighborhood. Jim, you let go of her now; I want her to meet some of the rest of us wives, and she'll never get away from you on her own."

"Known me too long, haven't you, Helena?" Big Jim chortled, and she said, "Much too," and put her arm around me and led me toward the pool, where a small crowd of women chatted and laughed together.

"What he needs is a spike heel in the instep, but he'll get that later from Precious." Helena smiled. "Your husband looks like he can hold his own."

"Thanks so much," I said. "He can. I never know quite what to do when something like that happens. Not that it does, very often," I hastened to add, thinking how smug I must sound.

"I would think quite often," she said. "It's just that Big Jim has an inflated sense of his own charm, to match everything else about him. I don't think you'll have to see much of either one of them. But your poor Aengus...it's a full year until the Olympics."

"Well, I can't thank you enough," I said. "I was beginning to feel like somebody's overdressed teenage daughter."

"You *are* pretty young," she said. "But there's not a woman here you couldn't hold your own with. You look very much like your grandmother; I'm sure people have told you. A truly wonderful woman."

"Yes," I said, my eyes prickling suddenly with the missing of Grand. "She was, wasn't she?"

After an outdoor buffet presided over by a white-clad chef in the only real chef's hat I had ever seen and served by pretty aproned maids, Big Jim herded the men of the committee away into the house "to tackle the business. You ladies just sit around the pool and look like water lilies."

"Back as soon as possible," Aengus whispered to me on his way inside.

"Don't hurry." I grinned. "A man's gotta do what a man's gotta do."

It was not an unpleasant evening. The pool looked lovely with its lights on and its little waterfall splashing over rocks, and the sweet night wind brought the surrounding garden to us. Most of the women were agreeable enough; some I hoped I would get to know better. We talked of what women always do when they are tighter in groups: children. Almost everyone had them. Almost everyone was lamenting about some rocky rite of passage or other. Precious Mabry smiled around and said, "I just don't know what it is, but we've never had a minute's trouble with ours. Nobody in Riverwood seems to. You'd think they'd be tempted to get into mischief now and then; most of us...them...have enough spending money to do it right. But they're angels, all of them."

Something flickered in my mind, something about the children of Riverwood. Carol Partridge. I could hear Carol's voice saying, somewhere and sometime, "Little zombies is what I think." I was surprised. I would have thought that children on this side of the river, especially Big Jim Mabry's children, would be plentifully spoiled.

Pretty soon the men came out to the pool to join us. Every one of them had that end-of-the-party-let's-get-out-of-here look on his face. Some of the women rose to join them, but Big Jim held up his hand.

"I just heard Aengus O'Neill here tell one of his Irish story things, and I want the kids to hear some of them. Makes the hair stand up on the back of your neck, he does. Precious, go round up those kids out of the basement and get 'em out here."

Aengus started to demur, but Big Jim overran him.

"They been down there all night practicing with their band. I want 'em to hear what real entertainment is."

Everyone clapped politely and sat back down. Aengus muttered something under his breath. Precious scuttled away to summon the boys.

Presently she came back with eight boys behind her. I stared. For a brief moment I thought they were octuplets. They all seemed to be about the same age, twelve or thirteen. All of them wore clean, pressed khakis and neat tee shirts, and all had clean, shining, carefully combed hair. At close range they did not look at all similar, but in the aggregate they were so alike as to be almost eerie. They nodded and smiled and spoke to everyone. Nobody shuffled or twiddled his fingers or twisted his baseball cap. Nobody wore a baseball cap. They resembled no teenage boys I had ever met.

"I didn't hear a peep out of your band," I said to Big Jim's son Jamie, who did not look as if he shared a single gene with either his father or his mother.

"We try to keep it down," Jamie said, smiling. "And it's not a rock band. Actually we're doing chamber music. We're not very good yet."

"You'd be surprised at how good they are." Big Jim beamed. "They even got me to a concert at Symphony Hall last winter."

The boys sat down on the rocks fringing the pool and looked expectantly at Aengus.

"You guys don't have to do this," he said. "Go on back to your music; nobody ought to have to listen to this stuff on a summer night...."

"No, sir," one of them, a boy named Toby, said. "We all want to hear it. We studied the Celts a little last year in history; I even named my dog Cuchulain."

"Did ye now," Aengus said, laying the brogue on like frosting. The boys all laughed.

"Then I will give you," Aengus said, "the stories of Chulainn, Cet Mac Mágach, and Conor Mac Nessa, lads all who were up to no good as mere boys but who yet brought honor and greatness to Ireland."

His voice slid, almost unconsciously, into the cadence I had come to think of as his fireside rhythm: It evoked fire; it lit fires; it called down fire from heaven. The boys fell silent; none of them moved. Aengus's voice rose and dipped and sang; his hands wove pictures in the air; his blue eyes followed the movings of long-dead yet living men.

When he finished, the boys rose as one and applauded long and loud. Aengus smiled. Big Jim nodded and beamed.

The boys sat down again and leaned in close to Aengus.

"Are there books about them that I could read?" one of them said.

"Can you tell us some more another night, maybe?"

"I have lots of books about the Celts; I'd be glad to share," Aengus said. "The library will have many more. And I'd be delighted to come and tell you more sometime."

I simply looked at him.

"I never saw such...adult young men, for their age. They're extraordinary," I said to Big Jim.

"They're good kids," he said. "All neighborhood kids. But you should have seen them when they were younger. Hellions. We thought we'd be getting them out of jail by now."

"Wow. What on earth happened?"

"Camp happened," Big Jim said. "Maybe you've heard we've got this little old camp up on Burnt Mountain, to the north there."

My head began to spin. Burnt Mountain. A camp on Burnt Mountain. A camp from which my father had never returned...

"Real old-fashioned camp this one is, none of this feel-good-about-yourself crap. Just swimming and boating and field games and lots of contests. Hiking. Tracking. Woodcraft. You know. Good counselors. Good headman, does everything. Even drives the bus."

"I've heard the bus," Aengus said, "and the kids singing."

"Right. The damned Cannibal King. Know it by heart, I do. The head taught them that. Old Nog Tierney."

Aengus raised his head and looked at Big Jim.

"Nog Tierney? An Irishman, then."

"Don't know about that. Didn't look Irish. Looked like an ol' Georgia upcountry redneck. Kind of hookwormy."

"Tir Na Nog. An old Celtic land where you're supposed to live forever. Pretty obscure. I don't think anybody but an Irishman would know it."

"Well, that's interesting. The camp is named Camp Forever. We got the land from the old man about thirty years ago, and he gave it to us free on the condition that we name it Camp Forever. Beautiful land, wild and unspoiled, goes on forever on the back side of old Burnt, where nobody else is. Got a big spring-fed lake. Matter of fact, I guess I'm responsible for it. I was up there about thirty years ago hunting, just me and the dog, and ran into this guy. He told me it was his land, and I said I hadn't meant to trespass, that it was beautiful land. One thing led to another, and I told him I lived here in this new community, lots of young families and children, and he said, 'Make a good camp, wouldn't it?'

"And that's how we ended up with Camp Forever. I kept thinking that eventually he'd want some money for it, but all he ever asked was to drive the bus and hang out with the boys. Finally I made him take fifty thousand dollars and sign a regular contract. Free land just made me nervous. So I guess I own it now, but there's no question of who ran it. He was a rough old guy, but you'd be surprised at what all he knew. More than an old dirt farmer, that's for sure. All this stuff about the old days and the old times. I kidded him some about going to college. Swore he never did. The kids flat loved him. And when they'd get back from camp, they were different kids. Nobody ever had a scrap more trouble with them. When he got too old his son took over. He's who we've got now, and just like his dad he is. Even named Nog. I couldn't have told one from the other if this one hadn't been a sight younger. Kids are crazy about him, too."

"So this Nog number two is the camp head now?" Aengus said.

"I guess you'd have to call him that," Big Jim said. "We've got a bunch of good counselors; kids fight to get on at the camp. And we've got a director, or that's his title, anyway. Been there several years, but I don't think I'm going to keep him on. He can't get along with Nog, though I never met anybody else that couldn't, and keeps running to me complaining about him. Says he's too 'free with the boys,' whatever the hell that means. I've stayed up there a week or so at a time and I never noticed him being what you'd call free with them. He just knows so much about the place, and he tells them all these stories about the land and the old folks that used to live on it. The kids love it. There's just something about him that—I don't know—reaches out to you. Always interested in what you've got to say, laughs and jokes like a kid himself sometimes. But he's got plenty of sense, just like his daddy did. I guess you'd just have to know him to see what I mean."

"I'd like to know him," Aengus said. "I'd like to see that camp."

Again, I stared at him in the silence.

"Love to have you," Big Jim said. "Maybe come up now and then and tell some more of those stories. Be a real hit around a campfire. We could put you up. We've got good dormitories. Want to give it a try, say this weekend?"

"Yes," Aengus said, shimmering.

We rode almost all the way home in silence. Then I said, "Aengus, are you out of your mind? You know nobody we know hangs around with that Riverwood crowd."

"Tir Na Nog," he said slowly. "The Land of Forever Young. Awfully obscure myth for an old Georgia mountaineer to know. I'd just like to see what's going on up there."

"You'll be sorry," I said, smiling in the dark.

I've never forgotten that.

CHAPTER

15

On Friday morning after our dinner with Big Jim Mabry, I woke soon after 6:00 a.m., my hair drenched with sweat, my nightgown twisted around me, the damp sheets nasty on my bare flesh. Hot. My God, it was hot. We had not used the air-conditioning system; it had been a cool spring and there was almost always a little night wind off the river. But as if a great internal engine had simply stopped somewhere in the earth, everything had stilled and the monstrous heat had slid in ghostlike.

Beside me, Aengus slept on, immovable and serene, as he always did. No air stirred on my nakedness; there was an overhead fan, but we had not used that, either. I had only to get up and turn the wall switch on and we would have moving air, but somehow I could not make my limbs move; I felt as if something vital had bled out of them and into the heat.

It isn't supposed to be really hot near water, I thought crossly, feeling betrayed by the river. I lay thinking about this. My father had always said it when my mother complained about the heat in Lytton. And we had had vicious summer heat there; I remembered that we had, but somehow I could not seem to feel that long-ago heat now. I had never really felt it. I know my father didn't, either.

"You two were born without sweat glands, I swear," Mother said petulantly. "It's not natural."

I could remember no really hot days at Sewanee, either. The Mountain and the Steep undoubtedly had something to do with that. And camp? My mind slid slowly, reluctantly, back to the summers at Camp Sherwood Forest. I did not want to go there, had not for years gone there, but I was too listless to pull my mind back. There had been water there, of course, the lake, and I remembered the cold of it, and the clean, fishy smell, and even the sun-scorched planks of the dock under my back and legs.... Nick. Oh, God, Nick. Had I ever seen sweat running down his face? I could not remember sweat, only the face.... And after, in the top bunk... No, there had been no sweat.

I got out of bed and pulled on shorts and a tee shirt and went, barefoot, down the driveway to the mailbox on the street. I would read the paper and have my coffee on the veranda, and perhaps by that time a breeze would have sprung up. I really did not want the air-conditioning. I hated the feel of a closed house in summer.

I had just pulled the newspaper out of the mailbox when I heard the grinding and shifting of gears and the surly growl of a big engine starting up our hill from the river. I stood still and watched. I thought I knew what it would be, and it was: the bus that took the little Woodies to camp. It was a regulation bus size and either new or freshly painted; its white enamel gleamed in the hazy sun. *Camp Forever* was written in dark blue script on its side. It was the most tasteful bus imaginable, I thought sourly.

As it drew alongside me I heard the children singing, "The Cannibal King with the big nose ring fell in love with a dusky maid...." Lord, didn't they know any other camp songs? What was wrong with "Ninety-Nine Bottles of Beer on the Wall" for instance? Only it would have to be lemonade, I guessed. Or, of course, Co'-Cola.

As if cued, the children all looked at me as the bus lumbered past, but none waved except the bus driver. He turned his face to me and smiled and held up a forefinger, as country people often do by way of greeting. He had a pleasant, snubbed face, red and peeling from sun, and a thatch of ginger hair showed under his Camp Forever cap, which was turned around bill backward. I lifted my hand in return, and he went back to his driving and to singing lustily, "And every night in the pale moonlight across the lake he'd wade...." They ground out of sight up the hill toward the expressway, but, " 'Aye-oomph! Aye-oomph! Aye-oomph-tiddy-i-dee-aye-ay!' " floated back to my ears as if reluctant to let go of me.

When I got back to the house Aengus was in the kitchen making coffee.

"Hot enough for you? As I don't believe I have ever said to you, have I?"

"No, you haven't, and yes, it is," I said. "It's really awful. I don't remember heat like this before."

"And you born and bred in Georgia?" he said, handing me a cup of coffee. "Turn on the air-conditioning, for God's sake. Or go jump in the river."

"I don't want to do either one," I said childishly, and then laughed. "What I really want to do is sit here and whine."

"Well, whine away, my dear. But I'm turning on the air when I get home and no arguments. We could maybe go out to dinner."

"I don't want to do that, either. Oh, I saw your camp bus when I went out to get the paper. Mighty fancy for a kids' camp."

"Consider whose kids," Aengus said. "Did you see the driver? Big Jim said he was new."

"Yeah. He looked about thirteen and was singing 'The Cannibal King' along with the rest of them. Somebody ought to teach those kids some other camp songs."

"Maybe I'll do that when I go up tomorrow night," he said. "Really nasty ones, like 'Roll Your Leg Over.'"

I remembered then that he was going up to Camp Forever at Big Jim's behest to tell Celtic tales to the Riverwood young. For some reason this made me crosser even than the heat.

"If you can sit around a fire in this you're a better man than I thought," I grumped.

"I thought you thought I was already a great man."

"I do. Don't listen to me. I guess I got up on the wrong side of the bed."

243

"There's no wrong side of a bed with you in it, babe," he said. He kissed me on the cheek. "Gotta go shave. Just some cantaloupe would be great for breakfast."

"I don't have any," I said with satisfaction, but he had gone into the bathroom and could not hear me.

I fiddled restlessly with answering letters and making a shopping list, then took a cool shower and pulled my heavy roan hair back in a ponytail and felt better.

Just after lunch Carol Partridge called.

"Thayer? Listen, could you possibly take Bummer for a while this afternoon?" she said. Her voice was not her own; it was tight and cracked.

"Of course I can," I said. "Is anything the matter?"

"No...yes. Ben and Chris are in Juvie; the police just called. I've got to go get them out, and I don't want to take Bummer down there."

"Oh, Carol, what happened?"

"The little bastards and their cronies went into that ratty little grocery place next to the theater up in the multiplex and pointed water guns at that crazy old fool who runs it and ran out with three huge boxes of fudgesicles. And when the old guy ran after him they shot him! With water pistols! Of course he called the police before they even got out the door, and he knows most of them, and at first he was going to press charges. Oh, God, their father is going to sue me for custody; I know he is. Anyway, if you could just oversee Bummer, this shouldn't take me long. I just have to pay their fines and spring them."

"Send him on. It'll be a joy. And come by when you get back, if you can. I'll give you a drink."

It was scarcely fifteen minutes before Bummer came trailing through the hedge to the veranda, dragging a kite behind him and licking an ice-cream bar.

"Hey, Thayer. Miz O'Neill," he said. "I was going to fly this kite, but Mother says there's not enough wind. Did you know my brothers are in the juvie? They stole a bunch of fudgesicles. This isn't one of them," he said matter-of-factly, looking down at his melting bar. "This is vanilla. Theirs were chocolate. I don't know what happened to them."

I hugged him, wincing at the sound of "juvie" coming so easily out of his ice cream–smeared mouth.

"I heard," I said. "I'm sorry. Maybe this will calm them all down a little."

"Fat chance," he said. "Would you like to go over to my house and go swimming?"

The thought of the broiling sun on the pool apron and Bummer's inevitable shouts of "Marco Polo!" roiled in my stomach.

"I don't think so, thanks," I said. "But you know what I'd like to do? I'd like to go to the theater up at the multiplex. I think Harry Potter's on."

"Oh yeah," he said. "That'd be cool. I've seen them all, but I'd like to see them again. Is it the one where their teacher turns into a werewolf, or the one where all those brains come floating at them?"

"We'll soon see," I said. "Me, I vote for the brains."

"Well, the werewolf was pretty cool, too. They had to fire him because of it, but he was really a good guy."

"I guess some werewolves are," I said, and we went up to the multiplex and dove deep into the chilled air and the utter

enchantment of the boy wizard and his friends and their sor-
ceried world. At some point I thought, This would be the way
to live. Where nothing that happened really surprised you,
because it was all magic anyhow. And even if it was bad, a
brave kid with round black glasses could come and fix things.

When we got home, Aengus was there, drinking iced tea
on the veranda. Bummer went immediately into his Harry
Potter reenactment, and I slumped gratefully into a rocking chair. It was still breathlessly hot, but the long shadows
over the browning lawn gave the illusion of coolness. I had
scarcely finished a glass of iced tea and given Bummer some
lemonade when Carol came through the hedge.

For one startled moment I thought she had somehow fallen
into water. Her hair was drenched, plastered to her head. Her
shirt and slacks were sticking to her skin. Her face, too, had the
greenish-white, puckered look skin gets when it has been a long
time in water. I rose to my feet; so did Aengus. Bummer, soar-
ing high above Hogwarts on his broom, did not notice.

"Carol..."

She looked down at herself and then forced a smile. It
might have been a rictus of pain.

"Just to put the finishing touch on this glorious day, the
air conditioner in the SUV is out and we've been stuck in Friday afternoon traffic for over an hour."

"Sit down, and let me bring you something cold...."

"No," she said wearily. "I've got them under virtual house
arrest next door, but I don't know how long I can enforce it.
You were wonderful to take Bummer."

She was about to crumple, perhaps literally.

"Let me come home with you and Bummer," I said. "I'm not heavy-duty, but I've got staying power. I'm good backup."

She shook her head. "No. I think tonight's covered. All the other parents are hanging tough on this; none of the kids are going out. But I might need Aengus sometime late tomorrow. Just a stern man's face, like showing the flag. They need to realize I've got resources, too...oh, God. This shouldn't be happening. I shouldn't even think about getting you all involved in my problems with my damned children."

She dropped her face into her hands.

Aengus went over and put his arm around her shoulder. "I'll be your resource whenever you need me, but I can't tomorrow night. I promised Big Jim Mabry I'd go up to that camp of his and tell tales around the fire. But any other time."

She leaned into him, nodding her head that she understood. Then she lifted her head and her face suddenly blazed.

"Aengus, can you get Big Jim to take the boys into that camp? I know it's supposed to be just for their kids, but it sounds like just what Ben and Chris need. The way those kids change...Aengus, please. If you ever wanted to do anything for me, do this one thing. Big Jim can make that happen; he may be the only one who can! I could pay—"

"Hush," Aengus said, hugging her again. "Hush. There's no question of anybody paying anybody. Of course I'll ask him. But I thought they hated the idea of camp—"

"I will get them there if I have to do it at gunpoint," Carol said. From her tone I thought she well might.

Bummer came trotting up, covered in sweat and grass stains.

"Hi, Mom. We went to see Harry Potter. It was the werewolf one. Did they put handcuffs on Ben and Chris?"

"Oh, Bummer, of course not! Come on. We've got to get back."

They turned to go home and I said, "Listen, why don't I come over and keep you company tomorrow evening for a little while? Aengus is staying over and it's the first time he's ever left me alone."

I looked at him and smiled; he grimaced and then smiled back.

"I'll bring supper," I said.

"I'd love that," she said, managing a watery grin. "I'll make dessert. We can slide it under their doors."

Over dinner Aengus and I talked about Carol and her children.

"I don't really know how bad it is," I said. "I don't know what kids do today. I know she's convinced her ex will sue for custody if this goes on. No matter how she jokes about them, I know that she's crazy about her kids. I wish I could think of something we could do to help her. Maybe it's just their age...."

"It's bad enough," Aengus said. "Bad enough at least to make me glad they aren't mine. The police and the famous juvie aren't just mischief level. They'll be in real trouble if they get involved with the cops again. Those kids just don't realize how good they've got it. Carol is a sweetie, and they have a great house, and a pool—"

"And a father who just took off and left them flat," I said.

"Yeah. There's that. Half the problem, at least. Still...I don't know if that camp is the answer."

"I know; it's enemy territory. But if there *is* such a real difference in the kids who come back from it..."

"I'll ask, of course. Meanwhile, I'm going to turn on the air and send you to bed. You've had a tough day. I need to fiddle around with whatever I'm going to do tomorrow night, but I'll be up before long."

But by eleven o'clock he had not come to bed and I could stay awake no longer. The blessed cool of the air conditioner and the freshness of the new sheets I had put on the bed claimed me as surely as sleeping pills would have, and when I finally woke the next morning he was in the shower singing something mournful and Celtic and the clock said 8:15.

When he left for Coltrane he was carrying, in addition to his briefcase, a small weekend bag. It looked as if it had seen a great many weekends in its life. I knew that he was spending the night at Camp Forever, of course, but still that bag spoke to me, absurdly, of loss.

He saw my face and put his arms around me.

"I can drive back tonight, you know."

"No. It's a long way, and those mountain roads...and besides, the most fun is after the campfire, anyway."

"That's right, you did campfires at that camp of yours, didn't you? And what possible fun did you get up to after your campfire, seeing as they were all preadolescent girls?"

I stood still in the darkness of our early-morning foyer and heard a slow, deep voice saying, Didn't anybody ever tell you that Zeus was a serial rapist?

Nick Abrams's voice.

"Not much, to be honest about it," I said, my face going hot.

"Then I won't, either. See you in the morning, love. Take you to brunch at the Ritz if you like."

He kissed me and was gone out the front door. In the open doorway the heat eddied and coiled, and then retreated as he shut it. Another hot day, then. My heart sank.

And then I thought, What possible difference can it make? and went to take my own shower and feel my way into this barren day in which he was not coming home.

By the time I had been at Carol's house for an hour or so that evening, the sky blackened and lightning forked and thunder crackled, and we fled onto her screened porch just as the first great drops fell, sizzling on the pavement around the pool.

"Thank God," she said. "I think if this heat breaks, everything might get back to normal, or nearly."

Chris and Ben and Bummer scrambled out of the pool and dashed into the house.

"Stay close, guys!" she called after them. "Dinner in less than an hour!"

Nothing from Ben and Chris, except the sounds of the doors to their rooms slamming. Bummer called froggily that he was going to play video games in the den.

"They're still mad, I take it," I said. "Chris and Ben, I mean."

"Of course. It was obviously my fault that they were impelled to shoot an old man with water guns and steal his fudgesicles." She sighed.

Then she turned her yellow head and looked at me. "They're really good kids, Thayer. I don't know what's gotten into them this year. It's just such a *major* change. And I don't even know exactly when it started. It's funny about the big life changes, isn't it? That you don't even realize that they've happened until long after, and then you can't remember when. Or what happened that might have touched them off."

I put my arm around her shoulders and pulled her close on the big glider on the porch. She was all bird-fine bones and a steady, tiny shivering. Outside, the rain poured straight down, making its own music and sending us the intoxicating smell of wet earth and grass.

"Things can change back," I said. "I don't think anything is written in stone, Carol. They *are* good boys. You all will laugh about this someday."

"Way better than crying," she said. "I'm glad I have you around, Thayer. All my other friends in the neighborhood have kids, and there's always a little of the Well, at least *my* kids didn't get hauled down to Juvie, going around. How nice to have a friend with great good sense who doesn't have kids yet."

I said nothing. This was an entire subcontinent that I meant to keep unexplored.

I had thought I would be restless that night and sleep poorly, but with the air off and the windows open and the cool murmur of the retreating storm outside, I was asleep before I even had time to miss Aengus.

I slept late, until almost ten, and jumped out of bed thinking that perhaps he had gotten an early start and was already home, letting me sleep in. But he was not in the house, nor outside. I put on jeans and a shirt and went out to tend my battered flowers.

He was not home by lunchtime, either. At two o'clock he called to say that he was not getting in until about six.

"The steps to the swimming float are busted and I told Nog that I'd help him fix them before I left. It won't take very long."

"Oh, Aengus... isn't there somebody else up there who could help him?"

"Not at the moment. Big Jim left early this morning, and the older counselors have lit out for Atlanta. It's their afternoon off."

"Do they just go off and leave all those little boys by themselves?"

"Nog can handle them," he said. "They idolize him. He just needs another pair of hands for the float. I'll be home soon."

This last was said rather crisply, and so I said only, "Fine," and we hung up.

He was, indeed, home by 6:00 p.m. He came into the kitchen, where I was making gazpacho, and hugged me from behind and swung me around.

"You really must have had a good time," I said, laughing, as he put me down and finished up with a little riff of a dance. I cocked my head at him. I had perhaps seen this Aengus once or twice before but not often: joyous, gleeful, every inch of him lit with a living fire. He seemed at once distracted and as focused as a burning glass. He could not seem to be still. I stood just looking at him, afire in my kitchen, smelling the smoke of his burning.

"Wow. Can I go with you sometime?"

"Well, I will be going again, I think, maybe once a week. Those kids are incredible. It's as if they were created for the sole purpose of hearing these old myths. I never saw anything like it. But I don't think you could go. Strictly for the menfolks. No women allowed except on Parents' Day. Besides, it's not exactly comfy. I'll tell you about those top bunks sometime."

At the dishwasher, I froze for a long moment.

He came up behind me and kissed me again, on the neck.

"Believe me, our bed is a fine sight better."

"Oh," I said. "Did you remember to ask Big Jim about Carol's kids going to the camp? She's really between a rock and a hard place with them."

He took his arms away, and I heard him walk over to the counter on the opposite wall. For a long time he said nothing, and then he said, "Yeah. Big Jim said for her to come by anytime and they'd talk about it."

"Oh, that's great. Will you call her and tell her?"

Again he was silent, and I turned and looked at him. His face was closed, his fires out.

"I'm a bit fagged out at the moment. Will you call her?"

Still looking at him, I picked up the telephone on the counter. What had gotten into him so suddenly?

Carol was ecstatic.

"Give Aengus a big hug for me," she said. "I'm going over there right now."

Aengus wanted a shower and a nap, so I put the gazpacho in the refrigerator and poured myself a glass of wine. I felt fidgety and dislocated, not quite sure of where I was, nor why I felt that way. I gave Carol another hour and then called.

"How did it go with Big Jim?" I asked when she answered.

There was a long pause, and then she said in a voice so strange and robotic that I would not have known it was hers, "He's going to take them. I'm going to drive them up tomorrow. Bummer, too."

She said no more, so I said, "That's wonderful. How on earth did you manage that?"

Another long pause, and then the robot voice said, "Don't ever ask me that again, Thayer."

Shocked and sickened, for there was no mistaking her meaning, I went to the door and stared out into the twilight. I thought about our conversation yesterday afternoon, about change. About how you could never tell precisely when it happened.

"You were wrong, Carol," I whispered. "We do know when it happens. You know when it happened for you; you know the precise moment. I knew, really, when Aengus said he was going up to that camp. My mother knew when she came back from the family camp on Burnt Cove, on her honeymoon. And Aengus knew when he came home from camp today, knew that a great change had happened. He was vibrating with it."

Camp. Camp Forever.

The camp on Burnt Mountain.

CHAPTER

16

In the middle of July I took a job. It was actually just a part-
time job, selling books up at the little independent bookstore at the end of the small mall that housed the multiplex.
Its name was Ephemera, which probably made no sense at
all to anyone but its patrons, of which there were not a great
many anyway. It could not and did not try to compete with
the immense, rapid-fire disgorging machines like Barnes &
Noble and Borders. It had a small inventory of quirkily wonderful books, by time-faded and contemporary authors, and
there was no one on its staff who was not eccentric, immersed
in books, and knowledgeable about them to an astonishing
degree. I did not consider myself any of these things and was
grateful when they hired me, but as Simon Morganstern, its
owner, said, "You're young enough and presentable enough
and smart enough to kick our image up a notch without scar-
ing off our old customers."

Ephemera had a tiny café and a cat, as well as an old-fashioned cash register on which we did business. Its espresso machine, probably one of the first ever made, honked and hissed and whistled before delivering of itself a shot of inky, sludgy espresso, and the cat, Moriarity, was not a cuddly lap creature but a cranky presence that regularly spat at anyone who tried to pet him. I had been intimidated by everyone and everything at first but soon grew to love the customers and the espresso machine and Moriarity and the kinds of books we carried and, most of all, the people of Ephemera. It was almost like finding my lost tribe. The pay was abysmal but enough, as Aengus said, to help us through September, when my kindergarten teaching job began. And the job got me out of the house during his working hours, so that he would have no distractions. Aengus, that summer, was writing a book, but for a long time I did not know that.

Aengus's first trip to Camp Forever had started us down a crazy path, so thicketed with the unexpected and the unimaginable that I could not see beyond its first curve. At first it was just his intensity, his sense of manic joy when he came home from Burnt Mountain. I had seen those before, on a smaller scale; it was still a part of Aengus. But soon he began to go two and then three nights a week. I drew the line at weekends, or I think he would have gone then, too.

"I'm married to you. I'm not married to Carol. I want to spend at least some time with you," I had said when he suggested that Carol and I find something to do together on weekends, especially since all three of her boys were at camp now.

"Take up golf," he said. "She plays well, I hear. Or have a

tea or something and get to know the rest of the Bell's Ferry women. You know, Thay, you really don't have many friends."

"That's because I've always been with you, since you've known me, anyhow," I said, stung. It sounded, incredibly, like he was trying to get rid of me, only simply that could not be. This was Aengus. This was Aengus and me. Married under a tree on a mountain by a witch.

I did not worry a great deal about it, not at first. When he was with me, he was still totally *with* me. We still laughed at the same things.... We still gardened and sweated and cursed the heat and made fun of each other's grubby face. And at night, in the big bed that still floated almost alone in the huge space on the third floor, he turned to me as eagerly, made even hungrier and more joyful love to me, cried out my name more often than he ever had.

Only now it was in Gaelic.

"*Tainach! Alainn, nas aille....*"

"English, please. This way I'll never know whose name you're really calling."

"I'll be calling no other woman's name, ever," he said softly into my damp hair.

And I do not think that he ever did.

Still, this new Aengus was a frequent burr under my saddle.

"What is it about that camp, Aengus?" I would say. "What does it have that holds you so? Why can't I share it?"

He would look at me thoughtfully.

"I think...it's the way the boys *receive*, Thayer. I can't quite put my finger on it, but they seem so hungry for the old ways, the old tales. I'm just now realizing that I never really knew what teaching was. To...to have something that seems so necessary to someone else, to really give it...It's as if these kids are missing sort of a vital nutrient or something and I have it and can give it to them. It's...heady stuff. I don't find that at Coltrane. I've never found it at any other school; if I did, I'd apply there in the blink of an eye. But I haven't run into it anywhere, except at this camp. Oh, I know, it's just a summer camp; it won't last past the end of summer. But there hasn't been anything else like it...."

"You haven't really looked, darling," I said. "Maybe a school for younger people."

I had thought until now that his college work had absorbed him fairly well; it had seemed so at Sewanee. But this was serious business. We would have to address this....

It was also the first inkling I had that I was not the be-all and end-all of Aengus's prowling heart. The moment I realized that, I realized also that it had been a foolish thing to assume in the first place. Nobody could be absolutely everything to anyone else. Not in real life, anyway.

But Aengus has been to me, some small hidden voice deep within me whispered. Hasn't he? But if, indeed, that was not possible, then what else was it that filled my heart? For it *was* full. Had been, since we met. I would have known if there had been empty space there. There had been long, aching times when emptiness howled before I met him. I knew that territory. I did not live there now.

But still...but still. Where was this path down from Burnt Mountain taking us?

I brought it up with Carol Partridge one morning. We

were in her kitchen, surrounded by small mountains of vegetables. She was leaning against the counter poking fretfully at a pile of glorious purple eggplants.

"I started putting all this crap up when Walter first told me about his cherished childhood Thanksgivings at Grandma Partridge's," she said. "Apparently the old bat didn't have anything to do all year but put up vegetables. It never seems to occur to me that I don't have to do it anymore."

"Would you miss them if you didn't have them?" I said.

"No more than I miss him, and that ain't much."

"Do you miss not having the boys around?"

"Of course. Bummer especially. But I couldn't have let things go on like they have been. I just hope that famous camp is the answer. I paid way too high a price for it not to work."

"I know," I said, and hugged her. She was tense and still in my arms, and then loosened all over, and melted into me. She had said almost nothing about her meeting with Big Jim Mabry, the one that got her boys to Camp Forever, but she knew that Aengus and I knew the gist of it. The first time we had seen her after the incident, I had said, "You could probably take him to court or something for that," and she had simply given me a dead look.

"I didn't say no," she said. Her voice was so lifeless that it was frightening, and after she had gone I said, "It's simply unbelievable to me that a man who's being talked about as our next governor could do a thing like that."

"I should have thought it out better before I told her I'd talk to him," Aengus said. "But still, all she had to do was say no."

"I don't think she thought that was an option," I said

slowly. "I think that when it comes to your kids, you just do what you believe you have to."

"Maybe so," he said slowly. "I'm just glad it's not my problem."

"What if it was?" I said. "What would you do if your kids were behaving like that?"

"Send 'em to Camp Forever." He smiled.

"Yeah, but you wouldn't have to fuck Big Jim Mabry to get them in."

"Thank God for small favors. I never heard you say 'fuck' before, Thayer."

In Carol's kitchen that morning, after I had hugged her I said, "When things started to go wrong with you and Walter, was it just small things every once in a while, that you hardly noticed, or did it all just blow up at once?"

"Hiroshima from the get-go," she said, and looked at me keenly.

"What's Aengus up to, up there on that damned mountain? I know he's up there a lot," she said.

I did not know how she knew that Aengus went often to the camp, but I did not doubt that she did. Probably everybody on Bell's Ferry Road knew. It was simply the way the world of women worked. My mother had shown me that.

"I don't honestly know," I said slowly. "Probably nothing worrisome; I'm inclined to blow things out of proportion. It's just that he's up to two to three nights a week now, and I think he'd like to go weekends, though he hasn't exactly said so. He was never away from me before. And when we do talk, at home, or rather when he does, it's getting to be all about the old stories, the old gods, the old Ireland. I know he's an expert on the Celts, and I know he loves teaching them, but all this... I feel like some night I'm going to get in bed with a naked man wearing a gold torque. I've said that to you sometime before now, haven't I?"

She looked down at her bare brown feet and then up at me. "Don't go up there with him, Thayer," she said. Her voice was low and level.

Deep in my head I heard Grand:... Don't let him take you there with him. What else had she said? Something about losing him to moonbeams and sea mist...

"I couldn't if I wanted to," I said, striving for a lighter tone. "No ladies except on Parents' Day."

"Which is coming up soon, and to which I am not planning to go."

"Why not?"

"Because I hear Big Jim puts on a tremendous fireworks show up there on Parents' Day, and I'm afraid if I went I'd stick a rocket up his ass."

I went home from Carol's feeling considerably better. She could always do that to me.

When I crossed through the hedge to our back lawn I saw that Aengus was home, sitting on the veranda with his feet up and a legal pad on his lap. He was busy scribbling away. When I touched his shoulder he looked up at me, smiling vividly. I saw that the fire was in him again; it flickered in his eyes and lit his face.

"Wha'cha doin'?" I said, kissing the top of his head. "School out early?"

He put his arm around my waist and pulled me down into his lap. The legal pad went sprawling.

"I'm writing a book," he said.

I could make no sense of what he had said. It was the first I had heard of it.

"You're writing a book...."

"A book of Celtic myths for kids. Nobody's ever done it, that I can find on the Internet. Or at the library. I never saw anybody take to the old stories the way these kids have. This book will make us a fortune. I know I'm right about this."

"Aengus...honey...do you know what it takes to get a book published? You have to know the editors, and have an agent, and...oh, I don't know...there are all these contracts and things. I have no doubt in the world it will be a wonderful book, but I think it takes a lot more than that...."

"Big Jim knows editors and agents. He's calling around. He says I'll probably have an agent sometime this week. He thinks this book would sell like hotcakes. The boys do, too. I'm going to read it to them chapter by chapter, around the campfire. Maybe make fiction of the old tales. I'll probably be up there a little more often now, but..."

"How are you going to find the time?" I said in a voice like crumpling paper. "Do you think you can teach and still write in the afternoons? It's a good month or six weeks till my school starts, and you'll be swamped with work. What if you lost Coltrane?"

"Thayer, this isn't going to take forever. Camp closes in September; I hope to be almost done with it by then. I can handle Coltrane without batting an eyelash or find another

college, if it comes to that. Big Jim knows every college president in the Southeast. We've talked all this out, baby. He and
I both think it would help a little if you got a temporary job,
and if we needed a little extra, you could borrow some of that
trust money Grand gave Lily for any kids that come along...."

"I won't be having any kids, Aengus," I whispered, my
heart making great loops and dives almost into my stomach.
"You know that. And what's all this Big Jim stuff? I thought
you thought... he was an obnoxious ass...."

"We'd get the trust if we adopted. Who's to say we can't
do that? We just don't have to say when. And as for Big
Jim... you just have to get to know him, Thayer. Nobody on
this side of the river has ever given him a chance. This will all
work! I feel it way down in my bones."

I sat still and boneless in his lap. Could he be... oh, what?
Delusional? Unhappy enough to want to destroy his world
and totally rearrange it? It was my world, too....

But Aengus was not unhappy now. He seemed happier at
this moment than I had ever known him. His arms were hard
around me, and his hands caressed my breasts and stomach
as they often had in his moments of joy. Happy the way a
gleeful child is happy. Totally, deliriously happy.

"I'll go make some lunch," I said. I wondered if this manic
joy could possibly last.

For the rest of the weekend, at least, it did.

On a mid-August day of such sucking, enervating heat that I
felt frail and sickened by it, I was walking across the first floor
of the big main library downtown, thinking despairingly of

263

the four-block walk to the garage where I had finally found a parking place. Parking downtown in Atlanta is a municipal joke at the best of times. Parking downtown on a Friday afternoon around rush hour is insanity. Parking downtown on a Friday afternoon around rush hour in ninety-seven-degree heat is close to self-immolation. Even in the stale-cold vastness of the library my summer dress was sticking to me. By the time I got home it would be indecent. This past summer had been a comatose animal of a season, bloated and corpulent and pumping out heat like a giant furnace. It was my first experience with an urban summer, though our stone house in the woods was about as cool as it could get, all things considered. I shifted my heavy book bag over my bare shoulder and thought that I would get out of my car and crawl straight into Carol's pool without even going home first. There was no need to make dinner. Aengus was at camp.

We were slow at the bookstore and I had taken the afternoon off to come downtown to research early Celtic swords for Aengus but had paused on the way out and then crammed my bag full of old Mary Roberts Rinehart mysteries. I had been through most of them at Grand's house when I was a child. They seemed to me suddenly, on that afternoon when the entire steaming world shifted sickly under my feet, the most comforting and coolly bloodless sustenance I could think of. I could fall asleep literally soothed into another world, one of faithful servants and fine linens and grand old summer houses in places like Bar Harbor and haute murders solved by plucky ladylike governesses or even the plucky daughters of the great houses themselves. I grinned to myself. Most of them would begin with something like "If we had known then what we do now about the theft of old Mrs. Thornwood's garnets..." Yes, in the big bed alone under the milky smear of stars Mrs. Thornwood's garnets would comfort me like a shabby teddy bear.

I settled the bubble more closely around my head and put out my hand to open the massive bronze front door.

The bubble. Somewhere around the time that Aengus had told me that he was writing a book—perhaps the same day—I had been given a bubble to wear. It enclosed my head like a snow globe or a diver's helmet, invisible to me and everyone else, but so irrefutably *there* that sometimes I could not imagine that other people did not see it glistening around my head like a great shield. I thought that I could touch it if I put up my hand to do so, but I never did. I knew when it was there. It came when I needed it.

I was sometimes unaware of the need, but when it settled down, hurtful noise became a murmur, and sharp edges outside it softened, and faces that came too close and wanted too much from me became faces outside a goldfish bowl. They might bump the bubble, but they could not reach me and I could hardly hear them.

A subterranean part of me knew that the bubble was my own protective device, and not necessarily a healthy one, but it did not matter. Inside was safety and the kind of dreaming contentment that had wrapped me during my earliest days at Sewanee.

I was certain that in some way Grand had sent the bubble.

Behind me, faintly because of the bubble, a voice said, "Thayer? Thayer Wentworth?"

I stood still. The bubble cracked and a fire-shot long-ago summer night flooded in. Sensations smote me as if I was being whipped with the smell of pines and cold lake water nearby, guttering smoke from a dying campfire, the rustle and murmur of restless little girls, fire heat on my face and legs and the chill of a mountain night on the back of me. And a deep voice out of the dark across the fire where a small group of boys lay sprawled.

This voice.

I opened my mouth to speak, and for a moment nothing came out, and then it did.

"Didn't anybody ever tell you that Zeus was a serial rapist?" I whispered, and turned around.

We simply looked at each other. Brown. He was still brown. The dark copper hair still fell over his face; the eyes under the long straight brows still seemed deep and dark as well water; the spattering of freckles was still strewn over the angled cheekbones. The only thing missing was the raw pink skin of the straight nose under peeling brown and the chipped front tooth. Only a faint webbing of wrinkles at the corners of his eyes spoke of the passing of time. But time had passed.

"You've still got hair in your eyes," Nick Abrams said in a voice I could barely hear, and pushed the tangled strand away from my forehead with a large brown hand I knew like my own.

I still said nothing. I could not quite manage it yet. He wore khakis and a faded blue Yale tee shirt and his arms were full of rolled blueprints.

He cleared his throat.

"Where did you go?" he said.

"Why didn't you write?"

He took a deep breath and let it out, and then said, "I did. I wrote every day. I called, from Paris and Siena. Both times they said you had moved away. They said you didn't want to hear from me...."

"Who is 'they'?" I said in a torn, almost inaudible voice. But I knew who.

"I guess it was your mother."

I felt myself sway, felt my bag of books start to slide out of my arms. Felt his arms go around me, to steady me. They were bare and warm, as if he had recently been in the sunlight.

"Of course it was my mother!" I said. I laid my head down on my arms, at the table to which he had steered me.

Of course. I could see her as clearly as a figure done in violent strokes of ink behind my closed lids. Answering every phone call: "No, I'm sorry, she doesn't live here anymore." Going every day to the post office and dropping his latest letter into her handbag. Had she burned the letters? Did it really matter?

"She never could get past the name Abrams," I said into my arms. My words had no breath behind them.

"Oh, God." He began to laugh. "She could have gotten so much worse than Abrams."

I raised my head and looked at him. "She did," I said. "To her mind, she did."

He looked into my bag briefly. "Celtic armor and Mary Roberts Rinehart?"

It was very strange. One side of my mind wanted to respond as I might usually have done, with something quick and supple; it was an odd combination. I would have laughed about it with Aengus. But I could think of nothing, almost literally.

"One is for my husband," I said finally, lifting my head. "The other one is mine."

"I don't imagine I have to ask which is which," Nick said, smiling. His smile seemed to grow until it filled my entire field of vision. I closed my eyes. The smile was still there. So were the freckles; I could have charted them like stars. Only the faint crow's-feet were new, but somehow they were where they should be.

"Mine's the Mary Roberts Rinehart," I said thickly. My head was spinning, and my face and mouth prickled. "My husband doesn't read mysteries."

He was silent for a moment, and then he said, "Thayer? Are you all right?"

"I think so," I said in a small voice. "It's very hot. I should go home, probably. My husband...Nick, I have a husband. Did I tell you that?"

"Yes," he said. "You did. Look, I think we'd better sit down someplace and get you some coffee or something. You look like you're about to hit the floor. God, I hope it's not me...."

"No," I whispered. I felt as if I were underwater, naked

and drowning. The bubble was gone; not a shard of it remained. I did not remember when it shattered. When I first saw him, I supposed. When I first heard his voice...

"Have you got time? I just can't let you leave like this...."

"I have time," I said. Where did this child's trembling voice come from?

We went out of the vast, book-smelling cool and into the blazing street. Passersby crowded into margins of shade. He held my elbow. In a few minutes we turned into the lobby of a nondescript fifties hotel that had, I knew, apartments on the top floors. The air inside was stale and glacial, smelling of carpet cleaner.

"You live here?" I said. "In Atlanta? Somehow I thought you lived somewhere like California, or maybe back down on St. Simons. I thought I'd know it if you were here...."

"No. I've got an apartment here because I'm designing part of the Olympics complex and our firm thought I ought to be on the spot. I live and work in New York, actually. Have since I got out of Yale."

"You did go to Yale, then...."

"Yeah. Did you go on to Agnes Scott?"

"No, I went to the University of the South. Sewanee. It's on a mountaintop in Tennessee. They call it the Domain. You'd have liked it, I always thought."

"I've heard of it. The Domain... sounds like you."

"How so?"

"Oh... kind of mystical, maybe. A little magical."

"I've given up magic," I said, trying for lightness, and failing.

He was silent till we got off the creaking elevator and I had followed him from the dim, sauce-smelling hallway into a large room blazing with afternoon light and very nearly empty.

"Did you give up magic when...you and I didn't get together?" he said quietly, settling me onto the couch. "Because if you did, I really may have to go kill your mother...."

"No. I guess what I mean is that I've learned that most of the time when you think you've found some magic, you really haven't...."

He didn't answer and went into the spartan kitchen. I was glad. The direction our talk had veered into frightened me.

I sat on his low blue couch and stared out the huge uncurtained glass windows at the immensity of Atlanta rearing itself up around us. He had very little furniture, but stacks and stacks of books and plans and sketches were scattered all over. Apparently he worked at what should have been the dining room table; it was a mare's nest of drawings and sketches and crumpled tracing paper. On a counter between the kitchen and living room stood a photograph of two very small girls, hardly past babyhood, with balloons on a seashore.

When he came in with coffee for me and a drink for himself, I pointed at the photo and said as brightly as I could, "Yours?"

He sighed and sat down beside me.

"Yeah. Beth and Carrie. They live in California now with their mother. I don't see much of them unless I go out there. It's not working out very well."

There was bitterness in his voice. I had never heard it before.

"Why did you get divorced? I mean, if you did," I said, and blushed furiously. Why could I not stop my tongue? This was not my territory now.

He was silent for a while, and then he said, "Yeah, we did. I guess it was because it was sort of—what came next. You know, you meet, you marry, you have children, you get divorced...."

I did not say anything. There seemed nothing to say. It was too late; too much lay between us; we had gone so far down such widely divergent paths....

I looked up at him helplessly.

"Who did you marry, Thayer?" he said.

"I married an Irishman. His name is Aengus O'Neill. He's a professor of Celtic mythology at a college here. Coltrane. He's writing a book now."

"Children?"

"No," I said. "I don't have any children."

He studied my face and then said, "What's your husband's book about?"

"I don't know anymore," I said. "I don't see him very often."

And to my horror I began to cry.

We sat in the big room until the lights of the city began to bloom, and by the time the sky had darkened completely I had given him most of my life after him. I could not stop the words, except the part about the baby—his baby, ours—and the subsequent illness that had left me barren. I knew that

271

that would be simply too painful for him to hear and for me to say. Later. It could come later....

But there could not be a later. How could there be? There should not even have been this much, this afternoon.

I stopped talking. My tears had dried, though several tissues around me on the sofa were damp balls and my voice was a drowned croak. I did not think I could have possibly drawn Aengus clearly enough for Nick to understand him, all that complexity, all that passion now skewing so inevitably toward obsession. All the very real magic that once had shimmered around him, and still sometimes did. It was I who had lost the magic, not Aengus.

After a time Nick said in a low voice, "We shouldn't be sitting here talking about this."

"I know," I said, tears starting again. "Of course we shouldn't."

"I mean...we should be catching up on what we did today. We should *know* what we did all those years. We should have done it together."

I moved jerkily on the sofa. It was time for me to go. It was way past time.

"I have to go home, Nick," I said.

He did not urge me to stay. He said, "I don't know yet exactly what I should do about this, but I think I have to do something. I can't...know you're so unhappy. I just can't. We should talk more; maybe I should meet him...."

"Oh, please, Nick." I cried softly. By this time we were standing by my car in the parking lot and he was holding the front door open for me. His face was tired and sharpened; there was anger in his voice. He seemed decades older.

"Please don't feel you have to do anything." I almost wept again. "I shouldn't have unloaded all this on you. My God, you get a lot for your nickel with me, don't you? I can work this out. Aengus and I can. You've got your own row to hoe. And I haven't really been fair to him; he's so much more than all that...."

Nick put his hand over mine on the steering wheel. I could feel him on every inch of my skin. Safety. His touch was, as well as so many other things, the warm, engulfing feeling of safety.

"I'm here for several more weeks, Thayer. We'll figure something out. Just don't go away again. Promise me that."

"Where would I go?" I said, putting the car into reverse to back out of the parking space. My foot trembled on the pedal.

"I'll see you soon. I want you to call me when you have some free time. If you don't call before long, I'm going to call you. I mean that, Thayer," he said.

"No," I said. "You can't call me. I mean *that*."

"Thay..."

I looked at him. Tears stood in his eyes. In the neon-flashing lights of the underground parking garage they shimmered; a tiny trickle started down one sharp-planed freckled cheek. Grief and guilt flooded me, and I felt, suddenly, a cold emptiness deep inside me where our baby had so briefly lived.

"Oh, God!" I cried out, and stamped down on the

accelerator. My car shot accidently backward. I slammed it into forward gear. I did not look back.

I snapped the bubble in place before I even got out of the garage. Outside it the entire world howled and hammered and shrilled. Inside it there was the old, soothing peace. Just outside the globe the faces of the two men who had defined me loomed close. They were talking. Talking. Talking to me.

It was not the time to hear them.

When I pulled the car up into my cool, green-tunneled driveway, I saw that a light on the third floor was on. Aengus was home, then, but his study door was closed and I knew that he was oblivious to all but the old ones who moved with magic through dark air. He did not hear me.

I slipped into bed without washing my face, clicked off the bedside lamp, and buried my head under the creamy linen pillows we had gotten for a wedding present. I still can't remember who gave them to us.

CHAPTER

17

I woke late the next morning and scrambled, sleep stunned, out of bed before I realized that it was Saturday and I did not have to go to the bookstore. I sat back down on the edge of the bed and shook my head hard, several times. I had not thought, when I had slipped between the covers last night, that I would sleep at all, but I had, deeply, not waking once, until five minutes ago. Aengus was not in bed beside me, but he seldom was this late. I wondered if he had slept on the sofa in his office, as he sometimes did when he worked or read late. I thought I would get up and go and find him, but the world was still heaving and rolling like a ship's deck under me, and I sat back down and stared into the gloom of the big bedroom. I thought if I got up and turned on the lights and opened the drapes the room would flood with morning light and my thoughts would slide back into their ordinary morning progression of Let's see, what do I have to do today? Who am I going to see? Do we have anything special planned?

But I did not move. For a long time I wanted absolutely no sense of the day and what it held. After last evening's time with Nick, I did not think there could be any more ordinary days. But neither could I imagine what there could be in place of them. I could not think at all.

"Maybe I'll sleep a little longer," I said to myself, and was preparing to slide back under the covers when I heard the Volvo's engine start up outside. I leaped up and ran barefoot down the stairs and out through the veranda to the driveway, my nightgown fluttering around me. Aengus saw me and stopped backing out of the driveway. He opened the window on his side and leaned out and grinned at me.

"Who have we here, fluttering like a butterfly in her shimmy at nine o'clock in the morning? I wasn't sneaking out; I just didn't want to wake you. I thought you must really be tired; you were dead to the world."

I put my hand out tentatively and touched his arm. It was warm and still a little damp from his shower. There was a cup of coffee in the holder between the seats. He reached up and covered my hand with his. I drew a deep breath. It was truly Aengus, Aengus in the morning as he always was, with lines smoothed out of his dark face and his blue eyes clear. I could already smell the sun on the pines and feel it on my bare shoulders and arms. I smiled; I could feel the smile trembling a little on my mouth.

"Morning," I said. "Where you going?"

He reached out and smoothed the hair back from my face. I knew it was wild and tangled.

"Up to camp," he said. "I've just about finished the book. I started the last chapter early this morning. I want the boys to hear it before I finish. The last chapter of anything always carries the payload. By the way, where were you last night?"

"I ran into a friend of mine from camp when I was at the library," I said. "We spent longer than I meant to catching up."

It was precisely what I'd meant to say: the truth and no more. There had seemed to me no reason for Aengus to pursue it, and I doubt that he would have if I hadn't felt my mouth opening and words tumbling from it: "He has an apartment in the old Findlay building around the corner from the library. We went there because there wasn't any-place to sit in the library and it was so hot...."

Aengus said nothing, and I pulled my arm away from the open window of his car and said, "I've got to get dressed. I can't stand around all day out here in my shimmy."

"What was his name, your friend from camp?" Aengus said in a smooth, polite voice. I sighed, not because I thought he'd make a thing about my having seen a male friend but simply because I did not feel like standing in the sun explaining the whole thing. That had been last night. This was this morning. Last night was over.

"His name is Nick Abrams," I said. "You know who he is. I haven't seen him since the summer before college. He's an architect in New York, and he's down here to do some stuff for the Olympics. Housing and things..."

"Oh, yes. The sainted Nick Abrams. He keeps cropping up, doesn't he?" Aengus said. "I think I'm on this program thing with him next week. The mayor has asked some of the people from the represented countries down to see what we've got in the way of facilities for families and I'm representing camps for kids and doing some kind of program with some of the boys. Your guy's name is on the list; I guess he's showing off some of his housing."

"That's terrific," I said, smiling at him. "You didn't tell me."

"I just forgot. All Big Jim's doing, of course. It's next Thursday night at that little amphitheater out at Cantwell Park. You have to come; it'll be another chance to catch up with your friend."

"Of course I'll come, but not because of him. Because of you and the boys. Do you know what you're doing yet?"

"Probably something from the book. We'll decide today, maybe. I think we can make something really special of it."

His face glowed. I had not seen that light lately.

"I miss you, Aengus."

"I know. I've been away a lot. But it's ending, and I think this book is going to be important for us. I truly believe it is, if these kids are any indication. Can you and Carol find something to do tonight? We'll take next weekend and go somewhere special. Maybe up to Gatlinburg or over to Cades Cove. I've never seen either."

"Oh, Aengus," I said, "not more mountains. Not for a while. Could we maybe drive down to the beach?"

"I don't see why not. Lean in here and give me a kiss. I've got to be up there by ten thirty. I'll call you tonight after the reading and let you know how it went."

"Please do. I feel like I don't even talk to you anymore."

"Well, after camp is over I can arrange to talk your ears off and you'll be sorry you ever said that."

He kissed me softly and fully on the mouth, and I swallowed a huge lump in my throat.

"Of course it's Aengus," I said to myself picking my way over grass stubble edging up between the bricks. "My husband. Aengus. The man I love, the man I chose. The man who chose me. I did nothing at all yesterday but run into an old friend."

By the time I had showered and dressed it was almost noon and Grand's bubble was firmly in place again. I would make something special for tomorrow night, I thought. I'll ask Carol and maybe the mayor and his nice wife. I ought to ask Big Jim and what's-her-name, too, but I'm not going to. Aengus sees enough of him up at camp.

I got into my little Mustang and started the engine, smiling at the obedient, throaty purr. It was six years old but immaculate and shining with new green paint. It had been Big Jim's son Markie's car until his father had bought him a new Porsche on his eighteenth birthday, and I had been grateful when Big Jim passed it on to Aengus, who passed it on to me.

"I'm not driving Big Jim's little boy's cast-off car," he had said stubbornly. "But we need one for you and this one is in good shape. It sort of looks like you."

"How so?"

"Oh … neat. Curvy. Aerodynamic. Sporty. This old Volvo makes you look like the Salvation Army coming to collect cast-off furniture. It would any woman."

"And it doesn't you?"

"I don't care what I drive, as long as I bought it."

"Well, I have no scruples about that. I think it's a great little car."

And it had been.

The next Thursday night I sat with a crowd of perhaps five hundred people on the uncomfortable old wooden seats of the small amphitheater at Cantwell Park. It was tucked behind a much larger one, one that seated perhaps five thousand people, where great occasions of municipal state took place, and traveling road companies of popular musicals, and sometimes even productions of the Metropolitan Opera. I remembered live elephants and horses and chariots pounding thunderously over the stage; my father had taken me to see *Aida* when I was small, and I never forgot it. Magical, those great panniered and jeweled beasts, their gray hides somehow gilded, with people singing ecstatically from their swaying backs. Magical, too, the painted chariots sweeping in behind them drawn by matched pairs of horses in feathery headdresses, dust rising from their golden hooves, with a dense green canopy of Georgia oak leaning over them and above them a great moon sailing alone in an indigo sky. And over it all, glorious music swelling to the stars...

I never forgot that night. This smaller amphitheater just behind the big one was even more deeply sunk into the woods, yet from it you could hear the faint blatting of automobile horns and see, in the distance, the nimbus of Atlanta. I realized, sitting there in my VIP seat beside the mayor's smiling wife, that this was its magic, this very proximity of our everyday world, encasing this place like a fairy egg but unable to seep into it. Here, the incredible, the unimaginable; just outside, home and comfortable banality waiting for us.

The audience was an appreciative one. They clapped and smiled and nodded when the mayor announced that this evening he was proud to be able to show our international visitors some of the amenities that awaited families from their countries who would be visiting Atlanta. I don't know how many nationalities were represented that evening, but it was definitely not an Atlanta or even a Georgia crowd; besides the flow of conversations in many languages, there were spates of dignified clapping and laughter and murmurs of "ahhhh-hhh" and much nodding and smiling at one another. No one whistled between their teeth, favored us with Rebel yells, or wriggled and whispered loudly when boredom set in. These people, as the mayor made plain, were here to find out what was available in this storied southern city for their country-men to live in, eat, drink, look at, listen to, and amuse their children with. Most of them knew Atlanta only from *Gone with the Wind* and seemed pleased to encounter no enslaved pickaninnies and booming cannon. They would, said the mayor, see plenty of hoopskirts and pillared mansions, and that seemed to feed the *GWTW* thirst.

We had seen displays and film clips from the movie people; sampled restaurant fare from every sort of eatery, from barbecue ("Ah, bobbycoo!") to the city's most elegant victuals; watched a panorama of sports vignettes, from the Atlanta Braves, to the Falcons, to the myriad Little Leagues, tennis, sailing, skating, boating, swimming, amusement parks, fairs and festivals, and house and garden tours. ("Scatlitt!" a young girl's voice behind me cried when the hoopskirted hostess of a palatial local home bared her teeth for the camera.) By this time the crowd was utterly captivated with this paradise of the Deep South; even I was clapping until my palms stung.

"And when your athletes come to compete, here, in part, is where they'll live," the mayor's voice intoned. "I give you one of our country's most renowned young architects, Mr. Nicholas Abrams, himself a Georgia native, and the unparalleled housing he has designed for them."

The stage lights fell and a solo spot illuminated a lectern. My heart slid into the icy pit in my stomach. I was appalled. I'd known he would be here; it hadn't, by this time, seemed to matter too much. It would just be Nick, showing off the houses that had been captured on the untidy rolls of paper and crumpled sketches I had seen in his dining room.

Just that.

But this was going to be more. My heart and stomach knew it before my brain did. The lectern was empty, and then Nick walked onstage from out of the darkness and stood in front of it, hands in his pockets, smiling at us. I felt rather than saw the smiles all around me. He wore a seersucker suit and a rather rumpled tie, and his shock of dark hair, lit by the overhead lights, hung as usual a bit over his eyes. His teeth flashed white and his rangy frame seemed to sprawl a little, and for some reason he was utterly irresistible. You could feel the wave of low laughter move through the crowd; it was affectionate laughter. I drew in my breath sharply. It was as if he stood floodlit on a stage for no one but me; the crowd around me faded away and I looked down at the man I had loved and fancied that he looked up only at me.

"He's attractive, isn't he?" the mayor's wife whispered. "My husband thinks very highly of him. I believe he's trying to lure him down here permanently."

"He'd be a great addition," I said pleasantly. My face burned in the dark.

From the stage Nick's microphoned voice said, "When I was a kid, I thought everybody used to live in trees. I was convinced that Adam and Eve started it in the Garden of Eden, and that we only gave it up about the time we started wearing suits and ties. I still think the best place to live is in trees, and so I designed the housing for our Olympic competitors so that everyone would live under and sometimes even up in trees. And because Atlanta is basically a city of trees, I've very graciously been given permission by the city to locate this housing in the woods and around the lake in Piedmont Park. Like this."

On the screen behind him flashed a module about the size of a freight car. It was made of a soft-weathered copper shimmering material, with one entire wall of very slightly tinted glass or plastic. Inside, at one end, a lower, curved wall of a dark gold metallic tile enclosed a sleeping space and a compact brushed-steel bathroom. Outside, in the open living area, deep burnished built-in leather couches and a small kitchenette fitted jewel-like. The floor was a thick deep shag rug in mixed-metallic colors that I thought was made of leather, and on the opposite end of the room was a wall of shelving with books, a TV set, and a pull-down movie screen. Soft ivory shading could be pulled down to cover the larger window wall, and the top was skylit so that sun- or starlight could flood in. The module was simple and beautiful. Nick clicked a button on the lectern and a deep curve of forest around the lake in Piedmont Park, in the city's heart, bloomed on the screen. It was a night shot, and the glowing modules hung in the trees, were stacked three and four deep in the open glades, and ran like lanterns along the paths that circled the lake. Above them the woods were a chiaroscuro of flickering light.

There was a concerted soft gasp, and then applause broke out. It was a fantastic forestscape hung with magic lanterns. My eyes filled with tears. I would have loved to live in that forest-set city of light even if it had not been Nick's. It was magic made entirely from the earth. Practical magic. Around me people began to stand. I stood, too. On the stage Nick grinned even more widely and bowed from the waist.

"I like 'em, too," he said. "The city has agreed to give us a spur rail line that will connect to Peachtree Road and the rapid transit system there. No competitor will be more than five miles away from every bar, restaurant, and theater from Buckhead to the airport. When the Olympics are over they can be transported wherever they're wanted. I know one family that's putting one in the backyard for the in-laws. I think another few will make a small apartment complex up in the foothills. I'm putting one in the country outside Manhattan for my kids. At any rate, they're all spoken for. Which is not to say I wouldn't whomp any of y'all up a few more if you ask."

He smiled again and walked offstage. The applause went

on for another few minutes. It was hard to say whether it was for Nick or his luminous housing.

"My goodness," the mayor's wife said. "That was lovely. Isn't your husband doing something to represent the camps? He'll have to go some to beat that. Big Jim says it's bound to be spectacular, though. Something to do with mythology, I think?"

"Probably," I said, trying to keep my voice neutral. "But I have no idea what it is. He says the boys will have the last say in it."

"Sweet of him," Mrs. Mayor murmured. "I believe he's next after the one about the transit system, isn't he?"

I looked down at my program. The last line read "Mythologist and Folklorist Professor Aengus O'Neill, representing Camp Forever."

"Looks like it," I said.

I was suddenly afraid. I could not have said of what. I wished with all my heart that I could slip out of my seat and run to my car and go home. I wished that Carol was sitting beside me, ready to pat my hand or puncture the night with her reassuring laughter, whichever was called for. But the sainted Walter was in town, and she had gone to dinner with him to strike another blow in the long custody battle. I had seen her before she left; she looked cool and chic and altogether respectable in dark blue linen with her hair pulled back smoothly and high-heeled spectator pumps.

"You'd get custody of any child in Atlanta tonight," I'd told her. "Why don't you bring him to see that thing the mayor's doing out at Cantwell Park for the Olympics? Aengus has got some of the camp kids in his presentation for Camp Forever; I should think even Walter would like that."

"Are you kidding?" she'd snorted. "Aengus probably has them playing trolls or something. We're going up Saturday to see the boys...if Walter's still speaking to me, that is. You can tell me about it tomorrow."

I laughed and agreed. But I wasn't laughing now, waiting as the perfunctory applause for the dust-dry show of street routes and city vehicles sputtered to a halt.

"Oh, Aengus," I whispered to myself, "keep it in this world, please. Keep it as real as Nick's."

And shocked myself even thinking it.

Instead of Aengus, Big Jim Mabry walked out onstage, smiling and nodding to the scattered applause.

"Before Dr. O'Neill's presentation, I'd like to tell you all about Camp Forever. I had the honor of purchasing the land, from a fine gentleman named Nog Tierney....Nog, come on out here."

The thin, sandy-haired, snub-faced bus driver I had seen ambled onto the stage, a Camp Forever cap in his hands, wearing blue jeans and a tee shirt and work boots. He nodded but kept his eyes on his boots. He was a picture of humility, but something about him was—false. This man was not humble.

"Anyway, to make a long story short, this is his son, and he 'bout runs that camp for me. He and Dr. O'Neill, who is going to show us how Camp Forever got its name. Take it away, Aengus!"

The two men left and the stage lights dimmed until it was totally dark. There was no light at all except the cold, pouring light of the full moon and the faint, glowing bubble that was Atlanta. There was no sound except for the monotonous non-noise of faraway traffic and a muffled kind of thumping that sounded as if it was coming from behind the stage. There was hardly any whispering in the crowd. We simply sat in the dark and waited for Aengus.

One spot came on over the lectern. A dense ray of light in which dust motes danced. It looked solid enough so that one might climb it. No one stood in it. And then, from offstage far right, a great drum began to beat. Long beats, thundering, echoing. Very slow beats. To me, up in mid-audience, they sounded muffled and unreal, but they filled the amphitheater and the woods and sky around it. A march, I thought, my neck hair prickling.

A death march.

Oh, Aengus, no. No, *please.*

As though it had manifested itself out of the sound, a figure came onto the stage, slowly, walking in time to the drumbeat. It was tall and oddly luminous, a very faint presence walking through darkness on the echoing vibrato of a drum.

He stepped into the light and there was a great exhalation from the crowd. It was not wonder and perhaps not quite shock; it was something older: a tribe catching sight for the first time of a being that might or might not be one of its gods. All I could think was that it was a waiting sound. I could hardly hear it over the slow throat hammering of my heart.

287

He wore nothing but a sort of one-shouldered singlet that looked as if it might be made from the hide of some pale animal. Where on earth would Aengus get such a thing? It came to the tops of his knees, and the shoulder that it left bare was gilded with some sort of thin wash...ink? Paint? His legs were gilded, too, and he wore short, soft boots that folded over, of the same skin. Around his neck was, what I knew now, a gold Celtic torque; this one did not look to be my necklace. His hair was pale and stood up in thick spikes, and he had a pale gold mustache. Aengus? Who was this gilt man? He was a wild thing, a wild man; he had no ken with my world or this place or even this or any other century that might easily be recalled. If I could have articulated it, I think I would have said that my husband gave off such a huge and potent spoor of pure otherness that there was nothing to do but regard him with silence and fright. He must have known this. How could he not? What would he have us do, this audience of his friends and fellow Atlantans and travelers from so many countries of the modern world? Aengus on this night called to no other world that could have been named. We all felt it. I know that as surely as I have ever known anything.

The last coherent thought I had was, Not even Carol could laugh at this.

Aengus's Irish brogue was never stronger: "Here," he almost sang, "at the foot of Ben Bulben lies the Stone Age cemetery of Carrowmore. Here the ancient Celtic hero Oisin met Saint Patrick, to lament the loss of lusty pagan Ireland, and here, under a great cairn, lay Maeve, the Celtic warrior queen of Connaught. And here, on these heights whipped bare by wild Sidhe, the wind off the ocean, also dwelt Niamh, the pale nymph who rode away with Oisin to Tir Na Nog, the Land of Forever Young, beyond the sea."

He paused for a moment; the great drum continued. Then he threw back his head and closed his eyes, lifted his arms to the sky, and chanted in a queer, trilling, flutelike voice:

> The host is riding from Knocknarea
> And over the grave of Clooth-na-Bare;
> Caoilte tosses his burning hair,
> And Niamh calling *Away. Come away:*
> *Empty your heart of its mortal dream.*
> *The wind awakens, the leaves whirl round,*
> *Our cheeks are pale, our hair is unbound,*
> *Our chests are heaving, our eyes are agleam,*
> *Our arms are waving, our lips are apart;*
> *And if any gaze on our rushing band,*
> *We come between him and the deed of his hand,*
> *We come between him and the hope of his heart.*
> The host is rushing 'twixt night and day.
> And where is there hope or deed as fair?
> Caoilte tossing his burning hair,
> And Niamh calling, *Away, come away.*

As he chanted, the drum quickened, and from the wings, one by one, four crude chariots with round wooden wheels came, drawn by what I supposed to be the camp's ponies, hung with tinkling trinkets and tossing their heads, on which appeared to be crows' feathers fastened in their forelocks. In the small painted wooden chariots, two boys stood back to back. They were all gilded and torqued like Aengus, and as the front one handled the reins the one behind raised a great shield painted with golden runes and shook a long lance. By the time Aengus had finished his chant and dropped his head, all four chariots had stopped in a line onstage and the boys stepped out to face the audience. They, too, wore tunics, and torques, but unlike Aengus, they were barefoot. They stood in a perfect line before their chariots while the bored ponies stamped and flicked their tails, looking off into the distance above the audience. The drum stopped. No one spoke. I did not hear a single person in the audience even draw a breath. No one moved.

Then the drum gave one last tremendous, echoing boom and the boys all drew from their chariots and held up to the audience four dripping, severed heads.

Even in the last row, you could have told they were papier-mâché. No human had ever walked the earth wearing heads like these. Nevertheless, they were…horrendous. The boys held them by long strands of blood-gummed black hair. Empty, hollow eyes stared. Open mouths screamed silently; half-severed tongues lolled out of them. Blood or ketchup or whatever—it did not matter—spattered the floor of the stage and pooled there. Still the boys and Aengus did not move or speak. My eyes registered that the two boys in the last chariot were Chris and Ben Partridge, even though my mind did not until the next day.

High up above me a woman took a deep, rattling breath and screamed, a long, terrible scream. Several others followed. A great general noise like a gust of wind started up in the crowd.

I jumped up out of my seat, nearly tripping over several people, and ran as hard as I could to my car out in the parking lot. There under the cold, clean, high-riding moon I vomited until I almost fell to my knees. I heard no more sound from the audience far behind me. When I stopped the car in our driveway all I could hear was the monotonous, heat-thickened sound of the cicadas and my own breath, sobbing in my chest.

CHAPTER

18

I let myself into the house with fingers that shook so badly that I dropped my keys twice. I did not turn on any lights. I stopped in the kitchen, trying to think where to go. My mind took a frantic, scrambling tour of the house, but I could think of no place in it as sanctuary, no place that was mine alone, nowhere that I could not see Aengus also. Aengus with his false yellow hair and lilting, inhuman voice, Aengus and his warrior children with the dripping heads...

I walked through the dark kitchen, my heels clicking on the beautiful river stone floor, and up the stairs and into our bedroom on the third floor, with the silver-blooming stars and the cold moon pouring their radiance down through the skylight onto the wide bed. Its pale bronze comforter was rumpled; I remembered I had sat there to pull on my unaccustomed heels. I stepped out of the shoes, slumped down onto the bed, and drew myself into a tight ball. This way,

I thought, nothing could pierce me through my heart or stomach.

I thought that I would cry, sob, wail aloud, scream out my grief and sheer disbelief, but I did not. I lay still and contorted, my face pressed into a pillow. I could only manage small, quick breaths, and I could not move except to shake my head very slightly back and forth, my lips rubbing the silky fabric, whispering, "No...no...no...no...."

The phone rang and I let it ring itself out. When it rang again I reached over and took it out of its cradle. Its insistent buzzing intermingled with the night-drowned throbbing of the cicadas outside the open windows, and after a while both faded into a kind of rhythmic, primal undersound, like the beating of a heart in a body deep in coma. The sound of life. The only sound of life.

I didn't fall asleep, but gradually my clenched-shut mind opened just enough to let the memory of the night seep behind my eyes. I found that I could not banish the images. I thought that I would have them forever, perpetually bobbing over and above anything else that came into my mind.

I will have to die, I thought, because I cannot tolerate that. That cannot be what I see when I think, Aengus. Of course I would think of Aengus; I would see Aengus every day; how could I not think of him? I would see him tomorrow night or the next; we would go about our lives; we would go to the beach, he had said we would do that.... We simply had to get past this night first, and then we could go back to being us, Thayer and Aengus....

The tears came then, wild torrents of them. I knew that

I did not think we could get past this night. Not and still be us. I did not know who I would be when I got up off this bed again, and I had no idea on the living earth who Aengus would be. Had I ever known?

"I want my mother!" I cried aloud, in the sort of extremis of grief of a devastated child. It is an old cry, as old as the world, a cry of utter loss, of howling helplessness: "I want my mother!..."

I knew that I did not want my mother, that my mother was the indirect architect of this anguish. I even knew that under any other circumstances I might have laughed at the sheer incongruity of it. But now it was not funny, only terrible, a cry for surcease where there was none.

I curled back into my ball. Over my ragged sobbing I heard Carol's voice, as clear as if she stood there: For God's sake, Thayer, it was only a skit. It was only one of Aengus's damned Celtic myths. Granted, it was pretty ugly to see, but...

Is that all it was? Can it be that that's all people thought it was? I begged her silently, desperately.

No, Carol said, her voice darkening. That's not all it was. It was...beyond human. It was an obscenity.

I began to cry again. A lassitude deeper than any fatigue I had ever felt weighted my body. I wanted to get up, to run out of the house, to run, run like the wind, down the street and to the river, to the cold, swift-running river under the bridge. I wanted to plunge in and be cleansed....But I could scarcely move. I could only cry.

A weight sank down on the bed beside me and two arms

came around me, lifting me up, pulling me in. I tried to tear myself away; how could he even think of touching me after what he had shown me?

"Thayer," Nick Abrams's voice said into my hair. "Thayer. Come here, baby. Come here to me."

I began to cry, sobs torn from deep in my belly, a weeping like vomiting. It was past midnight when I finally lifted my face from his shoulder. The salt weight behind my eyes began to lessen. I knew the time because, somewhere in the storm of my grief, I had heard the midnight whistle at the paper mill far downriver. It was faint, but you could hear it on still summer nights like this, with only the cicadas for competition.

The last time I heard it I had been lying in other arms. Except for inarticulate murmurings of comfort, Nick had not spoken to me again. Now he brushed my wild, damp hair back from my wet face and said, "Is he coming here tonight?"

"No," I said thickly. "He'll be at the camp tonight and probably tomorrow night, too. We . . . we were going to drive down to the beach on Saturday. . . ."

"Not on my watch, you're not," he said, drawing me back into his arms and resting the side of his face against mine. He kissed me softly on my forehead and cheek and rocked me gently, as you would rock a child.

"We need to talk about this, Thay," he said into my wet hair. "I don't want you to be around him right now. I'm not really sure he's sane. I'm not quite sure what to do about it, but if you'll let me I want to—"

"Nick, no," I said feebly. "He's not...That simply wasn't him. I don't know what's happened to him. That business tonight wasn't the Aengus I married. It was...I don't know...his interpretation of one of his Celtic things. He's always said the boys love them; I think he just...lost sight of where he was and who he was performing for—"

"I think he's nuttier than a fruitcake and bloodthirsty as a tick. You left; I saw you go...you don't know what went on afterwards. The crowd just went crazy. Women were crying, and you could hear the booing to Peachtree Road, and Big Jim and the mayor both stood up and tried to smooth it over, and then your sainted Aengus came running out on the stage and let out this...I don't know, war cry or something...and shook his javelin at the crowd, and drew that dirk thing out of its sheath and you could hear the boys crying offstage, and one of the ponies got loose and took off up the hill toward the highway, and that chanting of his got higher and higher....Security came and led him offstage, but by that time the audience was pouring out of the exits....They didn't take him to jail, I heard later, but there are some pretty pissed parents around here, I can tell you. I thought you'd be here, and I didn't want him coming home to you, so I...well, anyway, I let myself in. Your back door wasn't locked."

"How did you know where I live?" I whispered, the awfulness of the scene washing over me. Oh, God, Aengus...

"I looked you up in the city directory right after you left my place the other night. And I drove out and took a look. It's a nice place, Thay. Somehow I knew you'd live in the trees. . . . I can't see him living here, though. Anybody who could conceive of that monstrosity . . ."

"Grand gave the house to us," I said. Talking hurt my chest. "It was a poem, Nick. He was using a poem to explain how the camp got its name. The old Celtic words Tir Na Nog mean 'the Land of Forever Young.' He always has his students reenact things, legends and myths and things, when he can—"

"I know Yeats, Thayer," Nick said. I could feel him smile faintly against my chest. "Yale has a pretty fair English department. Yeats doesn't make it any less . . . ugly and brutal. If he truly didn't know how this thing could affect the audience, not to mention the boys, he might have considered what it would do to his wife. Jesus! I think they call it borderline personality; I'd call it psychotic. It doesn't matter what anybody calls it; you can't live with that man, Thayer. If you don't live with me, you at least can't live with him—"

"You don't know anything else about him!" I almost screamed it at him. *"You don't know how he's always been with me. . . ."*

"I don't need to know anything else about him," he said softly.

"Oh, Nick." I wept, drained and lost. "I'm so cold. I feel so dirty."

"Come here, love. Come with me," he said, almost whispering.

I let him pull me up off the rumpled bed and walk me into the bathroom with his arms around me. I stood still, trembling, as he unzipped the white linen sheath I'd worn and slid me out of my underthings. His hands were warm and sure. I closed my eyes. I thought that it had almost felt like this when my father had helped me get ready for my bath. Almost...

Warm water sluiced over me, and I abandoned myself to it. I stood, eyes closed, as it soaked my hair and engulfed my body. He simply held me still and let me receive the water. Pretty soon I felt a bath sponge full of creamy soap and bubbles start gently over my body, and leaned backward in one of his arms as the other washed me gently, gently, all over. Not until he turned off the shower and said, "Okay, now step out," did I open my eyes and look at him. He was dressed in his seersucker pants and his white shirt, unbuttoned, with its cuffs rolled up; the front of him was soaking wet. His dark hair was pasted damply over his face.

I got out and stood on my bath rug, naked and almost unaware that I was. The terrible shivering had stopped. I felt, simply, steamy warm and as scrubbed clean as a child. My knees buckled, but I smiled at him and he smiled back.

"Feel better?" he said.

"Yes. When did you get that chipped tooth fixed?"

"The minute I got home from camp my father had me in the dentist's office. When did you get those boobs?"

"When I got...," I started, and then stopped. Not there. I would not go there with Nick Abrams.

He knew, though. He stood still, his finger tracing my breasts very, very softly. My knees almost gave way. I knew that finger, that brown hand. I had known it first....

"But you didn't have it," he whispered. He knew that, too.

298

My eyes closed again.

"No. My mother took me to a doctor.... He said... It was so early, Nick.... He said it was... damaged...."

"It wasn't... his,... then."

I could not see his face; I would not open my eyes to see his face. "No. This was... right after we left camp...."

After a long silence, he said, "Did you want it, Thay?"

I nodded my head, feeling the hot tears roll again down my cheeks.

"I wanted it more than anything. More than anything. I'd never have let them take it, no matter what, but the doctor said... he said I needed hydrating and he put a needle in my arm and when I came to it was... just gone. And then I got an infection and I was awfully sick for a long time and after I got well I found out I couldn't... not anymore...."

"And all this time I was calling and your mother was telling me you didn't want to see me and that you'd moved away. Your mother..."

"I guess so."

"May God damn her to hell," Nick said without any inflection.

"Aengus didn't care," I sobbed. "He said we'd adopt. And I didn't think I'd ever see you again...."

I looked at him then. His face was contorted with pain, and tears ran down his brown face. I could not bear his pain. It was worse by far than any I remembered feeling.

He took my robe from the hook on the back of the bathroom door and slid it around me. I turned into his arms and simply laid myself against him, letting him take my full weight. I wanted to absorb this pain, all of it...the tears; the anger....I wanted them to seep back into my body from his. I wanted his grief for that child that never was to come back into me. I thought, I cannot let him hold the pain of a child that wasn't and my own pain, too. He can't carry *that*. He still held me closely, but I could feel that his muscles had gone slack and heavy.

"I'm mostly over it," I said into his neck. "I do all right with it now."

"Oh, God, sweetheart," he whispered, "I am so sorry." He picked me up and carried me into the bedroom and put me down on the bed and pulled the covers over me. He sat down beside me.

"We'll have a baby, you and I," he said softly, smiling at me. It was his old smile, slow and full. "There are more ways than one, you know. But you'll have to decide what you want before we can...I'm sorry, baby, but that will have to happen."

I began to shake my head back and forth, in sheer fatigue.

"I don't expect you to decide tonight, but it's something that you'll have to settle with yourself. Do you think you'll be able to do that? I can walk away from you if I have to. If that's what you want. But I can't come back again if I do. You know that, don't you?"

"I know that."

"You go to sleep then. I'll stay right here beside you till morning. I have to be in Macon by noon to get a project started....It's a big one or I'd cancel, but I'll be back late tomorrow night and you don't have to see him until Saturday, do you? I'll come back tomorrow night and stay...."

I could feel sleep taking me down like a riptide. I put out my hand and he took it and I whispered, "Thank you," and he whispered back, "Sleep tight, baby," and I slid far down where nothing but his breathing could reach me.

CHAPTER

19

The light from the skylight beat directly down on my face when I woke. I knew that it was mid-morning. I knew, too, eyes still shut tight, that Nick had been here beside me all night. I reached over and touched the bedcovers on the other side of the bed; they were rumpled. If I looked over it would be the imprint of his body that I saw.

I sat up and looked around the room. Everything was in order; even the clothes that I had worn to the amphitheater last night had been put away. There was no sign of anyone, not even me. But the entire room pulsed with Nick. We had not made love, however; I remembered that.

Not yet, he had said.

Was I sorry?

Yes.

Could I make the choice he had told me I needed to make? No. Not yet. Dear God, not yet.

Then when? Ever?

I was suddenly sick of it all. I wanted my ordinary life back. I needed normalcy as I needed food to eat and water to drink. I am not going to think about any of this until tomorrow, at least, I thought. I am going to clean the house and go into work this afternoon and maybe call Lily and see what she and Goose have been doing. Maybe I'll even ask them up over the weekend. That way I won't have to talk to Aengus about anything much, at least for a while, and maybe by then I'll know what I need to do next. I think it's a pretty safe bet we aren't going to the beach, though. In the meantime, I'll call Carol and see if she'd like—

Then I stopped. Carol would know about last night by now. About Chris and Ben, half-naked and gilded with paint in homemade chariots, holding up severed heads that dripped fake blood onto the stage before five hundred people. And about Aengus, keening to the sky about gods with their hair afire, who had led them there.

I doubted that Carol would be eager to talk to me. I went in to make coffee and found a note on the counter, weighted down with a Yale money clip. There was a telephone number scrawled on it.

"Call if you need me," it said. "Don't go up there till I'm back. We need to talk."

For some reason it annoyed me.

"The one I need to talk to is Aengus," I said to the note. "I owe it to him to find out what he was thinking with that stuff last night. It could have just been...a benign idea that didn't work like he thought it would, or...something. We don't know what he had in mind. I'm going to call him. I should have done it last night."

He should have called you last night, Nick's voice said in my head.

"Shut up," I said aloud, and sat down on the counter stool and dialed the number for Coltrane College. I glanced at the wall clock. Eleven thirty. He would be supervising sophomore English class now. I knew that I should wait until lunch break, but I didn't.

A woman's voice I did not know answered. It was not Patricia, who usually manned the central Coltrane line. This voice sounded younger and was thick with an accent I could not quite decipher.

"Dr. O'Neill, please," I said. "I think he's in sophomore English now, but I really need to talk to him...."

"Docker O'Neee?"

"Dr. O'Neill. Aengus O'Neill. This is his wife."

"You wait pliss." I heard papers ruffling.

"We got no Docker O'Neely."

"Oh, for... Can you ring Dr. Thornton for me?"

Craig Thornton was the school's vice president and a close friend of Big Jim's. We had met him on several occasions.

"Craig Thornton," his no-nonsense voice said when the new receptionist finally managed to ring his number.

"Craig, this is Thayer O'Neill, Aengus's wife," I said.

"Well, Thayer, what a nice surprise."

"I hate to bother you in the middle of the day, but I really do need to speak to Aengus, and I wasn't having much luck with your new receptionist. I wonder if you could..."

For some reason I stopped. For a long time he did not reply. Finally I said, "Craig?"

"Thayer, Aengus hasn't worked here for the past three weeks," he said in an oddly formal voice. "He left us on a Friday without notice. I thought surely you knew...."

"No. No problem, though. Thanks," I said brightly and stupidly, and hung up.

I sat at the counter for a long time, holding the phone and staring out into the blazing flower borders of the backyard. Finally I put the phone down and picked up Nick's note and started to dial the number he had written on it and then pushed it away. Then I picked up the phone again and got midway through Carol's number and hung up. There seemed no one right to tell.

The number for Camp Forever was written on the wall calendar that hung over the phone mount. It was scrawled in big red Magic Marker strokes, in Aengus's hand. It had been there most of the summer.

I did not dial it.

I went into my bathroom and splashed cold water on my face and then looked into the mirror over the vanity. In the dim light I looked back at myself. It was a much younger me than now. Me just out of a cold lake, shaking water drops from my hair and smiling a smile of pure joy. Joy given, still unearned.

Young. Young.

I knew that if I could see just a bit further into the mirror I would see Nick Abrams, smiling back at me.

I whirled and ran out of the bathroom and lowered the

blinds in the bedroom and curled up in the middle of the bed again, and pulled the still-rumpled covers up over me. I was asleep in less than a minute. When I woke again, the sun had slid past the skylight and rich late-afternoon light washed over me. Nothing in this blazing, barren day had touched me. Suddenly it seemed the silence would kill me. I would choke on it, smother under it. I needed a voice in my ear like blood in my veins, it hardly mattered whose.

I was midway through dialing Carol when I heard her voice behind me and turned to meet her. She was coming in from the veranda, dragging a white-faced, protesting Bummer with her, and her face was terrible to see.

"Carol!" I cried, starting toward her, my arms out. "My God, what..."

She was gasping so she could hardly speak. Her face was slack and paper white, and her eyes were enormous and red rimmed.

"Can you take Bummer?" she managed to get out. "Can you keep him for a little while? I have to go...I have to go..."

She doubled over my kitchen counter and I caught her with one arm and put the other around Bummer. He nestled into me like a small animal, a pet dog or cat.

"Sit down before you fall and tell me!" I cried.

Her yellow head was down on the counter, and she shook it back and forth. "Can you take Bummer? Can you?"

"Of course. Now sit up! I'm going to pour you a splash of bourbon—"

She turned her blighted face up to me and shook her head again. "No. I've got to drive. I've got to go up to camp! Right now! I've got to get Chris and Ben. Bummer hitchhiked home…hitchhiked, Thayer, down that whole goddamn mountain, seven years old and he…"

"*Carol…*"

"Something terrible is going on up there. Oh, I know about last night, that's bad enough, but Bummer told me… other things. Terrible things. Monstrous things. I have to get them home—"

"*What? What things?* I haven't heard of anything at all going on at the camp that shouldn't be, I mean—besides last night, and that was just…Carol, Aengus would know! Aengus wouldn't let anything happen to any of the—"

"*For God's sake, Thayer, Aengus is part of it!* Just like last night! Bummer doesn't lie! Why else would a seven-year-old hitchhike down that mountain by himself? He didn't even know where he was! It took him all day long—"

"Baby, just let me call Aengus. We can clear this up with one phone call—"

"*No…you can't!* And I can't call my boys! Aengus is the one who threw all the cell phones into the lake two or three nights ago. They had a ceremony about it.…"

I sat down beside her slowly, my breath gone, and simply stared at her. This could not be happening. This was not possible. Bummer had had a bad dream. There was no way on earth that my husband would throw all the cell phones at Camp Forever in its lake. No matter what Carol and I thought about the dreadful amphitheater scene last night, the boys meant too much to him; they were the listeners to his tales.…

"Carol, I want to go with you up there. Whatever it is, I can help—"

"The only way you can help me is to keep my son safe! Can't you even do that for me? And if not for me, for Bummer?"

"Yes," I whispered. I was nothing against this unleashed passion of fear and fury. "Yes, of course. We can watch TV and eat popcorn, or maybe just nap till you get back. But really, you must let me call. This can't be—"

"I'm just going long enough to get my boys into my car and come home! Lay off me, Thayer!"

"But if there was any kind of . . . danger—"

"Oh, God, Thayer, they don't want me! They just want the boys!"

"They? Who is—"

But she was gone through the hedge before I could finish my sentence. I heard her car's engine growl into life. I heard the shriek of its tires taking off down the long drive, and then heard nothing at all.

Bummer sat still on the stool beside me, leaning against me. I looked down at the top of his head. It did not move, and I could hear long, slow breaths and feel the warmth of them on my skin through my tee shirt. Asleep. Okay. I'd tuck him into our bed and watch television beside him, and if he woke up we'd have a snack, and maybe he'd tell me about the terror, whatever it was, on Burnt Mountain. And then Carol and the boys would be back with embarrassed explanations, and we could all sleep then. And tomorrow Aengus would be home. . . .

Carol's voice rang in my ears. I shook my head, hard. *No...you can't!...*Aengus is the one who threw all the cell phones...

I carried Bummer, a dead and somehow sweet weight, into the bedroom and pulled the comforter up under his chin and sat down on his other side and called Aengus's cell phone. He did not answer. When I dialed the camp's main number there was no answer, either. Well, all right, then. It was, after all, the dinner hour. And Aengus could have put his phone down anywhere; I was always running after him with it.

I dialed Carol's cell then. Again, no answer. I got up and tiptoed out into the kitchen and there it was, on its side on the counter where she had been sitting. This was all ridiculous. It was like a bad suspense movie. We would all laugh about this later. When Bummer woke up I would simply ask him what had so frightened him. Chances were we could work it out right here at home, before Carol and the boys even got back.

He did not wake until about nine. The night was still suffused to the west with the sunset's last flush. Out beyond the veranda the night creatures were tuning up: the sonorous burr of cicadas; the soft *cronk* of the big bullfrog who lived by the creek in our woods; the sleepy hoot of the small owl who lived back there, too. Soon the sinuous stream of bats that lived in the lightning-hollowed tree behind Carol's house would come flowing home. Soon there would be a late moon rising. Late moon rising...it sounded like a folk song, and not a terribly happy one.

Bummer yawned hugely and stretched, and then looked at me across the comforter.

"Thayer," he said. "Am I at your house?"

"Yep. You've been sawing wood for a few hours. Are you hungry?"

"Yep. What is 'sawing wood'? Do you have any French fries?"

" 'Sawing wood' is snoring. You're a great snorer. Olympic material. I've got a few French fries, but they're frozen. They wouldn't be as good as fresh ones."

"That's okay. I put ketchup all over them anyway. Is my mother back yet?"

"No. She hasn't had time to get there and back yet."

"Oh, okay," he said. I went and nuked the frozen fries and brought them to him on a plate with a glass of milk and the ketchup bottle. I walked stiffly, feeling trapped under thick ice where no light penetrated, nor any feeling.

Just before the last French fry disappeared he said guiltily, "I almost forgot. Would you like some?"

"No, thanks. I've already had a bite."

"Mama says I have the manners of a warthog. I'm not quite sure what a warthog is...."

"Not very pretty. But I never heard they had bad manners."

I was silent for a little while as he finished his milk. Then I said, "Bummer?"

"Yeah?" He looked up at me milkily.

"Do you think you could tell me about what scared you so up at camp? I can't reach anybody up there, and your mother left her cell phone here, and I can't think who else to call who might know if things are okay. I guess I could call Mr. Mabry...."

"Nah, I heard Mrs. Mabry say that Big... Mr. Mabry was taking her out to Hollywood, California, with him when he went on business. She said she wasn't going to do a thing but lie around the pool at the Bel Air Hotel with all the starlets, and Mother said Mrs. Mabry would fit the Bel Air like socks on a rooster.... Well, she didn't say it to Mrs. Mabry, you know. She said it later."

"I bet she did," I said, biting back a grin. "But about camp..."

He drew in a long breath and exhaled it slowly. It was such an adult gesture that my heart squeezed. I put my arm around him, and once more he leaned against me.

"Late at night when we're all supposed to be asleep the bus driver—you know, Mr. Tir Na Nog—comes to our bunks and he... stoops down and sings this kind of song, real low, and then he puts his mouth down on somebody's mouth and he... sucks. You can hear him sucking. Then he goes on to the next person, and the next, until he's done it to everybody in a cabin. And in the morning they're all different. They're all polite and nerdy like. My brothers are different now. I think I was supposed to be soon. He hasn't gotten as far as my bunk yet."

"Bummer... why don't they wake up?" I breathed in shocked disbelief. Oh, dear God...

"I think they put stuff in our dessert," he said. "I always take mine back to my bunk, but I don't eat it. I don't like anything but vanilla, and we don't ever have that."

He would say no more. I simply sat and held him, rocking him back and forth, my stomach roiling with the poison that had leached into this summer night. It couldn't be true, of course. It could not be true.

But how could a seven-year-old make up something like that? And hitchhike eighty miles on a mountain road to escape it?

Bummer slept again. I could seem to do nothing but rock him.

Near ten he lifted his head.

"I want my mother," he said.

"I do, too," I said. "Let's go get her."

Ordinarily I never in the world would have said such a thing to this frightened, sleepy child whose mother had not come back down the mountain. But this was not an ordinary time, and I was not the ordinary me. I did not even know who I was. I knew what I needed to do, though. I reached for the phone to call Nick, and then I stopped. I would *not* call *anyone* to tell them I was going to see my own husband, as if I was afraid of him. Nor to tell them that Carol Partridge had gone there and not come back. We were grown women. And especially, I would not call Nick. Set Nick against Aengus? The thought was unbearable.

I put Bummer into the front seat of the Mustang and belted him in and wrapped him in a thick sweater and laid the comforter over him. Then I got in and started the car. It growled deeply and happily: Road trip! Going up a mountain!

"It's a long way," Bummer said drowsily.

"I know. I know most of the way, but you'll have to help me later. I'll wake you up when it's time. Go back to sleep, Bummer. The dynamic duo is on the job."

I saw the flash of his teeth, and then his head dropped into the comforter and he was asleep before I turned the Mustang onto the interstate heading north.

The road up Burnt Mountain was familiar to me, though I could not remember the last time I had been on it. Even in the darkness my hands on the wheel made the necessary turns almost without thought. There were fewer and fewer cars, and then, higher up into the thinner air, there were none. All around us was a surrealistic moonscape; I could not quite comprehend the fact that I was driving through it in a car with only a sleeping child beside me. It was not like driving in the world. It was as if we had somehow drifted into a magical, dark forever. Well. That would be fitting on a night like this, wouldn't it?

I passed an old sign set into the woods beside an over-grown trail that led deep into the limitless woods: *Camp Edgewood: 3 Mi.*, it said. I didn't look down the old camp road, overgrown now with young mountain trees. But my heart raced down to the summer camp I imagined there and found again the days at Sherwood Forest—of cold, sun-dancing water; long afternoon shadows; crowded, clamorous evening meals; dark magic beside the leaping campfire.

And Nick. And Nick.

I knew that I would never turn down that road.

Near the very top of the mountain, I slowed the car and Bummer woke.

"I don't know the way from here on," I said.

"Go all the way to the top and take the little road to the left that goes down the other side," he mumbled, yawning.

I had never been all the way to the top of Burnt Mountain. When we reached it, I paused a moment at the scenic overlook and looked out. The whole of the valley that stretched all the way down to Atlanta lay bathed in light from the iron moon. In the far distance the city lights prickled like fireworks.

"That's the Sturgeon Moon," Bummer muttered sleepily. "I learned that at camp. They're big old fish. I don't think we have any of them down here. Take that road up there and it goes all the way down to camp. There's a sign."

A little way down on the other side I saw it, a neat white sign on a stone post that read: *Camp Forever.* I turned onto the gravel road. Bummer slept again. I drove, breathing hard, thinking nothing at all.

Far down the little road there was a large clearing where a sprawling log building sat. Beyond it I could see more small log structures…bunkhouses, a pavilion, a boathouse…and the moon-burnt sheet of the lake. I stopped at the clearing edge and, leaving Bummer in the car, got out and walked on dead feet toward the buildings. All the other buildings were dark, but a dim porch light burned on this one, that pale-urine light on pines that spoke of every camp in the woods everywhere. Aengus stood under it, his arms folded across his chest, leaning against the porch railing. His black hair shone like a helmet in the faded yellow light, and he was smiling his puckish, V-shaped smile. He wore shorts and a tee shirt that read *Camp Forever* and flip-flops and looked so like a teenager that I drew in my breath sharply. All around me unreality hummed like electricity.

"Aengus?" I whispered.

"I thought you might come," he said. His voice was light

and full of a kind of suppressed glee. His was a voice I did not know, somehow a piece of this forest.

"I'm looking for Carol Partridge," I said, feeling as if I was speaking to someone I had never met. "Bummer and Ben and Chris's mother; you know Carol. She...she said she was coming up here. She said there was something wrong. She left Bummer with me, but that was hours ago and she hasn't come back....Aengus, what's wrong up here? Bummer needs his mother...."

The night was wild and cold on the back of my neck.

Aengus didn't move, or stop smiling.

"Well, she was here, Thayer," he said. It was kind of a drawl. "A few hours ago, I think. She was half-crazy, spouting all kinds of nonsense about things her kid told her, the little one. About people stealing kid's childhoods, I think it was...sucking their childhoods out of their mouths. Real imagination that Bummer has. He ran off earlier today. I was glad to hear he got home okay. I told her he'd be just fine with you. Told her you'd have made as good a mother as she was, probably."

Aengus shook his head smiling ruefully. "I never saw that side of her. A real hysteric. When I wouldn't unlock the dormitory where her kids were she said she was going to the police. I told her to go right ahead, the only police with jurisdiction over this camp are the ones in Terrell County, barracks right down the road. Chief is our caretaker's cousin. That seemed to upset her even more."

"Aengus...where is Carol now?" I whispered. Nothing about this silent, moon-drowned place was right. Nothing about the man I had married was right.

"Don't know," he said. "Like I said, she was here, but she's gone. I never saw her leave. The other guy told me, the bus driver, old Nog. She said some god-awful things to him, said she'd come back up here and shoot him if she had to. Upset him so his son had to come get him. I don't think he'll be coming back. Said his heart was hurting him. Probably had a heart attack, old guy like that. She probably killed our bus driver, if you want to know what I think."

I could make no sense of this. I shook my head. My husband smiled and smiled.

"Aengus... I've seen that bus driver. He's not a day over thirty. What do you mean, 'old guy'?"

"Looks young, doesn't he?" Aengus smiled. "Some of those old Irish families have the knack. Tir Na Nog, remember? The Land of Forever Young? Celt-Irish, that is. Some say they stay so young they never die. Naturally, anyway. Feed off kids' childhoods, they do."

He shone in the faded light like a candle.

"The children...," I whispered.

"Oh, everybody's okay. Sleeping like babies. Never heard a thing. Counselors, too. I called her husband and told him what she said, and he's coming to get the two older ones tomorrow. I told him he shouldn't worry about Bummer, that you probably had him. He said he'd call you in the morning. I doubt if he will, though. I guess he figured somebody or other would look after him. I don't think he cares who, as long as it isn't him. You could just tell he doesn't like the kid. He's right. Kid's a menace."

"Carol went back home, then?"

"Well, of course," he said, widening his eyes at me. The moon danced in them. "Where else would she go? Went screeching out of here like a bat out of hell when I wouldn't let her take the boys."

Cold flooded me. I did not feel, on this haunted night, that Carol Partridge would be coming home. I could not have said why, but I was suddenly terrified for her. This place called Forever had swallowed her.

"Do you do it, too?" I whispered.

"What on earth are you talking about, baby?" he said.

The smile never wavered. His whole being radiated joy. A mad sort of joy. I turned and ran for the car, stumbling and slipping on fallen pine needles.

"If you've got Bummer, I need him!" Aengus called after me. "He ought to be here. He's got almost two weeks to go yet. She paid for him. He's not done yet!"

I ran faster. I reached the car and threw myself into it and turned on the ignition.

Behind my eyes I saw my grandmother sitting on our porch at home, smiling up at a young Irishman I had just introduced her to.

"Oh, Grand! I let him go too far after all," I whispered. It was only when Bummer spoke that I realized I was crying.

"Why are you crying?" he said. "Where's my mother?"

"I'm not crying," I said fiercely. "We'll find your mother."

I jerked the car around and roared off up the gravel road toward the main road over the mountain. Behind me I could hear Aengus calling, "I need that kid, Thayer!..."

At the top of the mountain, at the overlook, I stopped and pulled the car down behind the tree line.

"Where are we going?" Bummer said. He was crying, too.

"We're going to wait here a little while; then we're going to a place where we'll be safe. There's a man there who will take care of both of us. His name is Nick; he's a very old friend of mine. You'll like him. He'll like you, too."

"But my mama?"

"He'll know what to do," I said. "He'll know exactly what to do."

I heard the bus then. I heard the grinding as the gears changed and the growl of the big motor climbing as it neared us. It was coming fast up the mountain.

"Mrs. O'Neill...," Bummer began. I clapped my hands over his mouth and drew him down beside me on the seat. I crouched low. It was dark behind the tree line, but the moon was bleeding light, and I could see clearly up to the road. I saw the bus with *Camp Forever* scripted on its side careen past us. I saw the man who had been my husband, but who was now wedded eternally to older, darker things, in the driver's seat. His black head was thrown back, and his face was suffused with rapture. He was singing, singing as the bus flew past on the summit of Burnt Mountain.

I fancied that I could hear the song, and perhaps I did. Perhaps I would hear it forever.

"The Cannibal King with the big nose ring fell in love with a dusky maid...."

Epilogue

The beaches on the coast of Georgia are broad and gentle, the sand not Caribbean sugar white but a mild, soft gray like the breast of a dove. The beach on which Nick had built our house was a perfect semi-circle of shell-strewn sand. High dunes shielded it on either side from the other houses on East Beach. It was a beautiful site. It had been in his family a long time, he said. He had always known his home would be here.

I lay in the high sun of autumn and looked out to sea. At its edge Bummer splashed, throwing a Frisbee to a Labrador puppy he had named, for some reason, Walmart.

Bummer came up and sat beside me, dripping seawater. Walmart shook himself all over and rolled in the sand.

"When's lunch?" Bummer said. "Walmart's hungry."

"Soon as Nick gets home," I said. "He's out at the Frederica site now."

Bummer leaned into me and I put my arm around him.

There was a good bit more flesh over his ribs now, and his tanned body was warm. Two years had carried him out of small-boyhood. He had been with us here for three weeks. He came to us more and more often. His father, busy with his older boys, had little time for Bummer. I knew that his time with his mother was strictly circumscribed by the new custody decree his father had filed for and won. Aengus had testified well. My heart hurt for Carol, but I heard nothing from her. When Walter had taken her to court and gotten custody of the children, she had moved back to her mother's home in upper Montclair.

She had been back at home next door when Bummer and I got home from Burnt Mountain that night, but she would not speak of Camp Forever and what went on there. She never did. Indeed, we spoke little at all. She did not return my calls, nor answer my knocks when I went next door to see her. I don't know if she felt I was still too deeply connected to Aengus for her to trust me or if some essential Carol-ness had simply been burned out of her on that night and she did not know me anymore. In a very short time there was a custody hearing and the boys were gone, and finally she was, too.

We did not see her again. Calls arranging Bummer's visits to us came from Walter. I had started to call her several times at her mother's home, but always Nick said, "Let it be."

"But Nick, it's Carol. . . ."

"Let it be, Thay. Anything to do with that damned camp is poison for her."

We talked of it very little.

"Did Big Jim know all that, do you think?"

"God, no. He'd have had apoplexy. And of course he'd have closed the camp."

"And the boys—did they stay, you know, like that? Perfect?"

"No. Two or three of them have ended up in Juvie. They're just boys. It's all they ever were. The rest was just moonbeams."

Oh, Grand.

I did not know if Camp Forever was still there now. I did not know where Aengus was. He was still up in those empty woods when our divorce was finalized that winter; he did not contest it and I did not see him again. He was wherever there was magic, I thought sometimes. If there's any magic left. The hole he left in my heart will always be there. Magic, for me, had largely slid into it and was lost.

Bummer and I were both silent. I looked out to sea once more. There was magic here, perhaps, where earth, air, and water, those three great elements, came together. This beach was a wonderful spot for looking. You could see the empty blue horizon to the east. You could see the thick island forest to the west. To the south you could see the small curve of the St. Simons Island pier and, beyond it, the breast of the island as it slid out of sight into the sea toward Jekyll Island.

But you could not see north. And in any case, I never looked, not north. Not toward the first abrupt green peak that marked the dying of the Appalachian chain.

Not toward Burnt Mountain.

About the Author

Anne Rivers Siddons is the author of seventeen *New York Times* bestselling novels, including *Off Season, Sweetwater Creek, Islands, Nora Nora, Low Country, Up Island, Fault Lines, Downtown, Hill Towns, Colony, Outer Banks, King's Oak, Peachtree Road, Homeplace, Fox's Earth, The House Next Door,* and *Heartbreak Hotel.* She is also the author of a work of nonfiction, *John Chancellor Makes Me Cry.* She and her husband, Heyward, split their time between their homes in Charleston, South Carolina and Maine.